I'll Be Waiting for You

ALSO BY MARIKO TURK

The Other Side of Perfect

I'll Be Waiting for You

Mariko Turk

LITTLE, BROWN AND COMPANY
New York Boston

This book is a work of fiction. Names, characters, places, and incidents are the product of the author's imagination or are used fictitiously. Any resemblance to actual events, locales, or persons, living or dead, is coincidental.

Little, Brown and Company
Hachette Book Group
1290 Avenue of the Americas, New York, NY 10104
Visit us at LBYR.com

First Edition: April 2024

Little, Brown and Company is a division of Hachette Book Group, Inc. The Little, Brown name and logo are trademarks of Hachette Book Group, Inc.

The publisher is not responsible for websites (or their content) that are not owned by the publisher.

Little, Brown and Company books may be purchased in bulk for business, educational, or promotional use. For information, please contact your local bookseller or the Hachette Book Group Special Markets Department at special.markets@hbgusa.com.

Library of Congress Cataloging-in-Publication Data
Names: Turk, Mariko, author.
Title: I'll be waiting for you / Mariko Turk.
Other titles: I will be waiting for you
Description: First edition. | New York : Little, Brown and Company, 2024. | Audience: Ages 12 & up. | Summary: While mourning her best friend, Natalie, an aspiring teen paranormal investigator, stays at the purportedly haunted Harlow Hotel, where she finds more than she expected.
Identifiers: LCCN 2023003656 | ISBN 9780316703444 (hardcover) | ISBN 9780316703437 (ebook)
Subjects: CYAC: Grief—Fiction. | Best friends—Fiction. | Friendship—Fiction. | Interpersonal relations—Fiction. | Haunted places—Fiction. | Hotels, motels, etc.—Fiction. | Japanese Americans—Fiction.
Classification: LCC PZ7.1.T8745 Il 2024 | DDC [Fic]—dc23
LC record available at https://lccn.loc.gov/2023003656

ISBNs: 978-0-316-70344-4 (hardcover),
978-0-316-70343-7 (ebook)

Printed in the United States of America

LSC-C

Printing 1, 2024

To Andrew

chapter one

It's our last night in Estes Park. Imogen and I are making the most of it—hanging out in the lobby of the Harlow Hotel, scarfing down a bag of Cherry Sours, and communing with the ghost of Agnes Thripp.

"Agnes," I say with my mouth full, leaning over the Ouija board and touching my fingers to the planchette. "You're an upstanding woman. A real straight shooter."

Imogen snorts, clapping a hand over her mouth like she doesn't snort-laugh all the time. "Why do you sound like my dad?"

That sets off my giggle reflex, and then we're in a full-on laughing fit. We're doing a good job of pretending the best part of summer isn't about to be over. Pretending it isn't wildly unfair that best friends only get to hang out for two weeks in June and then basically not see each other until school starts, all because one of them is a genius destined for the Ivy Leagues and the other one is me. But we can't pretend forever.

"It's why we come to you, oh wise Agnes," I continue. "With a question so important, the answer could change everything."

Imogen's smile fades as her eyebrows quirk up—half-curious, half-wary.

"Should Imogen go to piano camp this summer, even though it sucks and she hates it there?"

Imogen throws a Cherry Sour at me as she sinks back into the leather chair. "I knew it."

"It's true, though." I slide the planchette toward her. "You *do* hate it there."

"Of course I hate it there. It's *Midsommar*-level creepy. Everyone acts all bright and happy, but they're secretly planning to bludgeon you. Metaphorically."

I nod, remembering all the times she FaceTimed me from a bathroom stall last summer, hiding from the ultra-competitive piano camp kids who smiled sweetly while negging her into the ground. "So don't go."

"I have to go. My parents expect me to, and I know what you think about that, but I can't just not do it."

"Well, I already asked Agnes, so..." I tap my finger on the beat-up Ouija board resting between us on the polished coffee table.

"Fiiiine." Imogen sighs, resting two fingers on the

planchette and fixing her gray eyes on me. "But for the record—"

"Shhh. Let Agnes think," I whisper. My voice blends with the hum of tourists drifting around the Harlow Hotel lobby, admiring its old, spooky vibe. The dim lighting casts off the crimson carpet and mahogany furniture, giving everything a reddish glow. There's a taxidermied mountain goat staring eerily from the front corner, its glassy eyes somewhere between sinister and sad. The walls are lined with photographs of the mediums who founded the hotel in the late 1800s, making it a center for supernatural exploration. They all practiced Spiritualism, a religion that believed the dead could communicate with the living.

Nowadays, more people come to the Harlow Hotel for elk mating season than for séances. A family-friendly resort surrounds it, with rental cabins, a crafts center, tennis courts, stables, and mini golf. But the Harlow—bless its creepy little heart—leans into its Spiritualist history, preserving its antique look, playing up its haunted status, and employing a resident medium, who has an office in the basement and pretty decent Yelp reviews. Imogen and I have never gotten to spend the night here—it's way too expensive for that—but at least our cabins are nearby on the resort, only a quarter mile up the hill.

Imogen's leg bounces up and down as she stares at the planchette. "I know you're going to move it."

I almost snort this time. *Obviously*, I'm going to move it. Who else is going to do it, a ghost? Don't get me wrong,

I love spooky stuff. I played "Possessed Girl" at Terror in the Corn last Halloween. My one and only life plan is to become a TV ghost hunter on *Ghost Chasers* so I can travel to cool, creepy places with host Joshua Jacobs—the hottest human being on the planet—while occasionally shouting things like, *Something touched me!* and, *Oh my God, what was that?*

But I don't believe in actual ghosts. It would be great if when you died, you became a transparent version of yourself that could walk through walls and send cryptic messages and finish unfinished business. I just don't believe it's true.

I didn't get out the Ouija board to contact a ghost. I did it to make a point, and my point is this: Imogen should finally stand up for herself and tell her parents she's not going to piano camp, aka the thing she hates but her parents ship her off to every year so she'll be a more attractive candidate to Ivy League schools, aka the schools she'll get into anyway because she's the most brilliant person ever.

Seriously. She's on track for valedictorian. She can explain cryptocurrency in a way that makes sense. In seventh grade, when we had to write a short story for English and I dared her to write hers about a cannibalistic bunny named Beaniford, Mr. Quinn read it out loud to the class. Such is the power of Imogen Lucas's brain.

But instead of trusting in that, her parents ship her off to piano camp for three weeks every summer, and after that, coding classes and debate intensives and any other awful thing they think will up her chances. It totally ruins our summers.

The only reason I get to spend any time with my best friend over the summer is because, when we were eleven, we decided to take matters into our own hands. At a sleepover one night, we Googled around and found a *Wall Street Journal* article that said unstructured time in the great outdoors could improve the brain's executive functioning. I convinced my mom that it wouldn't be manipulative if she *casually* brought up the article to Imogen's parents at the next PTA meeting, and then *casually* mentioned that we rent a cabin in Estes Park—the tiny town at the base of the Rocky Mountains—for two weeks every summer. Mom must have really sold it, because the Lucases started renting the cabin next door that very summer and every summer since.

Which means that for two weeks, Imogen is free. We can ride bumper boats and wander the winding trails. We can paint matching merman mugs and hang out behind the library downtown, in the secret, shaded spot we named Oasis. We can watch horror movies, sprawled on the thick woven rug in my tiny cabin bedroom, screaming at the good ones, laughing at the bad ones, debating what's scarier—ghosts or demons or aliens or slashers or monsters that are metaphors for real stuff, like depression or racism or the internet.

Imogen loves a good horror movie metaphor. She wants to write screenplays like that one day—stories that take the darkness of the everyday and translate it into monsters that make you think about the human condition. I'm more of an *Evil Dead II* kind of girl, personally. Give me Bruce Campbell gutting demons with a chainsaw arm over metaphors any day. Not that I won't be there to see all of Imogen's movies on opening day, bragging to anyone who'll listen about how she's my best friend.

"Natalie, come *on*," Imogen says, shifting in the leather chair. "I know you're going to move it, so just—" The planchette zips sharply to the corner of the board, the circular window coming to an abrupt stop over the bold print NO.

"Cheese and crackers!" Imogen gasps out, snatching her hands away like she's been burned. And then I die from laughter. Because in sixth grade, Imogen read the expression "cheese and crackers" in a book and started using it all the time until she realized it was British slang for testicles and stopped. But every once in a while, it still slips out.

Imogen is laughing, too, her cheeks pink with embarrassment because people are starting to look over, but we can't stop. Until a sharp, insistent sound splits the air.

Imogen's curfew alarm. Our last night is over. And no matter how much Imogen hates piano camp, no matter how much I try to convince her the world won't end if she disappoints her parents just this once, it won't matter. Tomorrow, our families will drive fifty minutes down the mountain back to Boulder, and then it's off to separate summers.

Imogen solemnly zips up her favorite hoodie. The white one that says ESTES PARK on the back, with elk antlers growing out of the letters and spreading onto the shoulders, like wings. I tug on my beaded bracelet, contemplating the rest of the summer. I can stay out later when I'm not bound by Imogen's curfew. I can play beer pong without her describing in detail all the bacteria that's swimming around in those Solo cups. But somehow, the prospect of late nights and guilt-free pong doesn't make me feel better. It only makes me feel bored and sad and basic.

"Thank you for communicating with us, Agnes," Imogen is saying, swirling the planchette around the board. "Goodbye." She blinks up at me expectantly.

"Really?"

"The box says if we don't say goodbye, the door to the spirit world stays open."

I sigh. I don't understand how Imogen can believe that.

"I know, I know." Imogen waves her hand in the air. "It's totally irrational, but we don't know the secrets of the universe. And we don't want to leave Agnes hanging." Her eyes slide to the photograph mounted over the stone fireplace. It's of Agnes Thripp—one of the psychic mediums who founded the hotel—sitting in a rocking chair on the wide front porch of the Harlow, staring into the camera.

What's cool about the picture is that it looks like there are dark flecks hovering above her head. When you look closer, you see the flecks are hummingbirds, flitting in between the feeders hanging from the awning. It's a famous photo because Agnes is the only person to have died at the Harlow Hotel. It was a big deal at the time, and the circumstances surrounding her death were publicized in all the newspapers. The Harlow still has exhibits about it sometimes.

"You don't have to say it out loud," Imogen says, finally tearing her eyes away from the photo and heaving her backpack onto her shoulders. "Just think it."

"Fine." I close my eyes. But I don't think it, not even a little bit.

We return the Ouija board box to the game shelf and walk out onto the wide front porch, down the steps, and through the front courtyard, setting off across the resort.

A dusky gray has settled around the pines and dirt paths. The tree-covered mountains surrounding us look soft and muted in the dim light, like a vintage postcard. In fifteen minutes, it'll be totally dark.

"Headlamp," Imogen says, adjusting the elastic band around her head and straightening the LED bulb in front as we pass the mini golf course. She reaches into my tote bag and pulls out an identical headlamp, the one she made me buy last summer at REI for "wilderness safety purposes."

"I'll just use my phone." I'm against headlamps on account of they look super dorky.

"No way." Imogen shoves it into my hands. "It'll be mountain dark soon."

I strap the thing on begrudgingly as we reach the Starlight Trail, the short, winding path that dips down into the trees, runs along the creek, and takes us back to our cabins.

The harsh, bright glow from our heads lights up every protruding tree root and stone as the darkness grows heavier, snaking its way through the branches.

Imogen is right—in the mountains, darkness is different. It almost feels alive. Like it breathes and moves and tugs on our shirts, brushes our skin.

It would freak me out more, if it wasn't for all the familiar landmarks along the path. The silver-green sage filling the air with a fresh, spicy scent. The little white yarrow flowers that look like bouquets shrunken down to Barbie size. We pass Harvey, the aspen with black scars in the shape of a goofy, smiling face. And Buttview, the flat rock we were standing on last year when we saw a hiker drop her pants to pee.

We're going up a slight incline when I notice Imogen's eyes are fixed on something up ahead. "What?" I ask, trying to see what she sees.

"Nothing."

We walk another minute in silence, and then Imogen stops suddenly. "Seriously, what?" I say before realizing where we are.

Agnes Tree. A giant ponderosa pine with a rough trunk shooting up into the sky, its bare, naked branches sticking out at odd angles all the way up, like the arms I used to draw on my stick people. Pine needles cover the higher, twistier branches that blend into the dark sky. Most importantly, there's a gaping hole gouged into the trunk about three quarters of the way up.

We discovered it our first summer in Estes Park. Imogen had been convinced there was something inside the hollow. She'd wanted so badly to climb up to find out if she was right, but was way too afraid of heights, the disapproval of park rangers, and broken bones, in that order. So, I'd climbed the tree. And the bizarre thing? There actually *was* something in the hollow.

An old hummingbird figurine, covered in dirt.

It was all we talked about for the rest of the trip. Imogen spun this whole story about how it was a message from Agnes Thripp. She couldn't wait to come back the next summer to see what other messages Agnes would leave for us. But when we came back, and I climbed up, all I found inside the hollow were rocks and sticks and dirt. And that was all we'd ever found every summer since. It was a huge letdown, even though I didn't believe Imogen's story.

"Aren't you going to climb it?" Imogen asks. She looks up at the tree and then back to me expectantly.

"What's the point?" I scuff my sneaker along the loose rocks. "Nothing's up there."

Imogen's mouth drops open. "But what if there is?"

"There isn't." We used to get the hummingbird out every time I slept over at Imogen's, just to look at it, and then Imogen would carefully tuck it back into the miniature wardrobe in her dollhouse. We hadn't done that in forever. "Don't you think it's time to move on?"

"Moving on is overrated," Imogen says, her eyes bouncing

frantically between me and the tree again. "Please? It's a just-in-case thing. Like how we said goodbye to Agnes with the Ouija board."

"Right," I say, a beat too late.

"Wait, what?" Imogen's tone is immediately tense. She always knows when I'm lying.

I heave a sigh. "I didn't say goodbye to Agnes. I didn't think it." It's quiet for a few seconds, the only sound a slow wind wandering through the trees. It picks up suddenly, lifting our hair, carrying the slight butterscotch scent of the ponderosa pine bark.

Imogen casts one last look up Agnes Tree, her face scrunching up like some sort of death match is going on in her head.

"Don't freak out—" I cut off when a clicking moth flits between us, making us both jump.

"Okay, okay, let's just go." Imogen breathes out, gravel scraping under her feet as she speed-walks down the trail.

I jog to catch up. "Dude, we're fine."

"This is how horror movies start," Imogen mutters.

"This isn't a horror movie. If it was, it would get terrible reviews."

"Shhh!" Imogen flaps her hands at me. "This is what horror movies *do*. They drag things out so the characters get all smug and say stuff like that. Like, 'This isn't a horror movie.' Like, 'Hahaha, nothing's going to happen to *me*.' It builds tension. And then *bam*. Agnes comes out of the dark, and her flock of demon hummingbirds peck at us until we turn into rabid human-hummingbird hybrids and flitter around these woods forever."

I blink at Imogen, her posture rigid, hurrying straight down the trail like Agnes and her hummingbirds from hell are right behind us.

This happens a lot. Imogen thinking real life is like a horror movie, where every little transgression will lead to an outrageous punishment. It's why she'll make amazing horror movies one day. But it's also why she always follows the rules. Because if we don't say goodbye to the spirit world, if she doesn't go to piano camp, if she doesn't always obey her parents, who knows what horrifying thing will happen?

The gap between us widens as Imogen hustles down the trail, and a familiar double wish settles over me. I wish Imogen wasn't so scared all the time. I wish I didn't have to miss her all summer.

And then I'm running off the trail before I even know what I'm doing. I heave myself onto a large boulder, cup my hands around my mouth, and tilt my head up to the sky. "Hahaha, nothing is going to happen to *me*!" I yell as loud as I can. "Do you hear that, Agnes? I'm *smug*!"

My voice lifts into the trees as Imogen skids to a stop and rushes over. "What are you doing?" Her voice is somewhere between a whisper and a screech.

"I'm showing you there isn't anything out here to be scared of!" I stretch my arms out wide and call out to Agnes again. I'm about to run out of breath when Imogen grabs my elbow, and I startle. She tightens her grip, the coldness of her fingers seeping through my flannel shirt.

"Okay, I get it," she says, still whispering. "It's irrational, but can we please go?"

I jump off the boulder, and Imogen keeps her hand on my elbow the whole way out of the woods. It's only when we see our lit-up cabins that she lets go. But I still feel the imprint of her fingers on my arm.

"You're the worst," she says. And then we start laughing at the same time. Because we're out of the woods, and nothing bad happened, and Imogen isn't scared anymore.

In bed later, I scroll through my Instagram, tapping on a selfie I took of us yesterday. We're on the Harlow's front porch, squeezed into one wicker rocking chair, leaning back as far as we can so we'll both be in frame. I snapped the picture at the exact moment we tipped back too far, the chair losing its balance for a second before we righted it again. Our reactions are perfectly captured. Me mid-laugh, Imogen mid-scream.

I'm about to put my phone down when a notification pops up. Imogen just commented on the rocking-chair photo.

cheese and crackers!!!!!

I respond with a row of crying laughing emojis. I put my phone down on the nightstand, smiling as my eyelids get heavier. Because even though it's our last night in Estes Park, there's always next summer. And the one after that.

But Imogen would say that horror movies do this, too.

Lull you into a false sense of security. A character does something smug in the woods, so you hold your breath, expecting the worst. But they make it. Everything is okay. You relax.

Then *bam*. Jason Voorhees bursts out of the lake. Nell Crain lunges from the back seat of the car. Carrie's hand shoots up from the rubble. And you scream even louder because you don't see it coming.

I don't see it coming.

And it's not a slasher or a creepy doll. It's my mom, standing at the foot of my bed, her face gaunt in the early morning light, telling me that last night, while everyone was sleeping, Imogen had a sudden cardiac arrest. Her heart literally stopped beating. And instantly, on the last night of vacation, in the dark of the mountains, she died.

chapter two

One Year Later

I'm going to have fun tonight. I keep repeating that to myself as I trudge up the Stein Incline—the steep residential street that leads to Dave Stein's house. Dave's parties are always worth the burning calves it takes to get there. I know that. Still, the hill seems steeper than usual. But I keep walking.

Because I'm going to have fun tonight.

Halfway up the hill, Liam Jeffries whooshes past me in a shopping cart, screaming his head off while cheers ring out from Dave's front lawn. I laugh, grateful for the distraction. People find all kinds of ways to roll down the Stein Incline. Bikes and skateboards first, then shopping carts, and then someone would go down on a swivel chair or a Roomba and need to go to the hospital.

When I finally get in the door, the bass vibrates in my

chest. I close my eyes, letting the familiar party noises wash over me. *I'm going to have fun tonight.*

"Nakada!" Raden Suzuki calls out, and I open my eyes, stretching my mouth into a smile. I make my way over to the dining room, getting hit with a chorus of "Hey!" and "Natalie!" and some unintelligible stuff from the drunker people.

I do a broad wave as I take in the cardboard boxes covering the dining room table and stacked on the floor, overflowing with pink and purple toys. There's a unicorn bed in the corner. A full-on, sparkle-horned, three-dimensional unicorn with a mattress in the middle.

"What's all this?" I ask as Raden offers me a beer. I wave it away. After one humiliating night last fall that started with me deciding I was ready to go out again and ended with me puking all over a potted begonia, I'm strictly no alcohol at parties. I'll fill a cup with water later and no one will know the difference.

"Stein's sister starts middle school next year, so they're giving all her little-kid stuff to Goodwill," Raden says as we plop onto the unicorn bed. He reaches into a box sitting on the edge of the mattress and pulls out a doll head with knotty blond hair and garish red lipstick smeared on her chin. His eyes go wide. "Yikes."

I grin. I like Raden. He's cute and funny and we sometimes kiss, but he never sends feel-it-out texts to see what else I'd be down for—hooking up or hanging out or whatever. Raden understands what we are.

I grab the doll head and hold it up. "Hello, lover," I say in my best demon voice.

Raden laughs but gives me a funny look. "Uh, hi?"

My smile fades as a wave of loneliness ripples through me. "It's from *Evil Dead II.*" I toss the doll head back into the box with a plastic thunk. I don't know why I did the reference. Of course he doesn't know it.

"I'll have to see it sometime. Lover." He elbows me in the arm.

I elbow him back, but the lonely feeling is still there. So I shoot up onto my knees, crack an imaginary whip, and shout, "Let's ride a unicorn, bitches!" Riley Adams and Emma Larue run over, bringing the rest of the dance team with them. Riley dives headfirst onto the bed, which sends it crashing into the wall, because apparently there are wheels on the bottom. We scream and laugh and more people pile on.

My shoulders and legs are wedged against everyone else's, the warmth of their bodies imprinting on mine, and I feel all right again.

I'm having fun tonight.

I promised myself I wasn't going to get all caught up in memories, but I can't help thinking about how far I've come from last summer, when I barely went out at all. For obvious reasons. I only saw people from school at the funeral and then by accident—in the ice cream aisle at Safeway, in the CVS parking lot, on the trails in Chautauqua. They'd glance at me and then look away, glance and away, wondering if they should approach. It was like I'd been abducted by aliens and now I was back, and I looked the same, but nobody knew what I was like on the inside. If I was still me or an alien in a Natalie shell.

When they did come up to me, they'd talk to me like I was a toddler, with soft voices and dragged-out vowels. *Heeey, Natalie. It's reeeeally good to see you.*

But then school started, and things changed. Guidance counselors started talking about college applications. The basketball team won a few games for once. The coffee shop a block away from school came out with a maple bacon doughnut. Everyone just...forgot. Which was weird at first. But then it was good. I could breathe easier without everyone watching me, talking in their quiet voices.

And then I started drifting. I slid in and out of groups depending on how I felt that day. I sat with the AP kids at lunch. I went to pep rallies with the dance team. I vented with the drama kids about physics. And at some point, as I drifted along, the sad eyes and awkward silences tapered off. At some point, everyone realized I wasn't an alien in a Natalie shell.

I'm still me.

And now it's been a year. The worst year of my life. For obvious reasons. But I went to therapy with Dr. Salamando. I had breakthroughs. I'm okay now. Good, even.

The karaoke crowd on the patio bursts into cheers, which means something really good or really embarrassing is about to happen. I get ready to drift.

"Later?" Raden lifts his mouth into a flirty smile as I scoot my way off the bed.

"Maybe. I'm starting my senior project tomorrow, and I still have to pack."

"You're starting that already?" Raden cocks his head at me. I get why. *Natalie Nakada* and *getting a jump start on the senior project* don't really go together. "Where at?"

I clear my throat. "The Harlow Hotel. In Estes Park? I'm going to film my audition for *Ghost Chasers*."

"Huh." Raden looks thoughtful. "The Harlow Hotel is that haunted place, right?"

"Yeah, *haunted*." I smirk, doing air quotes.

"You don't believe in ghosts?" he asks, his mouth tipping into a smile that looks a little sad. "Like, at all?"

"Nope." I could add that if I did believe in ghosts, if I believed that when people died, some part of them lived on, maybe last year would have been a little easier. But this is a party, and this is Raden, so I don't.

"What the hell is *he* doing here?" Emma Larue's voice rises over the noise, and I follow her gaze across the crowd to the living room.

Leander Hall is standing by the front door, rocking his trademark bored scowl. Everyone stops what they're doing to look at him, like he's Cinderella arriving at the ball. If Cinderella was a huge dick no one liked.

Confused whispers are circulating.

"Why is he here?"

"What is his *deal*?"

Valid questions. But like everyone else, I have no idea how to answer them. All I know is that Leander Hall moved here from New York at the beginning of the school year and started writing a column for the school paper called Truth Hurts, which basically consisted of articles that insulted everyone. In an article the day before the Homecoming game, he wrote about how high school football teams were "bastions of toxic masculinity." A few weeks later, on Chili Day no less, he criticized our school's "meat-centric" lunches, saying they contributed to climate change. In April, he wrote about how promposals blurred the lines of consent and perpetuated rape culture. *In April,* when promposals were literally happening every day.

It's hard to tell if he really believes what he's saying, or if he just likes making people mad, or if we're heading toward some sort of M. Night Shyamalan twist, where we'll find out he's an alien from Planet Pretentious and this is all a grand experiment to see if Earth teenagers can be annoyed to death.

Leander scans the room in his all-black outfit, looking like a disgruntled vampire, and not the cool Nosferatu kind. Suddenly, he stalks over to the table where Dave deposited all the random alcohol and snacks he scrounged up. He grabs a box of Pop-Tarts and a bottle of Dave's mom's wine, and strides out of the sliding glass door, disappearing into the dark of the backyard.

The noise kicks back up a few seconds later, but it's muted. "Someone ask him why he's here," Riley says, bumping my shoulder.

"Sure." The party mood has already taken a hit. I'm going to have fun tonight, and Leander Hall isn't going to ruin it. I follow his path through the sliding glass door, cut through the karaoke crowd on the patio, and head into Dave's huge backyard. A surprisingly cold breeze kicks up, spreading goose bumps over my bare arms. I shiver and squint into the dark, the trees making murky shapes in the distance.

I spot Leander sitting in an Adirondack chair next to a birdbath, tipping the bottle of pink wine into his mouth. I'm practically right in front of him before he blinks up at me.

"Why are you here?" I say, figuring I'll get right to it.

"Wow." Leander plunks his head back onto the painted wood. "That's a big question. It's pretty much *the* question, existentially speaking."

I open my mouth, but he's still going.

"Why am I here..." He stretches his long legs out in front of him. "For what reason was I put on this Earth? What's the purpose of my existence? You caught me off guard here, so I might need a minute to think about it."

I smile pleasantly, ignoring the gallon of sarcasm dripping from his words. His speech is slightly slurred, so I assume he's been drinking before he got here, but not so much that I'm in danger of being puked on. "I'll wait."

Leander shrugs, putting his hands behind his head and flicking his eyes to the sky. He stays that way as the seconds tick by, which is annoying because it makes me notice that his chest stretches the fabric of his T-shirt in a not unattractive way. His face isn't gross, either—all sharp cheekbones and big brown eyes. He even has the audacity to have good hair. It's the messy, brushed-forward look that's just haphazard enough to seem like it isn't styled that way on purpose. It truly hurts to admit it, but Leander Hall is sort of hot.

But I keep staring because I'm not breaking first. After a while, Leander shifts on the chair, and I think he's finally going to say something, but instead he tears open a silver package of Pop-Tarts and takes a bite. He chews for a full calendar year and then swallows.

"The frosted ones are better."

I roll my eyes. "Another hard-hitting truth from Leander Hall."

"Was there anything else?" he asks, and God, he's the worst.

"Yeah. Your articles suck."

"And why's that?" He's smiling, but it's sarcastic, like he knows I couldn't possibly say anything worth listening to.

"They're condescending," I say. The sarcastic smile stays put. Normally, I would just move on, but for some reason, I dig back through my brain to every Truth Hurts article I hate-read, trying to piece together what makes them so terrible. "It's how they're written. I mean, some of us might agree with the general points you make. But it feels like you're yelling at us for not knowing exactly what you know. It's demeaning. It makes us direct all our energy into hating you instead of thinking about what you're saying. You might as well write in all caps."

And just like that, the smile is gone. Leander's mouth looks altogether different now, with his lips parted in surprise. My mouth is open a little, too. I can't believe that all came out so coherently.

But I blink and Leander's standard bored scowl is back. He thunks the wine bottle onto the grass. "Why are *you* here, then?"

"Um..." I laugh a little. "I'm here to have fun. Like a normal person."

"You're having *fun*?" He raises his eyebrow skeptically.

"Yes," I say slowly. "Why is that so surprising?"

Leander shrugs. "Because you seem miserable."

My eyebrows shoot up. I try to think of a comeback, but I'm too distracted, toggling between irritation and something else—a squirming feeling in my stomach, like I've just gotten called out.

The karaoke music abruptly cuts off, casting a strange quiet over the backyard. I whirl around to see Dave Stein standing at the karaoke mic on the deck, waving his hands in the air.

"Hey, hey, everyone!" Dave's voice booms into the night. The karaoke crowd gathers around him as people trickle out of the house, shivering and rubbing their arms. "I just wanted to say, this year was truly amazing. You're all amazing."

"Booooo!" Leander yells from behind me, but it's buried by a wave of cheers.

"You guys," Dave goes on. "Next year, we're seniors." Even louder cheers. "And it's like, the time went by so *fast,* you know? That's why I want to slow down a minute. Take a second to remember someone really special who died on this day one year ago."

I stiffen. There's no way he's doing this.

"Imogen Lucas."

My mouth is open, but I can't move. I need to breathe. I need to breathe like Dr. Salamando said. Focus on the exhale, a forceful whoosh of air out. People are starting to look at me, but their faces are hazy, and the trees behind them blend into the charcoal sky. Everything has gone shapeless. Except her name hanging in the air. The absence of her that's suddenly as tangible as skin.

"She was, like, so smart." Dave is still talking. "And it's such a tragedy that she's gone. But I believe she's here with us tonight. I *feel* her here with us tonight."

Dave lifts his eyes to the sky, and all around the backyard, faces begin to tilt up, too. They nod and whisper. *Maybe that's why it's so cold. That's a thing, right? Ghosts and cold?*

It brings me back to myself. Enough to scrunch my eyes closed. Enough to almost scream "*BULLSHIT!*" into the night.

Imogen isn't here with us tonight. She had a rare and undiagnosed heart abnormality. She was born with it, and nobody knew. She lived her whole life not knowing. And then it killed her. She was gone even before they buried her at Green Mountain Memorial Park. She was gone the second her heart stopped beating a year ago.

"So, Imogen," Dave says, still looking up at the sky. "This one's for you." Somber piano chords play on the karaoke machine, and Dave sings out, "*I will remember you. . . .*"

And I can practically feel her standing beside me, smiling at Dave, not wanting him to realize how much he's embarrassing himself.

I shake the image away and whoosh out another breath. We're supposed to move on. I *have* moved on. And a silly, sentimental song isn't going to make me cry.

I shake out my hands. I can move again. And as Dave finally stops singing, I remember something.

The unicorn bed has wheels.

I'm walking, fast, through the yard, across the deck, and into the dining room. I put my hands on the unicorn's sparkly butt. As I wheel it clumsily to the front door, a crowd gathers. A few people help me fit the bed through the doorway and push it across Dave's front lawn to the top of the hill, the rest of the party following behind, chanting, "Stein Incline! Stein Incline!"

I stare down the long, steep hill, my stomach dipping. I've been down on a bike before, but never on a bed. No one's ever gone down on a bed. For a second, I wonder if this is a really bad idea.

And then a cold hand grips my elbow. I startle at the force of it, the chill of fingers seeping through my sleeve.

I spin around, and for one deeply unpleasant second,

I don't see anyone near me. Just the crowd, several feet away, gearing up to watch. But as I turn back to the mattress, I see Leander standing by the other side of the bed, giving me a look that says, *Really? This is what you're doing right now?*

I let out a breath. Leander grabbed my elbow. Once a buzzkill, always a buzzkill, I guess. I roll my eyes at him and hop onto the mattress. Raden and a few others give me a push, and I'm flying.

Like, really flying. It hadn't felt this fast on a bike. I close my eyes and feel the air blasting over my face, my hair whipping back, the sharp plunge in my stomach as I hurtle faster and faster down. Everything behind me fades away—the party, Dave's song, Leander's existence. It's just me and the hill.

I race past neat houses, gathering speed until the bed hooks a sharp left. I hold on to the unicorn's neck for dear life, trying to use my body weight to straighten things out, but I've lost all control. The bed spins out toward the sidewalk, and I imagine myself hitting the curb and being thrown into a mailbox.

And then, I'm slowing down.

The bed comes to a gentle rest at the bottom of the Stein Incline. When I stand up, legs shaky from the adrenaline, cheers come from the top of the hill. The cold breeze rustles my hair, and I feel lonely again.

I start back up the hill, but after a few steps, I don't want to go any farther. There's a strange weight on my chest, like something is pushing me back. I need to pack anyway, so I turn around and get into my car.

When I shut the door, the silence settles in around me, ringing strangely in my ears after all the noise of the party. I turn the key in the ignition and punch up the volume on the radio, thinking the steady rumble of the engine and the music will fix it. But all through the drive home, the silence only grows thicker and heavier. Like it has a body and is sitting right next to me.

chapter three

I'm staring at the half-filled suitcase on my bed when I hear Mom's footsteps padding down the hallway. "Down where?" she says, clearly talking into her phone. "On a *what?*"

Crap.

I grab a bunch of socks from my drawer and start folding them, trying to look like I have everything under control but am also too busy to talk. Mom gives a warning knock and then opens my door. Her long black hair is up in a damp, messy bun, and she's wearing the silky pink pajamas I got her a few years ago for Christmas. She calls them her "fashion jammies," which I both love and hate.

"Thanks for letting me know," Mom says into the phone as her eyes zero in on me. "Yes, I will. You have a good night, too." She puts her phone down carefully on the top of my dresser. "Well. *That* was an interesting phone call."

"Mmm?" I say, tossing a few folded-up socks into my suitcase.

"It certainly wasn't the kind of phone call I was expecting to get right in the middle of my Bubble Bath and Book Time, which, as you know, is sacred."

I do know that. Mom does education programming for Colorado Parks and Wildlife and spends most days traipsing through dirt and rocks with kids. Reading in the bathtub is how she "washes off the wilderness."

I sigh and put down the socks, knowing I'm not getting out of this. "Who tattled?"

"Mrs. Matsuda."

I blink at her. "The piano lady?" I forgot she lived on the Stein Incline.

Mom flicks her eyes to the ceiling. "Mrs. Matsuda is a complex human being with a vast array of experiences, but yes. Let's call her the piano lady because she taught you piano for a month."

I'd forgotten that Mom is basically president of the Mrs. Matsuda fan club. When I begged Mom for piano lessons after hearing Imogen play *Moonlight Sonata* at the sixth-grade winter concert, she was pumped I wanted to try something new. She got even more pumped when she found Mrs. Matsuda. She's Japanese American, like us, and she and Mom bonded over their love of hiking and natto bean sushi and old Japanese detective shows.

But then I sucked at piano, so I quit after a month. Mom and Mrs. Matsuda still get together sometimes, though, so I think I should get some credit.

"She was passing by the window when you came rolling down," Mom says.

"Oh. Was she mad?" I remember Mrs. Matsuda's house being super classy, with potted azaleas and nice-smelling candles. She probably wouldn't like the idea of a unicorn bed flying down her street.

Mom sighs. "She wasn't mad." Her voice gets softer. "She was concerned."

"Did you tell her I made it out okay? Like, seriously, no bruises or scratches or anything." I hold my arms out to prove it.

"She knew you weren't hurt, sweetie. She saw you get up and drive away. She was just, well, she was concerned that you did it at all. It's dangerous, and she thought maybe you were acting out because of... well, because..."

My chest seizes up. "Seriously?" I turn to my dresser, pulling out a fistful of underwear and cramming it into the suitcase. When are people going to realize I'm okay? I definitely don't need Mom questioning my state of mind right before I'm supposed to leave for the Harlow.

She's never been a fan of me going in the first place. She'd been floating the idea of going to the beach this summer instead of Estes Park, which I was on board for. But then Principal Roth held an assembly last month, telling us about how we'd all be expected to complete a senior project next year. Something we'd have to design ourselves that would give us a meaningful, hands-on learning experience in an area of interest. He'd even brought in all these people from places around the state to talk about why we should consider working with them.

Normally, I would have ignored it until next spring and then slapped something together as quickly as possible, banking on the fact that by that point, teachers would be so burned out they'd just wave me on through to graduation.

But then the weirdest thing happened. I was scrolling Instagram during that very assembly when I saw a post from the *Ghost Chasers* account, announcing their upcoming streaming show: *Ghost Chasers: Teen Investigators*. Each episode would feature a different high school student investigating local ghost lore. They invited "aspiring teen paranormal investigators" to send in audition footage.

Right as I was reading the details, Principal Roth introduced Dr. Bobincheck, the Harlow Hotel's director of community outreach. She said the hotel welcomed any students doing projects on historical or paranormal topics, adding that they'd get to stay in the dorms for seasonal employees, right on the hotel grounds. They essentially got to live at the Harlow for ten days. They also had to present their projects at the Conference for the Paranormal at the end of their stay, alongside "other researchers doing scholarly work on the supernatural." I almost went back to scrolling Instagram when she said that. Because the idea of me standing up in front of a bunch of "scholars" to present my "research" seems as ridiculous as the plot of *Killer Klowns from Outer Space.*

But then, Dr. Bobincheck mentioned that senior project students got to attend the Harlow's annual Spirit Ball, the biggest Halloween party in Colorado, famous for its outlandish costumes and all the "haunted" things that supposedly happened there, like music playing backward and lights cutting out. I'd always wanted to go to the Spirit Ball, to see the fancy costumes and figure out how they do all those tricks.

I emailed Dr. Bobincheck that night, spewing my love for the Harlow Hotel and how it would be the perfect location for an aspiring paranormal investigator to complete their senior project, aka filming an audition for *Ghost Chasers: Teen Investigators.* The next day, she got back to me, officially inviting me to complete my senior project at the Harlow Hotel from June 16–26. I almost couldn't believe it.

I'll slap together a barely passable presentation for the conference, which hopefully won't be a big deal. How many people go to those things, anyway? And in return, I'll get to go to a famous costume party and film an audition that could be my first step toward becoming a ghost hunter on *Ghost Chasers,* aka getting paid to travel to haunted places with professional hot person Joshua Jacobs.

It should be easy.

Imogen would say it sounds too easy. Like in the beginning of a horror movie, when some nice guy gets an amazing deal on a sprawling, creaky old house that definitely is totally fine and not evil at all, so he moves his family into it....

"Honey." Mom puts an arm around my shoulders, pulling me out of the hypothetical horror movie. She gently guides me to my bed and sits down beside me, hip to hip. "Were you? Acting out?"

"Everyone goes down the hill. It happens at every Dave Stein party. It's not a big deal."

"Everyone rolls down the hill on a bed?"

"They do it on all kinds of things. Plus, I don't know, *Leander Hall* was there, and Dave did this terrible karaoke thing, and I just...I thought it would be fun." I know my rambling isn't very convincing, but I'm suddenly too tired to think.

"What's a Leander Hall?" Mom asks, eyebrows furrowed.

"A pretentious jagoff." I'm relieved when Mom smiles. "Jagoff" is her favorite insult. She grew up in Pittsburgh, where everyone apparently said it. I figure a little pandering couldn't hurt right now.

Mom laughs through her nose and pulls the elastic out of her hair, the black strands falling loose over her shoulders. For a second, I think I'm out of the woods. Then Mom's smile fades. "I know you don't like to talk about it. But I know how hard the last year's been for you, and—"

"Mom." She's right. I hate talking about it. Because it was awful. There was last summer, when I'd have this recurring dream that Imogen was in my room, sitting on

top of her sleeping bag, watching me over the top of a book. *Are you awake?* she'd always say in the dream, and I'd open my eyes and blink at the bare stretch of carpet beside my bed, reality sinking in one second at a time. And I didn't just hear her voice when I was sleeping. It would echo in my head all the time. Like, I'd be listening to Taylor Swift singing about how impossible it is to move on, and Imogen's voice would say, clear as anything: *Moving on is overrated.*

Then there was the fall, when I couldn't sleep, and I'd lie in bed for hours, totally exhausted but never drifting off, and then the next day literally everything would infuriate me. I'd drop my toast onto the floor and slam the cupboard shut so hard it would shake. Sienna Poppleton would compulsively click her pen in English and I'd fantasize about stabbing it into her eye. My finnicky locker wouldn't open and I'd practically burst into tears. I was like a stranger all of a sudden. So emotional and out of control.

In the winter, Mom made me go to therapy with Dr. Salamando. I learned that my out-of-control feelings were normal. I was depressed and anxious, which made it hard to sleep, and then the lack of sleep made the depression and anxiety worse. I asked Dr. Salamando how to get better, and she told me not to ignore the sadness. She said that "the only way out is through." So I went through. Full force.

I told Dr. Salamando everything. How kind and smart Imogen was. How she snort-laughed whenever I told her a random anecdote, even if it wasn't that funny. How she was going to write all these brilliant stories that were going to change the world, and now they were just... gone.

How part of me was gone, too. The person I was when I was with her. Dr. Salamando asked me to describe that person, but I couldn't do it. I only had memories. Laughing impossibly hard at our inside jokes. Talking about random stuff for hours. Begrudgingly agreeing to watch a six-hour version of *Pride and Prejudice* at a sleepover and then getting super into it, staying up reciting the best lines. I didn't know how to distill all that, how to describe who I was with Imogen. She just made everything feel bigger sometimes. More exciting.

After a while, I broke down and told Dr. Salamando about the guilt that had been growing inside me since the night she died. The doctors had said the sudden cardiac arrest occurred because of an undiagnosed heart abnormality and that the only way to have prevented it was if she'd gotten screened. But still, I couldn't shake the feeling that I'd triggered it by doing the whole horror movie routine. I should have just climbed Agnes Tree, like she'd wanted.

We worked through that, too. Slowly but surely. And then, instead of just knowing that Imogen's death wasn't my fault, I believed it. I started sleeping more. I stopped hearing Imogen's voice in my head all the time. By spring, I didn't need therapy. I felt like me again. At least, the me I am without Imogen. I'd gone through all the awfulness.

And now I'm out.

I turn so I'm directly facing Mom, and I look her straight in the eye. "I'm okay now. I really am."

Mom takes a deep breath and blows it out slowly. "I know," she says quietly.

I raise my eyebrows. "You do?"

She nods, swallowing hard. "No one should have to go through what you did. Not at your age. But watching you work through it..." She puts her hand on her chest. "You're so resilient. So strong." She blinks away a tear building up in her eye and smiles. "You've always been like that, you know. I don't know how this sappy old soul made you. When you were a baby, I cried more than you did. And everyone said you needed a father, a male influence, blah, blah, blah. But nope. You turned out amazing anyway."

I smile. My dad was never really in the picture. His name is Devon, and he was an international student from Scotland who Mom met in grad school. I obviously wasn't planned, but Mom wanted to raise me and was okay with the fact that Devon didn't. Maybe I'll meet him one day, maybe I won't. All I know is that Mom has always been enough for me.

She tilts her head so it's resting on mine, the strands of our hair mixing together. From far away, our hair looks identically black. But when you look up close, when you see the strands mingled together like this, all the different, distinct hues are so clear. There's Mom's darker, jet-black glisten. My slightly lighter mahogany tones.

"You're *you*," Mom says, squeezing me to her side. "My strong, fearless girl."

The knots in my stomach loosen as I breathe in her words.

A minute later, Mom lifts her head and says, "But so help me God, if you ever ride a unicorn or anything else not meant to roll down a hill again, you're grounded indefinitely. Hear me?"

"I hear you." I give her a solemn nod.

"Swear on the book." Mom points to *The Big Book of Why* on the bottom corner of my cube shelf, and I sigh. When I was younger, whenever Mom was really serious about me not doing something again, she had me swear on *The Big Book of Why* because she liked the ritual of swearing on a Bible, but we weren't religious. It's been forever since she's asked, but I don't argue. I stand up from the bed and slide it out, seeing a flash of bright green behind it.

The cover of a book Imogen lent me a few months before she died. A play called *Arcadia*.

A complicated mix of sensations hits me all at once. The familiar dull ache when I see something that belonged to her. But also something sharper. A prick of remorse. A stab of disappointment. I swallow it down and quickly look away.

"I swear I'll never ride a unicorn or anything else not meant to roll down a hill again," I project, standing in front of Mom, my hand on the book.

Mom nods, satisfied, tossing *The Big Book of Why* onto

my bed. After she leaves, I plunk down on my bed, too. In the quiet of my room, I hear Mom's words again.

You're you. My strong, fearless girl.

I take a breath before springing up and packing the rest of my clothes and toiletries. I put all my ghost chasing equipment in my backpack: tripod, Mom's old Sony FX1 camera, my Mini Maglite flashlight, and my headlamp, which I tuck carefully into the front pocket. I stash everything by the door and get ready for bed.

I'm crossing my room to flick off the light when my eyes catch on something. *Arcadia* is lying faceup on the carpet next to my shelf, its glossy green cover shining in the light.

I must have jostled it when I pulled out *The Big Book of Why*, and then it slid off the shelf. I keep my mind carefully blank as I pick up *Arcadia* and put it back in its place, stuffing *The Big Book of Why* in front of it again. I turn off the lights and climb into bed, turning my thoughts quickly to tomorrow.

Because tomorrow, I'm going to the Harlow Hotel.

chapter four

October, eight months before Imogen dies

I study my reflection in the mirror, trying to figure out what's missing. I've got cakey alabaster foundation whiting my face out, dark smudges under my eyes, and a blood-stained white nightgown. But it needs something. It's my first time working at Terror in the Corn haunted maze, and I need to look perfect.

Footsteps clamber up the stairs. Usually, Imogen's stride is so quiet I can't hear her coming at all, so she must be excited about something. I'm wondering what it could be as I position myself in front of my bedroom door, fixing my face into a demented smile just as it swings open.

"Ahhhhhh!" Imogen's scream quickly morphs into a laugh. "You look amazing!"

"It's missing something, though. Right?"

"Hmmm." Imogen examines me, bouncing on her toes, her face slightly flushed. She *is* excited about something, which is odd because it's Saturday night, which means she has to play the piano at the Silver Lake Retirement Home, which she once described as "like *Hellraiser* but more painful." Not because she hates volunteering or old people or playing the piano. She just hates playing the piano in front of people. She told me that when she plays, it feels so personal, like she's putting her thoughts and feelings and—when she's really going for it—her soul into each note and phrase and trill. When she has to play for other people, it feels like they're reading her diary or pawing through her closet.

She doesn't even like playing in front of me. Sometimes she has to get her forty-five minutes of practice in even when I'm over at her house, and she always tells me to hang out in her room while she goes downstairs to the piano. I don't think she knows that I can still hear the notes—sometimes sunny, sometimes sad—floating around me. I don't think she knows that I listen, wondering what it's like to translate your feelings into music.

"What's with you?" I raise my eyebrow. "Why are you all happy?"

"Hold on, let me do this first," Imogen says, still bouncing a little. "You need blood on your face." She grabs the bottle of liquid blood from my dresser and unscrews the cap. "Around the mouth?"

"Too vampire. Streaks down the forehead?"

"Too *Carrie*. We need 'possessed girl' vibes without being too *Exorcist*-y. Ooh, I got it!"

I don't even ask what she's going to do. I just offer up my face, and Imogen carefully paints streaky lines of blood from the bottom of my eyes down to my chin.

"Perfect." I smile at myself in the mirror before turning back to Imogen. "Okay, so what's going on?"

Imogen pulls her phone from her bag and holds it up to me. "Boulder Community Theater is doing *Arcadia*!"

I gasp. I can only partially remember what *Arcadia* is about, but I know Imogen loves that play. "When is it? We'll go."

"No, you should audition!" Imogen squeals. The bouncing is more like full-on jumping now.

"What?"

"For the role of Thomasina!"

"Who?"

"Okay, okay." Imogen puts her hands out. "Let me go back. The play takes place on this big English estate during two different time periods—the early 1800s and the present day. In the 1800s, there's this girl Thomasina and her tutor, Septimus. Thomasina is a genius. She discovers all these scientific concepts by accident, just by observing the world around her. Like chaos theory and the second law of thermodynamics, stuff that won't be discovered officially for years. She and Septimus have all these witty, intellectual conversations about science and history and stuff."

"So...," I say slowly. "Thomasina's a genius? And that makes you think of me why?"

"Because! She's smart and fierce and funny and confident. Trust me, you'd kill her lines."

I furrow my eyebrows, staring at my bloody reflection in the mirror like it'll be able to tell me what Imogen is talking about.

"Anyway," Imogen goes on. "In the present-day timeline, these researchers find out that Thomasina died in a fire when she was sixteen. They track down her notebooks and find all her brilliant math and science work. And they're sad because she never got to grow up and discover more things, but they also realize that everything Thomasina found, all the theories she developed back then, was discovered again later. They didn't die when she died. They were found, piece by piece, by other people. There's a lot more that happens, but the point is, nothing is truly lost."

"That sounds..." I stop because I can't think of how to finish the sentence. It's a lot to take in. "Plays aren't really my thing, though." I've never been involved in the plays at school, and I haven't done any drama club stuff.

"Why not? You're a really good actor. Do your Terror in the Corn routine again."

I sigh but duck behind my cube shelf. After a few seconds, I jump out. "Go back," I hiss gutturally. "They'll kill you!"

"*See?* That was amazing! If there were Oscars for haunted corn mazes, you'd totally get one!"

"Okay, but a play is different than a haunted corn maze."

Like, a lot different. Plays are serious. Intellectual. More like something Imogen would do if she wasn't scared of public speaking.

"I'll lend you my copy of *Arcadia* so you can see what it's all about," Imogen says, blatantly ignoring me. "Auditions are this spring, and I really think you should do it."

I'm about to argue again, but all of a sudden, I'm imagining myself on a stage. Saying a bunch of smart-sounding lines. Pretending to be a prodigy making scientific discoveries and having intellectual conversations. An odd sensation forms in my chest—deep and warm and sparkling, like bubbles fizzing and popping and expanding inside me.

"Fine. I'll think about it."

"Yaaaaay!" Imogen squeals, doing a clumsy little dance. But then she glances at her phone, and her face drops. "I have to go soon."

She heaves a deep sigh and steps up to my mirror, smoothing a loose piece of dark blond hair back into the chignon at the nape of her neck. Her mom always makes her wear a low chignon whenever she has something "important" to do. Piano recital? Chignon. Eighth-grade valedictorian speech? Chignon. Dinner with extended family who literally could not care less about what Imogen's hair looks like? Chignon. Imogen always said it made her feel way too fancy, like she should be wearing gloves and a tiara, but of course she always did it without argument.

"I wish I could go with you tonight," Imogen says to her reflection.

"Then bail."

"I can't bail. Volunteering is an important part of the whole 'get Imogen into an Ivy' plan, and now that we're sophomores, my parents are getting really extra about it. They keep bringing up how Bea made the biggest mistake of her life by following her girlfriend to Johns Hopkins instead of going to Yale. The horror."

I scoff. I hardly know Imogen's sister, Bea, because she's ten years older and lives in Maryland. Imogen sees her on holidays and talks to her on the phone, but Bea doesn't come home that often.

"But, of course, *Imogen* would never do that." Imogen lapses into a spot-on impression of her mom, complete with gigantic fake smile and overenunciated vowels. "Imogen would never give up an Ivy League education for something as frivolous as romance."

I roll my eyes, running my fingers through my hair, trying to make it look stringier. "Does your mom think people don't have lives if they don't go to an Ivy? I obviously won't be going to one. Maybe I won't go to college at all. Does she think I'm going to be staring at a wall for the rest of my life?"

Imogen does a full-on gasp. "You might not go to college?"

"Joshua Jacobs didn't go to college."

"And that matters why?"

"It proves you don't need a college degree to become television's greatest ghost hunter."

"But college isn't just about finding a job. It's about finding yourself. Learning about the world. Figuring out your purpose." Imogen looks at me expectantly, starry-eyed and smiling, like she's straight out of a college brochure.

"My purpose is hunting fake ghosts with a hot guy."

"Your purpose is *not* hunting fake ghosts with a hot guy." Imogen opens her mouth to say something else, but she's cut off by the shrill beep of her alarm. She clicks it off and turns to pick up her bag, the enthusiasm from a second ago completely gone.

"Good luck tonight," she says, her voice sounding small. "You're going to be amazing."

"Good luck, too. It'll be over before you know it."

Imogen takes a wobbly breath and brushes her fingers against her left wrist. "Shoot. I keep thinking it's still there."

I look down at my own left wrist, encircled by a bracelet of white beads. Last year, Imogen got us matching ones at the Denver Art Museum gift shop. They're actually really cool—irregularly shaped, round white beads flecked with translucent spots, like hailstones, which is why she had to get them. Imogen has been obsessed with hailstorms ever since one hit us in Estes Park a few years ago.

It had been a clear day, and we were sitting out on the porch of the Harlow, sweating from the heat. And then boom, the ice stones started rocketing down from the sky. We ran inside and craned our necks up to watch. It felt a little bit like magic. Then Imogen spent the rest of the day looking up hailstorm facts on her phone, telling me all about ice particles and updrafts.

Imogen's bracelet broke a few days ago. We were walking out of school, Imogen fiddling with her bracelet like she always did, but that time, the elastic snapped, and all the beads plunked to the ground.

"I know it's dramatic," Imogen says, frowning at her wrist. "But I feel exposed without it. Like everyone knows I'm walking around with something missing."

I hold out my arm, waving my bracelet in front of her face. "Borrow mine. Maybe it'll help."

Imogen smiles a little and reaches out. But all she does is tug gently on the bracelet, letting it go so it snaps back onto my wrist. "I'll be okay."

I hate that her voice is so small, so scared. I can't make her stand up for herself. I can't stop her from going. But I can distract her. Maybe I can distract her enough so that she feels more brave. "I know what we need," I say, scampering over to my bed and picking up my phone. "The Song."

Imogen's eyebrows flicker up, even though she still looks like she wants to disappear.

I scroll through Apple Music and bring up Celine Dion's "To Love You More." It's our go-to hype song ever since my mom belted it when it came on the radio as she was picking us up from the movies one day. I'd teased her for it, but then Imogen and I adopted it as our own. It's basically five and a half minutes of balls-to-the-wall emotion.

I press Play, and my room fills with a sentimental violin melody, followed by Celine Dion's voice singing about a lost love. I sing along, giving some truly terrible vibrato. Imogen is singing, too, but she still looks deflated. "Louder!" I command.

Imogen smiles and closes her eyes, projecting her voice. Our favorite part is coming, the part where we go for it with everything we have. Imogen opens her eyes. We grab each other's hands and start spinning. *"I'll be waiting for you!"* we belt at the top of our lungs, laughing through the next line like we always do. *"I'm the one who wants to love you more!"*

"Wooooo!" I scream. We keep singing, gesturing wildly with our hands and arms, and Imogen doesn't look nervous anymore. Suddenly, she runs to my window and throws it open.

"Sing out the window!" she yells over the song.

I leap over to stand beside her. "Why?"

"Because..." She pauses. She has that focused, faraway look that means she's thinking of a story. "Because okay, if we sing it loud enough, it'll project into space. Like a broadcast. And it'll travel around for a hundred years out there, and some civilization, light years away, will hear it. And it'll make them laugh. And one of the aliens will come to Earth to meet the girls who sang the song. But we'll be long dead by then. But we won't really be dead. That's the whole point. Because a part of us will still be out there, singing The Song."

And there it is again, that sparkling feeling in my chest. I look out at the same stretch of sky I've seen out my window my entire life, but it seems different tonight. It's not just the sky anymore. It's *space* now, full of distant aliens who love music. Imogen could always do that: make the world feel bigger, full of wild possibilities.

I don't even mean to, but I picture myself onstage again, saying lines about science and history and how nothing is truly lost.

The chorus is coming up again. We take a huge breath, pressing our noses into my window screen.

"*I'll be waiting for you,*" we sing as loudly as we can. It strains my throat and rings in my ears. And some small, irrational part of me believes, just for a second, that the aliens are listening.

chapter five

Ten days until the Spirit Ball

The Harlow Hotel always looks bigger than I remember. You'd think everything in Estes Park would seem small compared to the Rocky Mountains. But the Harlow's gleaming white facade and red roof sprawl out against the mountains and sky, stubbornly trying to stand out.

"Are you completely and totally sure you want to do this?" Mom asks as I peer out the passenger-side window. She insisted on driving me because Highway 36 is narrow and winding. She also said she wanted the chance to chat since we'd be apart for ten days, but we were quiet the whole way up the mountain.

"I'm sure." I tear my eyes away from the window, running my fingers over the smooth white beads of my bracelet, feeling a quick burst of confidence. I can do this.

Mom clutches the steering wheel. "If anything happens, anything at all, call me. I'll come right back and pick you up."

"What's going to happen?" I ask, giving her a smile. Mom leans over to hug me, holding on longer than usual. Then I'm out of the car, dragging my suitcase up the steps to the wide front porch, breathing in the dry, pine-scented air.

I'm supposed to meet Dr. Bobincheck by the front desk in five minutes, so I hurry across the porch, past the shiny red hummingbird feeders and wicker rocking chairs and into the lobby. Where everything looks the same.

I let out a breath. Of course it's the same. Nothing about the Harlow lobby has changed in all the summers I've been here. The dark red carpet, the mahogany furniture, the dim lighting. The same smoky scent perfumes the air. The game shelf still lines the front wall. I spot the Ouija board box on the bottom shelf, stuffed in between Monopoly and Trivial Pursuit.

It's all the same except for one thing.

There's a strange silence hanging in the air. Like the stillness after the hum of the air conditioner goes off. Like the quiet in my car after Dave's party. Like someone turned off a vital, familiar sound.

It's even stranger because the lobby is filled with chatter from guests asking questions at the front desk, checking out the antique elevator, talking about Agnes Thripp's photo. But it all seems muted somehow, like the silence is trying to snuff it out.

I grip the handle of my suitcase, shaking away the bizarre feeling. And when I turn toward the front desk, I see something that makes it disappear in an instant. Leander Hall is standing there, looking just as unpleasantly surprised to see me as I am to see him.

Suddenly, he's all I can think about, and I don't know whether to be annoyed or grateful. I roll my suitcase across the carpet, glancing around for any pretentious-looking adults nearby who could be his parents. Maybe he's on a family vacation and will only be here a couple of days. "What are you doing here?"

"You really like asking me that question," Leander says.

A suitcase the size of mine is resting beside him, and I realize that the chances of Leander's parents sweeping in to carry him away are growing slimmer. "There's no possible way you're doing your senior project here," I say.

Leander shoots me his sarcastic smile. "I guess I'm about to expand your view of what's possible."

I sigh aggressively as I process this new reality. Leander Hall—Mr. Truth Hurts, the guy who showed up drunk to a party he wasn't invited to and grabbed my elbow for no reason—is going to be living at the Harlow for ten days.

"What's your project?" I ask before I can stop myself. I should just ignore him, and after he answers my question, I will. It's just that Leander Hall doing his senior project at a haunted hotel doesn't compute. He's way too serious, way too much of a killjoy for that.

"I'm writing an article on Agnes Thripp and her

influence on the American public's belief in Spiritualism," he says easily. "You?"

I'm stunned into silence as an odd, protective feeling washes over me. I know Agnes Thripp is a locally famous figure, but it sometimes felt that only Imogen and I knew about her. It doesn't feel right having Leander Hall poking around in her business. But it's not like Agnes Thripp is alive to care. I clear my throat. "I'm filming my audition for *Ghost Chasers: Teen Investigators.*"

Leander blinks at me. "Why?"

I never knew a single word could sound so judgmental. "Why are *you* writing about Agnes Thripp? Who are you trying to piss off now?"

I catch a quick eye roll. "This may shock you, but the primary goal of my articles isn't to piss people off."

"What is the *primary goal,* then?"

"To tell the truth. Even if people don't want to hear it."

"And you're the guy who sees all truth, I guess."

"No, I'm the guy who does research and doesn't pretend everything is fine when it isn't," he snaps, before going silent and then looking away.

I stare at him, having no clue how to respond. Seriously, what is his deal?

"Greetings!" a voice behind us calls, and we both jump. I turn to see a tall thirty-something white woman in a tailored navy blazer. "I'm Dr. Bobincheck, but you can call me Dr. B." I remember her from the senior project assembly.

Under her blazer I see a T-shirt that reads IT'S AN EXCELLENT DAY FOR AN EXORCISM. I like her immediately.

"You must be Natalie." Dr. B shakes my hand before turning to Leander. "And that would make you Leonard."

And now, I *love* her.

Leander clears his throat. "It's Leander," he says as I stifle a snort.

"Ah, right." Dr. B squints down at her clipboard, pulling a pen out of the voluminous bun on top of her head. "Sincerest apologies, Leander." She scribbles something on the clipboard before looking back up and waving a hand between us. "I see you two have already met. You're our only two senior project-ees this summer, so I'm sure you'll be seeing a lot of each other."

"Great," Leander mutters.

"Terrific," I say back.

"Let's start the tour!" Dr. B says chirpily, starting across the lobby. All through the porter taking our bags out to the dorm building and Dr. B's tour of the library and billiards room, Leander and I stay a healthy distance apart. But I can't help glancing at him a few times, watching him write notes in a leather journal, wondering why he's interested in Agnes Thripp and why he seems extra intense right now and why I keep noticing his eyes—how vivid they look when he's focusing on something. I mentally pinch myself. Noticing his eyes is the *opposite* of ignoring him.

"And here's our Agnes," Dr. B says as we circle back

to the lobby, gesturing to the photo mounted on the stone fireplace—Agnes Thripp in the rocking chair on the porch, a fleet of hummingbirds over her head. "She'll obviously be of interest to both of you because she's the most famous Harlow ghost." Dr. B nods to me before turning to Leander. "And because her life and especially her death played a role in shifting attitudes toward Spiritualism." Dr. B glances back at the photo and launches into the familiar story.

How Agnes Thripp was a well-known medium in her day who wanted to prove the existence of an afterlife so much that when she got pneumonia in the summer of 1920, she refused treatment. She wanted to die, to go to the other side so she could send back proof of it to the living. Agnes made a pact with another medium, her friend Cynthia Harding, that once she was on the other side, she'd send a message, thus proving that the dead could speak. On July 8, 1920, in Room 303 of the Harlow Hotel, Agnes died.

And Cynthia waited. She held séances attempting to call forth Agnes's spirit. She listened and looked for any messages, any signs, however small. There were newspaper reports following the story, both believers and skeptics eager to know the outcome.

Which was that Cynthia never got a message from Agnes. A lot of people took that as proof that the dead couldn't speak to the living. Some took it as proof that the afterlife didn't exist. Spiritualism was already on the decline, and stuff like that only made it less and less popular.

It made sense to me, why believers would stop believing after that. But Imogen always said that just because Cynthia never got a message, it didn't mean that Agnes wasn't out there somewhere.

There are other possible explanations, she'd say, brimming with conviction.

"There are other possible explanations," Leander says, tapping his pen against his notebook. I stare at him, my heartbeat quickening. I know, logically, that the words came out of his mouth. It's just that for a second, it felt like Imogen's voice, echoing from years ago.

"Yes, absolutely." Dr. B nods enthusiastically. "There are a lot of theories as to why Cynthia never got a message from Agnes. For example, perhaps time is different in the afterlife. Maybe a day on Earth is like a millisecond over there, and Agnes hasn't had time to send her message yet. There are even plenty of mediums who have sworn over the years that they *have* gotten a message from her. And Harlow Hotel guests claim to have encounters with Agnes all the time."

"What kind of encounters?" Leander asks, and I look up at him again because I thought he was interested in the real Agnes, not her fake ghost.

"Oh, all sorts of things," Dr. B says. "A whispered name. The thump of a cane across the floor. The hummingbird feeders swaying on a windless night. That one's pretty common. Agnes loved hummingbirds and was known to add more sugar to the feeders to attract them. Many guests watch the feeders closely, hoping to catch old Aggie trying to sweeten the water."

I'd heard similar stories about the feeders. I never believed them, of course. Imogen didn't, either, but she did believe that Agnes was out there somewhere. When we found the hummingbird figurine in Agnes Tree when we were eleven, Imogen spun that whole story about how it was the missing message from Agnes. I can still see her excited smile, her eyes impossibly bright behind the mint-green glasses she had that year, the ones that were a touch too big for her face.

I glance away from the photo to the two leather chairs around the fireplace. The mahogany coffee table resting between them, where we played Ouija last summer. The memory washes over me like a sudden blast of wind.

The screech of the planchette zipping across the Ouija board.

"Cheese and crackers!"

Laughter, loud and giddy and unrestrained.

"Natalie?" Dr. B is saying, looking at me expectantly.

"Sorry, what?" I say, breathing through the ache in my chest.

"Do you plan to focus on Agnes in your *Ghost Chasers* footage?"

"Oh, yeah. Of course." I have to. There are other supposed ghosts that haunt the Harlow—Spiritualists and maids and children. But it wouldn't make sense not to focus on Agnes when she's so tied to the Harlow Hotel's history.

"Good." Dr. B nods. "You shouldn't have any trouble

finding people to interview about her. People love talking about Agnes around here."

I try to smile as Dr. B turns to lead us downstairs to the basement level. It's more modern-looking down here, with bright overhead lights and a tiled linoleum floor. Relief seeps through me. Imogen and I never spent much time in the basement, so the whole place feels unfamiliar. Clean of memories. There are a few nondescript offices and a café called Jitter Beans with shiny metal tables and a hand-chalked menu of specialty drinks. I take a deep, coffee-scented breath, and the ache in my chest melts away.

Dr. B shows us the small staff cafeteria and the archives room, where Leander will hopefully be holed up for the entire time we're here. Then she shows us the door to the underground tunnel that runs between the hotel and the employee dorms. I stand on my tiptoes, peeking over Dr. B's shoulder at the rust-colored door, wishing it was open a crack. I've never seen the tunnel because you have to be an employee to get access, but it's supposedly one of the most haunted locations in the hotel. I'll have access to it now, which means I can feature it in my audition footage. And if I know anything about *Ghost Chasers*, it's that a dark, underground location is pretty much all you need to create the illusion that you've seen a ghost.

As Dr. B walks us toward the café, my eye catches on another door with a shiny copper sign.

MADAME ALTHEA: RESIDENT MEDIUM AND GUIDE TO THE SPIRITUAL REALM

I perk up even more. I've always known that the Harlow has a resident medium, but I've never noticed her office before. I'll for sure interview her for my audition footage. *Ghost Chasers* episodes always have at least one interview with a "paranormal professional" who talks about energy and frequencies, making the whole investigation seem more scientific.

I'm bringing out my phone to see if I can get her contact information when I catch Leander peeking inside the narrow window that runs alongside Madame Althea's door. It's covered with a lacy cream curtain, but Leander is ducking his head, trying to see through the gaps.

Great. Leander is going to want to interview Madame Althea, too. A not-completely-rational desire to interview her first comes over me, and I vow to email her as soon as I can.

After the tour, Dr. B leads us to a small metal table in the corner of the café. "Here's the part where I tell you the rules," Dr. B says as we all sit down.

"First and foremost, you're here to work on your senior projects. I'll serve as your supervisor, and you'll have check-in meetings with me, but the goal is for you to self-direct, so I'll be very hands-off. Since both of your projects concern Agnes Thripp, there could be some potential for productive collaboration. But in the past, collaboration has sometimes led to distraction, so remember that you're here for your projects, and not for anything else." She raises her eyebrow sharply, and I realize what she means by "anything else" at the same time as Leander. He winces and I scooch over in my chair.

"There's also the Conference for the Paranormal that you'll both be expected to present at on the last Saturday of your stay. Just a ten-minute summary of your project and what you've learned here, presented to a community of supernatural scholars."

My skin goes clammy as I picture a crowd of scholars blinking up at me, waiting for me to tell them what I've learned. I feel myself deflating until Dr. B mentions the Spirit Ball, reminding me that the torture of the presentation will be worth it.

"Last thing," Dr. B says, pointing over her shoulder to the rust-red door that leads to the employee tunnel. "Don't walk through the tunnel alone."

There's a heavy pause. I sneak another glance at Leander, but he looks as confused as I do. It's like Dr. B just gave us the Elder's Warning. The part of the horror movie where a local says to stay away from the woods/mines/abandoned amusement park/tunnel...

"I swear it's not as ominous as it sounds," Dr. B says with a little laugh. "The tunnel is completely, totally safe. It's just that it can be unsettling. The mind can play tricks. I suppose it's the whole 'being underground' thing. I don't want either of you to feel spooked here. So, I'd feel better about it if you buddied up and walked together, at least when it's dark out."

I would rather run into Hannibal Lector in a butcher

shop than buddy up with Leander Hall, but I say, "Okay," and Leander gives a vague nod, so Dr. B seems satisfied. With a wave and a reminder to get started on our projects, she heads into one of the offices. And it's just me and Leander again.

I run my finger over the metal ridges of the table edge, wondering how rude it would be to get up and leave.

And then Leander gets up and leaves.

"Jagoff," I mutter, not caring if he hears.

After Leander disappears upstairs, I drum my fingers on the table. The café has gotten quiet as late morning rolls around, but thankfully, it's not like the strange silence when I first walked into the lobby. I shudder just thinking about it.

But then I remember something Dr. Salamando said once. She said that the places we associate with people who have died can have a visceral effect on us, triggering memories and emotions and even physical feelings. That's probably what happened up there. She said some people avoid those places because they're scared of how intense the feelings can be.

I'm not scared. The Harlow Hotel is full of memories, but I can handle it. I *am* handling it. I just walked through the Harlow Hotel for the first time since Imogen died. The hardest part is over.

I feel my shoulders loosen up as I turn my focus to the *Ghost Chasers* audition. My camera and the rest of my equipment are out in the dorms. I look longingly at the door to the tunnel, but even though I have no intention of following Dr. B's "buddy up" plan, I also don't want her to see me ignoring her advice on the first day.

So, I go the long way. Back upstairs, through the lobby, and out onto the front porch, where the late-morning sunlight bounces cheerfully off the white rocking chairs. A few tourists are leaning against the railing, staring out at the green, tree-covered mountains and the silver-gray ones beyond. Patches of yarrow dot the edges of the Harlow's front courtyard, dipping slightly in the breeze, like they're waving at me.

A hummingbird buzzes by, hovering by one of the feeder ports above my shoulder, its wings a blur. It has a ruby-red neck, just like the crystal figurine Imogen and I found in Agnes Tree.

The one I'll never see again. After Imogen's funeral, her sister, Bea, asked me if there was anything of Imogen's I wanted. I immediately thought of the hummingbird tucked away in the dollhouse. It was both of ours, really, but we'd decided Imogen should keep it because she was better at not losing things. I wanted to ask for it, but Bea's sharp green eyes were red and swollen, and the smell of lilies in the church was making me nauseous, and I was so tired I felt like at any second, my bones and muscles would give up and I'd collapse onto the floor.

I said no. And now, it's probably gone. Donated or packed away in an attic in Arizona, where the Lucases moved.

The hummingbird suddenly zooms inches from my

face, and I take a surprised step back. It tilts its head and fans out its tail feathers before flying away.

My eyes follow it across the surrounding resort—the crafts center, the dining hall, the mini golf course. I'm still watching as it disappears down the familiar path that dips behind the trees, the Starlight Trail that took Imogen and me back to our cabins.

I stare down the trail for a long time, not knowing why, before I turn away.

chapter six

My dorm room is like a square pine box. Knots cover the walls, gazing out like eyes in the wheat-colored wood. There's a simple wooden desk, a matching dresser, and green-and-pink flowery curtains over the window. Dr. B mentioned on the tour that the dorms were built in the 1920s to accommodate seasonal hotel workers, and that the Harlow wanted them to be as homey as possible. I appreciate the effort, but the room has a stuffy, suffocating feel.

I shoot a quick email to Madame Althea introducing myself and asking for an interview, grab my camera bag, and head back out to the lobby to film, working out a script in my head on the way.

In the lobby, I find the best spots to film and wait for

lulls in noise and activity. Then I turn my camera around, selfie style, and press Record.

"When you step into the Harlow Hotel, it feels like you're stepping back in time," I say in a clear but hushed voice, starting a slow walk through the lobby. "A time when a group of Spiritualists visited Estes Park, Colorado, and heard the voices of the dead whispering in the dry mountain air."

I keep walking to the grand staircase and pan around the portraits hanging there. "The rich, spiritual energy they felt here is the reason they chose this spot to build a hotel for Spiritualists, a gathering place for mediums and all people who wanted to speak with the dead."

I walk to the stone fireplace. "Those Spiritualists have passed on themselves, but the spirit energy remains. There are many ghosts said to haunt the Harlow Hotel. But the most mysterious one"—I focus in on the photo mounted above the fireplace—"is Agnes Thripp."

I stop there and do it a few more times, trying out different pauses, emphasizing different words, taking different routes around the lobby.

The whole time, two front desk employees watch me, whispering to each other. When I finish, I hear a sharp "Psst!" and glance up to see them waving me over.

"You're auditioning for *Ghost Chasers*, right?" a college-aged girl with blond hair asks. She's got a nose ring and a name tag that reads CLARISSA.

"Yup."

"We've got ghost stories," Clarissa says, gesturing between herself and a guy who looks about the same age. "If you want to interview us."

"Really? That would be awesome." Interviews with locals are a key part of any *Ghost Chasers* episode. The team would hear their stories and then investigate the most interesting claims. "Is one of the stories about the tunnel?" I ask hopefully.

"Silas has a tunnel story. A good one." The girl elbows the guy, who gives me a telegenic smile.

"I'm still on shift now," Silas says, "but maybe tomorrow morning?"

"That would be gr—"

"Did you say you're auditioning for *Ghost Chasers*?" A middle-aged woman wearing a shirt that says I SPEAK ELK taps me on the shoulder. "Because the strangest thing happened to me last night. . . ." She tells me about a woman wearing an old-fashioned dress who was leaning against the porch rail. "She looked exactly like the woman in that picture." She points a finger at the Agnes photo over the fireplace.

A friend of hers joins us, telling us about how when she came out of the bathroom this morning, her bed was made, and she never makes her bed in the morning. They both assure me they would be willing to be interviewed, too.

I take their names and promise to interview them tomorrow morning, shocked at how eager everyone is to be part of a *Ghost Chasers* audition.

Even better, when I head down to Jitter Beans to edit my intro, the footage looks great. The shakiness of the camera fits in with *Ghost Chasers'* whole "I'm an intrepid ghost hunter" vibe. All I need now are the interviews with locals, some night vision footage of the tunnel, and a few breathless utterings of *Oh my God, what was that?*

This is going to be easy.

I sit back and refresh my email again, but still no reply from Madame Althea. I go back to editing and planning out questions for my interviews tomorrow, continuing to work while I eat dinner in the staff cafeteria and text Mom back, assuring her several times that everything is okay. Before I know it, it's dusky outside the window. I stretch and roll out my neck, checking the time on my phone and seeing it's almost eight o'clock. I gather my things and eye the door to the employee tunnel. Dr. B must be gone by now, so this could be my chance to check it out. But then I hear the noise from upstairs.

A swell of muffled voices, growing louder and louder. I shoulder my camera bag and head upstairs, the voices getting more distinct as I step into the lobby and see a crowd of people buzzing with excitement, heading toward the old billiards room. I go with them, catching snippets of conversation—"Madame Althea" and "spirits" and "vibrational frequency." I'm about to ask what's going on when I smack into something tall and firm just outside the pocket doors.

Leander.

"What's going on?" I ask him, mostly because I don't

want to think about the fact that after we collided, Leander automatically shot his arm out to steady me, his hand clasping my shoulder before he realized I wasn't falling.

"Sorry," Leander says, clearing his throat. It may be the dim lighting in here, but I swear there's a sweep of a blush on his cheeks. I know I'm staring, but it's so unexpected that I can't look away.

"Madame Althea is doing a free public reading," he says, glancing inside the billiards room. "She'll deliver messages from deceased loved ones to specific people in the crowd."

"Oh." I peek inside the room, too, taking in the brass lighting fixtures overhead, a few of them flickering like candles. I wonder if that's an on-purpose effect or if they just need new bulbs. There are chairs set out in neat rows and a small portable stage at the front of the room. I'm super curious to see what Madame Althea is like in action. And maybe I can catch her afterward and ask her in person for an interview.

When I look back at Leander, the blush is gone, and without another word, he strides into the billiards room, taking a seat in the almost-full front row. I watch him for a beat as he taps his pen on the leather journal he's always carrying around, twirls it around in his fingers, sticks it behind his ear, and then takes it out again. Like he's excited? Or nervous? Why does he even want to be here in the first place? I could see wanting to interview Madame Althea for his project, but what does her public reading have to do with Agnes Thripp?

God, I need to stop speculating about Leander Hall. And I really need to stop picturing how his face looked when he blushed, all soft and genuine, so different from the sarcastic smile I'm used to.

I turn my gaze away from the front row and head into the billiards room. There aren't any empty chairs left, so I sit at the far end of the long wooden bench mounted against the side wall. On the tour, Dr. B said this was where women used to sit and watch men play billiards. I run my fingers along the smooth, worn wood, imagining a bunch of bored women doing the same thing over a hundred years ago as they watched men poke balls with sticks.

Before long, a woman in a flowing yellow dress breezes into the room. The crowd hushes as she walks down the aisle and jumps spryly onto the stage.

There's something about her eyes that makes me stare. They're the palest kind of blue. So pale they almost blend into the whites. Her hair is striking, too. Waist-length and dark brown with strands of silver that twinkle like tinsel in the light.

"Welcome." Madame Althea's voice fills every inch of this old space, from the red carpet to the wooden ceiling beams. "Tonight, we open ourselves up to the world beyond our own. To those who walk among us unseen, to the spirits of the departed who wish to speak." She holds her hands out, palms up. "Let us welcome them."

A deeper quiet falls over the room, and I find myself holding my breath, even though I believe Madame Althea can speak to the dead as much as I believe Leander will lead the school in a rousing rendition of "We Are the Champions" at the next pep rally. But what can I say, she's good. She'll be perfect for *Ghost Chasers*, if she lets me interview her.

Madame Althea closes her eyes, breathing in and out a few times. The sound of it is peaceful, lulling.

"I'm connecting with a woman, a mother figure," she says, opening her eyes and placing a hand on her chest. "I'm sensing a weakness in the heart. And the letter *S*. A name that begins with *S*. Does that mean something to anyone?"

There's a pause, and then a man with salt-and-pepper hair sitting in the third row raises a shaky hand.

Madame Althea smiles warmly. "Hello. Please, tell us your name."

"Dan Callahan," he says, stopping to clear his throat. "My mother's name was Sharon. She died of a stroke five months ago, caused by heart disease."

The audience rustles, whispering and turning in their seats, as Madame Althea nods. "I'm getting a strong scent of roses. Does this mean anything to you?"

Dan's lips part in surprise. "Roses were her favorite flower."

More whispering. Madame Althea nods briskly, like she already knew. "Is there something you would like to ask your mother, Dan?"

Dan takes a few seconds to compose himself. "I lost something of hers when I was a boy. It was special to her, and I've felt terrible about it all my life. Of course, she said she forgave me, but she was a stoic woman. Never let what she was really feeling show. I have to know. Does she truly forgive me?"

Madame Althea tilts her head, and her eyes glaze over a little, like she's listening to a very faint voice. "It wasn't a ring, was it?"

Dan's gasp echoes in the dim room. "Yes!" The audience is louder now, murmuring among themselves. "Her wedding ring. I took it off her dressing table for a game I was playing—even though I knew it was wrong—and I lost it. My father had passed away a year earlier, so it was even harder on her that it was gone."

"Yes, she's with your father now. He's cutting in and insisting you stop feeling guilty." Madame Althea pauses again briefly. "And Sharon says of course she forgives you."

Dan starts to cry. He buries his face in his hands, his shoulders shaking as the man sitting beside him rubs comforting circles on his back. After a moment, he lifts his head to look back at the stage. "Thank you," he says, voice thick.

A hardness forms in my own throat. It feels like such a private moment, like I shouldn't be watching. I can feel his relief. He carried this guilt and doubt and sadness with him all this time, and now he's finally letting it go.

Madame Althea raises her arms once more, the audience quiets, and the reading continues. A woman wants to know if her friend who suffered from PTSD finally found peace in the afterlife (yes, her mind is finally free).

Another woman asks if her grandmother disapproves of her decision to pursue a career instead of have kids (no, it is the right decision for her). A man asks if his wife has reunited with their beloved dog on the other side (yes, Wanda and Lumpy are very happy together).

Each time, Madame Althea knows details that make the audience gasp and the question askers cry. Each time, there's that overwhelming sense of relief. And each time, I feel more and more uncomfortable, like I shouldn't be looking, like I shouldn't have come at all. The ghosts in this room aren't like the ones I heard about in the lobby earlier, who thumped canes and wore old-fashioned dresses and floated across the porch. These ghost stories aren't fun or spooky. They're just sad. I'm glad the people in the audience are getting comfort from what Madame Althea tells them. I'm glad they believe, I truly am. But it's not real.

As another audience member breaks down, my eyes drift again to Leander, pen moving swiftly across his notebook. I wish I could see what he's writing. There's no way Mr. Truth Hurts believes that Madame Althea can talk to the dead. Right?

Madame Althea raises her hands again. "We're almost out of time. But the room is crowded with spirits tonight. Let's hear what one more of them has to say."

I shift on the bench, more than ready to leave.

"I'm getting an *I*, the letter *I*." Madame Althea's voice floats out into the room, and her face turns melancholy. "It's a young spirit I'm connecting with. A girl."

I glance up as Madame Althea does the same pause as always, tilting her head like she's listening. "She wants to speak to her best friend."

My fingers tighten on the edge of the wooden bench, and I remind myself that none of this is real. But then Madame Althea looks at me, her pale blue eyes sparkling.

"Cheese and crackers."

chapter seven

I breathe in sharply, my heart pounding uncomfortably fast, like right after a jump scare in a horror movie, except not like that at all because there's no relief after. No laughing and sighing and thinking, *God, that was a really good one.* There's only my throbbing heart and a room full of people and my brain trying to remember what Dr. Salamando said about breathing when you feel like you're going to lose it. Focus on the exhale. Focus on the exhale. A forceful whoosh of air out.

Madame Althea blinks heavily, like she's coming out of a trance. She looks away from me and back into the audience, who is shifting around, half-excited, half-nervous. A few people have turned to look at me, including Leander, who's staring so intensely it almost burns.

"Apologies." Madame Althea holds her hands up to calm everyone down. "Sometimes when a spirit has a very strong desire to be heard, I let them speak for themselves. The result can look quite strange on the outside, but I assure you, it's nothing to be frightened of. Did that message mean anything to anyone?"

I glue my eyes to the floor as she scans the audience. I'm fine. Everything is fine. Mediums aren't real.

But how the fuck did she do that?

"No one?" Madame Althea smiles faintly. "Well. Spirits can be perplexing sometimes. If you think it might mean something, take it with you. It could become clear to you later."

The audience is still riled up, but Madame Althea thanks the spirits and brings the reading to a close. As soon as I hear clapping, I grab my stuff and bolt out of the pocket doors, back into the reddish glow of the lobby. But I need air. So I rush out onto the porch, leaning against the railing and whooshing out breaths, focusing on Dr. Salamando's voice telling me to release the overwhelming, unnameable feelings with each exhale. My heartbeat slows down as I blink out at the familiar dusky gray settling over the landscape, muting the rich greens of the pine trees.

Headlamp, I can almost hear Imogen say. *It'll be mountain dark soon.*

I shiver in the coolness of the night, forcing my eyes away from the Starlight Trail to stare at the outline of the Rocky Mountains in the distance, snowcapped even though it's June. I try to make my mind go blank, but it's hard when *How the fuck did she do that?* keeps blaring in my brain. I'm trying to calm down and think of rational explanations, when a memory nudges its way in. The summer before high school, walking through the Harlow Hotel's Spiritualists and Skeptics exhibit with Imogen.

"You don't believe that Agnes and the other Spiritualists could really *talk to the dead, right?" I ask.*

"Probably not all of them could. But maybe some?" Imogen pauses at a picture of two young women with dark, shiny hair, staring out at us. "Have you ever heard of the Fox sisters, Maggie and Kate?"

"Nope."

"Oh, it's a really good story. They were mediums who started the whole Spiritualist movement in the 1800s. When they were kids, they lived in this old farmhouse in New York. It was supposedly haunted. There was a rumor that years before, a peddler went into the house and never came out."

"Solid beginning. Continue."

"Maggie and Kate started hearing taps on their bedroom wall at night. They would say things like, 'If you're a spirit, tap three times,' and then they would hear three taps. They said it was the peddler speaking to them, the one who was supposedly killed in the house. People heard about what the sisters could do and wanted to see for themselves, so Maggie and Kate started talking to spirits in huge concert halls, where

everyone heard the taps. It was a big deal. They were booked for public demonstrations and séances all the time. National newspapers covered them and everything."

I look back up at the portrait, studying the sisters' solemn expressions. "They were eventually debunked, I'm guessing?"

"Well, yeah. Maggie later confessed that the whole thing was a hoax. She and Kate made the tapping sounds by cracking their toe joints."

I snort. "That's kind of amazing."

"But here's the cool part. Years after they died, some kids were playing in the Fox sisters' old farmhouse. And guess what they found in the walls."

I'm fully leaning forward now, dying to know.

"Bones," Imogen whispers. "A whole skeleton's worth of bones, right behind Maggie and Kate's bedroom wall, where they first heard the taps."

"The peddler," I say as goose bumps dot my arms. "Okay, yeah, that's a good story. It doesn't prove they were actually speaking to the dead, though."

Imogen shrugs. "Nope. But it pokes at your belief for a second, doesn't it? It makes you wonder. It's the final, eerie 'What if?'"

I scrunch my eyes closed. I don't even know why I'm thinking about this now because what happened in the billiards room was not a "what if" moment. It was a trick, and I don't care if I don't know how Madame Althea did it. I'm not falling for it. I turn around and stare up at the Harlow's white facade. I'm going back in. Because I'm fine, and mediums aren't real.

I stride back into the lobby, worming my way through the crowd. When I see Madame Althea outside the billiard room doors, swarmed by people, I look away. I still need her for my audition footage. But I don't want those pale blue eyes on me right now.

I make my way down the stairs to the basement, trying to focus on what I came here to do. I'll finally check out the tunnel, maybe get a few night shots. Then I'll head back to the dorms and play around with my footage some more.

"Hey." Leander stands up from one of the tables as I step into the nearly empty café. He casts a quick, assessing look over my face. "Ready to go?"

"What?" My voice sounds loud in the big, empty space.

"Dr. B said to walk back to the dorms through the tunnel together."

"We don't actually have to do that."

"I know. But I like Dr. B. Figured I'd at least try to do what she asked."

"You like Dr. B?" I remember the stony face he'd held all through the tour. She had also called him "Leonard," and I assume he's the type of person to hold a grudge.

"Yeah," Leander says slowly, like I asked a weird question. "She clearly knows everything about this place. Why, don't you like her?"

"*I* do. It's just... during the tour, it didn't seem like you did."

"What am I supposed to do, wag my tail?"

I don't realize how much pressure is still in my chest until it releases a bit. I almost laugh but stop myself just in time. "No, but you could try this thing I read about. It has to do with your mouth? You lift both sides up, so it makes a kind of crescent moon shape? I forget what it's called."

"Let me know if you remember," he deadpans. "Sounds intriguing."

We stare at each other for a few seconds. Leander breaks eye contact first, opening the door to the tunnel, and we step inside.

I take it all in. An overhead light blares down, illuminating the reddish-brown rock surrounding us. The dank smell, the low ceiling, the tree roots jutting out of the rocks every so often are all reminders that we're truly underground. That the only thing keeping us from being buried alive are 150-year-old beams.

Weirdly, it makes me feel lighter. The tunnel is my kind of scary. The fun kind. It's *Scream*, not *Hereditary*. *Evil Dead II*, not *Pulse*. It's Bruce Campbell gutting demons with a chainsaw arm, not *your mother forgives you* or *your wife is finally at peace* or *cheese and crackers*.

"What'd you think of the reading?" Leander's voice echoes sharply over the soft crunch of our shoes on the dirt floor.

"It was...," I start, snapping my bracelet against my wrist. "I don't know. I don't believe in mediums, so."

"Yeah." Leander twirls his pen around in his fingers. "I mean, even if you did, it was obviously fake. Madame Althea used all the most basic tricks in the book."

"Obviously." I snap my bracelet against my wrist again. I hate to feed into Leander's whole know-it-all persona, but I can't help it. "Like what tricks?"

We sidestep two kitchen employees heading back to the hotel. Leander waits until they're out of earshot before talking. "Take the first guy. Dan Callahan," he says quietly. "Madame Althea said she was speaking to someone's mother and that she sensed a heart issue and the letter *S*."

I nod, remembering Dan's shaky hand raising into the air.

"*S* is a really common initial for first *and* last names. And heart disease is the leading cause of death in America. Chances are, someone in that room would have a mother who died of a heart issue, and whose name, first or last, began with an *S*. And sure enough, someone did."

"Yeah," I say slowly, shaking off a wave of discomfort. Hearts didn't always kill people by surprise like Imogen's did. Hers was a shock, a rare case, a tragic fluke. But an older person dying of a heart issue was a lot more common. I make circles in the air with my hand. "What else?"

"So after that, Madame Althea made some educated guesses to get things going. She said she got a strong scent of roses." Leander looks down at me, eyebrow raised. "A mom having some connection to roses? That's a pretty safe bet."

I scoff. "Stereotype much? Moms like all kinds of flowers. My mom likes hydrangeas. She hates roses, actually. She says they're trying too hard."

"Ah, but...," Leander says smugly, raising his pen into

the air, old-timey nerd style. The urge to stab him with it is profound. "Madame Althea didn't say that roses were Sharon's favorite flower. She didn't even say that Sharon liked them. She said, 'I'm getting a strong scent of roses.'"

I think back, and he's right. "So... Sharon Callahan's favorite flower didn't have to be roses for Madame Althea to be right," I say, working it out. "Like, she could have worn rose perfume or something."

"Exactly. Or maybe Dan bought her roses for Mother's Day every year."

"Or maybe she was an international assassin, and her calling card was a single rose."

I expect an eye roll, but Leander's mouth ticks up at the corner. "Or she was an international assassin, and her calling card was a picture of Rose from *The Golden Girls*."

My eyes widen. Because this is the second time Leander Hall has almost made me laugh. And also because... "You watch *The Golden Girls*?"

He opens his mouth but doesn't say anything for a second, like he's deciding whether or not he wants to tell me. "Sometimes I have trouble sleeping," he says, putting his pen behind his ear. "I thought if I watched something boring, it would help. I picked it randomly, but it was actually pretty funny, so I watched an episode before falling asleep. I kept doing it, and now it's like a sleep trigger."

I stare at him, trying to figure out if he's kidding. "You can't fall asleep without watching *The Golden Girls*?"

Leander sighs, and suddenly I'm smiling bigger than

I have in forever. The image of Leander in his all-black clothes, falling asleep to spunky old ladies having adventures is flat-out sending me. The urge to stab him with his own pen fades, and I tuck the knowledge away in a box inside my brain. The "Things About Leander That Don't Make Me Want to Stab Him with a Pen" box.

"You see my point about Madame Althea, though, right?" Leander cuts in before I can say anything else. "She was really careful with her words so that there were a lot of ways for her to be right."

"Solid deflection. But sure. I see your point. It wouldn't work all the time, though. I mean, say Madame Althea was pretending to contact the ghost of my mom and she said she was smelling a strong scent of roses. I wouldn't be like, '*Oh yeah, that makes sense because my mom hated roses*'?"

Leander shrugs. "Maybe not. But people really want to believe they're communicating with their dead loved ones. Madame Althea uses that to her advantage. She can say something vague, and grieving people will do their best to make the connection, even if it's a stretch."

Again, he has a point. I take in a breath of the tunnel's close, earthy air, remembering the faces of the audience at the reading. So full of hope when Madame Althea threw out information about the people they loved. Then utter relief when she told them what they were desperate to hear.

Of course they wanted to believe they were communicating with the dead. For some, it was because things were left unfinished—there was a question they needed to ask, an apology they needed to give, a reassurance they needed to get before they could move on. For others, it was because they simply couldn't live with the idea that this person they loved was gone. Truly and utterly gone. So they believe in mediums. They believe the dead aren't gone, not completely.

I don't fault them for it. If I believed, even a little bit, that the dead could talk, I'd have gone to a million mediums by now. If I believed that Imogen was out there somewhere, snort-laughing and geeking out about movies and being way too nice to the other ghosts, I would try to talk to her every freaking day.

But I don't believe. Imogen isn't out there, waiting to communicate with me. I can't make myself believe anything different.

It's just that sometimes—like right now, as the tunnel walls narrow in and my chest tightens and every breath feels thick and heavy and gasping—I wish I could.

I wish I could believe.

I don't want to be underground anymore. I quicken my steps until I finally come out onto the curving dirt trail that leads to the dorm building. I gulp down the mountain air and throw my head back to blink at the sky miles and miles above me. As I stand here in the vast mountain dark, my chest opens up, my lungs expand. I feel both better and worse. Big and small all at the same time.

Leander's footsteps scrape the ground behind me.

He catches up and then we head down the path, the streetlamps lighting our way. I roll a smooth, white bead from my bracelet between my fingers, my breathing back to normal now. Maybe Dr. B was right about the tunnel playing mind games with people. At least now that I've been through it, it won't be nearly as unsettling the next time.

"What about the ring?" I ask, wanting Leander to keep debunking the reading. "Madame Althea knew Dan Callahan lost his mom's ring. How did she do that?"

"Oh, yeah. This one's interesting. Dan says he lost something special of his mom's. If he were to say that to you, and you had one chance to guess what it was, what would you say?"

He wants me to say jewelry. And even though it makes sense, even though he's been surprisingly not terrible on this walk, the desire to annoy him just won't fade. "I don't know. She could have collected stamps. Or Hummel figurines or baseball cards. I read something once about a woman who collected airplane barf bags. Women aren't just about necklaces and rings, you know."

"Really?" Leander does an exaggerated gasp. "So you're saying that jewelry commercials have been lying to me all this time?"

I roll my eyes, trying and failing to supress a smile.

"I know women aren't all about jewelry. But if you *had* to guess..." Leander pushes. "If your livelihood depended on you getting the answer right, what would you say?"

"Clown erotica."

And then a strange thing happens. Leander laughs. It's an unexpectedly gentle sound—soft and tumbling and oddly peaceful. It sends a bubbly rush of heat to my body, which my brain offers no explanation for. And then the sound is gone, lost in the expanse of sky and trees.

Leander clears his throat, seeming as surprised about the laugh as I am. "Anyway. Madame Althea probably figured the most likely answer was jewelry, so she picked one of the smallest and most easily lost kinds."

"Yeah..." I attempt to organize my thoughts, but I feel flushed and confused. Seriously, what is happening? I've already accepted the fact that Leander is hot, so I guess I could be physically attracted to him. But I don't feel that warm, bubbly rush when I hear Raden's laugh.

I focus back on the issue at hand. "Why didn't Madame Althea just say jewelry? Why take a risk and say it was a ring?"

"She didn't say it was a ring. She said, 'It wasn't a ring, was it?' "

Another trick.

"Saying it like that gives her lots of leeway," Leander goes on. "Because if Dan had said no, it wasn't a ring, she could have said, 'Right, I didn't think so.' And most likely, Dan would have given more information after that. Maybe he would have said, 'It was a necklace,' and she could have said, 'Yes, I sensed it was a special piece of jewelry.' "

"Either way, she doesn't look like she got it completely wrong," I say, catching on. "But if she *is* right, if it *was* a ring, it looks super impressive."

"Exactly. I bet she booked a ton of private readings tonight. That's the whole point of these free public readings anyway. To drum up business. So she takes calculated risks."

I picture all the people surrounding Madame Althea after the reading as we step onto the front porch of the dormitory building, which looks like an overgrown rustic cabin, with a brown exterior and green roof so it blends in with the trees. I lean against the wooden wall as Leander sits across from me on the porch railing. I'm smiling again. Because while Leander's obsession with the truth is usually annoying, it's incredibly useful right now. And I have to admit there's something thrilling about how he debunked Madame Althea's whole convincing show.

Or, almost all of it.

"The only thing that doesn't fit the pattern," Leander says, watching me carefully, "is the last thing. 'Cheese and crackers.' "

I make my face as blank as possible as Leander fixes me with his intense stare. He takes a breath, like he's gearing up for something. "Did that mean something to you?"

My chest tightens. I feel exposed, but also suspicious. "Why do you want to know?"

Leander rolls his lips together, considering me. Then

he jumps off the porch railing and circles around the side of the dorm, gesturing for me to follow.

I have no idea why, but I do. He stops under a pine tree several feet from the dorm, ducking underneath the lower branches. "I'm not really here to write about Agnes Thripp and Spiritualism," he says in a near whisper. "I came here to write an article that exposes Madame Althea as a fraud."

I blink at him. I don't know what I was expecting him to say, but it wasn't that. "What?"

"I had to come up with a decoy project because they wouldn't have let me come if they knew what I really wanted to do. Madame Althea is a big part of the Harlow."

I shake my head, trying to make sense of it. "Why? I mean, what's the point of exposing her?"

"The point is the truth," Leander says sharply.

"So, that's why you went to the reading tonight? To get evidence?"

"Yeah. I wanted to know what tricks she uses at cold readings."

"Cold readings?"

"Public shows where the medium doesn't know any information about the audience beforehand," Leander explains. "Hot readings are when the medium can find out information about the audience beforehand. Like, they access the list of people who bought tickets and look stuff up about them online. Facebook or Instagram or obituaries that mention their name."

I scrunch up my face, trying to process all of this.

"Madame Althea's reading was free, and anyone could come in," Leander says as a pine cone thuds softly into the dirt at our feet. "It was basically a cold reading, except..." He takes a breath. "She could have known that the senior project students might be there."

My eyes shoot up to his. And just like that, all the pieces click into place. The email I sent to Madame Althea, introducing myself. "Natalie Nakada" isn't a very common name, so she could have Googled me and found my Instagram. I imagine her scrolling through, seeing what I look like, reading all the comments on the pictures of Imogen and me: **Rest in peace. Gone but not forgotten. God called her back early.** She could have seen the last photo I ever posted with her, the one of us on the front porch of the Harlow, the one Imogen commented on.

cheese and crackers!!!

I gust out a sharp breath, like someone punched me in the stomach. *That's* how the fuck she did it.

Madame Althea probably figured a teenage girl talking to her dead best friend would be a dramatic way to end the reading. Really seal the deal.

"I don't think what Madame Althea is doing is right," Leander says, determination coursing through his voice. "She exploits people's grief. She makes them believe in something that isn't real. Some people think that's okay, that it's closure. But it's dangerous. I mean, the whole thing with Agnes Thripp not taking her medication because she wanted to prove the dead could speak? Believing in this stuff can get people to make bad choices."

He breaks off, shaking his head. "I want to tell the truth about Madame Althea and people like her. If you know something, maybe it could help me do that."

My jaw clenches as a confusing mess of emotions tangle up inside me. I'm grateful I know what Madame Althea did. I'm glad I won't be wondering about it all night. But I'm also pissed. Pissed at Madame Althea for exploiting Imogen's death for her own profit. Pissed at Leander for asking me about it. Pissed at myself because I know mediums are fake. I *know* that, and I still let Madame Althea mess with my head.

When I look up, Leander is watching me intently, hopefully. And a new source of anger creeps in. Was he only being decent because he wanted information from me? Is that why he told me about *The Golden Girls*, so I might tell him something personal, too? Was he faking that laugh that made me all warm and fuzzy?

I take a breath and try not to let anything show. "I have no idea what it meant," I say firmly. "I won't tell anyone about your top secret project but leave me the hell out of it." I turn and walk back to the dorm building, letting the door bang shut behind me.

In my pine box of a room, I change into my pajamas, trying to forget the whole night. I'm about to shut my laptop when a new email pops into my inbox.

Dear Natalie,

I would be happy to sit for an interview.

I'm available at one o'clock tomorrow in my office. I hope to see you then.

Warm Wishes,

Madame Althea

I read it three more times, my heart beating rapidly in my chest. Before I can read it again, I type out a quick response: Thanks. See you tomorrow. I hit Send.

It'll just be a ten-minute interview, and then I'll never have to see her again. I try to shove her out of my mind as I crawl into the stiff dorm bed and blink up at the knotty pine boards on the ceiling.

It's only as I'm drifting to sleep, listening to a moth click around between the window and the curtain, that an unsettling thought floats into my head.

My Instagram is private.

chapter eight

Nine days until the Spirit Ball

"So, I'm walking through the tunnel at about one in the morning," Silas says, scraping his shoe over the dusty floor. "And the lights suddenly go out."

"Ah." I nod at Silas. I'm trying to look engaged and investigative, but I'm mostly thinking about the fact that I'm meeting with Madame Althea in half an hour.

I've been thinking about it since last night, which is why I didn't get much sleep. The only theory I currently have is that Madame Althea somehow, via the mysteries of the internet, accessed my private Instagram. It's totally probable, but I want something more concrete.

"So, I get out my flashlight," Silas says, giving me a charming smile. "You learn to always carry a flashlight when you work the graveyard shift at the Harlow. I look around, and I don't see anything. But I hear someone whispering my name, all urgent-like. *Silas! Silas!*"

I stifle a yawn, hoping the camera set up on the tripod doesn't capture the strain on my face. "What did you do?"

"I said, 'What?' And then I feel this pressure on my shoulders, like someone is trying to shake me. Not violent, really. More like excited? And then my flashlight went dead, and I got the hell out."

"I see. The Harlow has a lot of ghosts. Do you have a sense of who you might have been encountering?"

"Agnes Thripp. For sure. Her whole thing is she wants to tell people she's here, you know? That she's communicating from the other side. No one believed it back when she died, and she wants to set the story straight. That's why she said my name and grabbed me and did the thing with the flashlight. She wants to be heard."

I smile my first genuine smile of the day. This is perfect. I mean, it's your standard vague ghost story, but it's perfect. It stars the most famous Harlow ghost, and it'll be a great segue into investigating the tunnel. I take a breath and let myself feel good about the work I've done today. I've been up and at 'em since 6:00 AM this morning, interviewing the women I talked to yesterday about the porch ghost and the supernaturally made bed. I caught a few people from the night staff as they got off shift and interviewed them, too. I have more than enough stories to establish the Harlow as haunted, and now I have my reason to investigate the tunnel.

"Thanks," I say to Silas as I turn off the camera and detach it from the tripod. "That was great."

"No problem. It's mostly true even. I mean, my name being whispered was probably Clarissa messing with me—she does stuff like that all the time, trying to freak people out. And the tunnel lights go off automatically at 1:00 AM to save energy."

I peer up at the glaring overhead light, my smile growing. Now I know exactly when to film in the tunnel.

"But the flashlight did go out. And I did feel someone touching me, and I don't think it was Clarissa."

I stop myself from saying it was definitely Clarissa. "Wow." I try to sound amazed as I pack the tripod away. By the time I zip up my bag, my mind is traveling back to Madame Althea again. I glance up at Silas, wondering if he knows anything useful.

"Hey," I say casually. "What do you know about Madame Althea? Like, do you think she's for real?" I try to look innocent. I remember what Leander said about Madame Althea being a big part of the Harlow. I don't want it to seem like I'm fishing for information about her, even though I totally am.

"I've only been to her once." Silas scratches at the back of his head, his whole relaxed vibe turning awkward. "Last summer, I turned eighteen, so I was old enough to get a private reading. I was taking this summer course online for college credit, and one of the assignments was to write a research paper on an ancestor of ours. I'm not big into research, so I thought, why not just ask Madame Althea to contact the dead ancestor I'm writing about and tell me all the stuff I need to know?"

I laugh because he's not kidding.

"So, I went into Madame Althea's office and said I wanted to contact my great-great-grandfather Dorian. I told her I wanted to learn all about his life. Madame Althea did her whole thing—closed her eyes, like she was listening. Then she looked right at me and said, 'Dorian is telling me that you should do your own homework.' "

Silas shudders a little. "Not gonna lie, it creeped me out. So yeah, if you ask me, she's the real deal."

I can't tell if he's messing with me. Maybe he has to say she's the real deal. Maybe it's part of the Harlow Hotel employee training to make up some story like that to hype up Madame Althea's abilities. It's possible.

I thank Silas again and hurry through the tunnel to Jitter Beans so I can watch the interview back. But when I do, my heart sinks. Silas's story is exactly what I need, but the footage doesn't look right.

It's way too static. Too much like the school news segments they play in homeroom every morning. It's because I used the tripod, I realize. It doesn't have the handheld shakiness of *Ghost Chasers*. No tension, no suspense. I sink back onto the hard metal chair and try to figure out a solution. I can't hold out the camera selfie style when I'm interviewing another person. It wouldn't look right. But neither does the tripod setup.

I'm blanking, but I don't let myself fall too far into hopelessness. I just need to make sure the Madame Althea interview is really good. If I have amazing content, maybe it'll make up for the way things look.

At one o'clock on the dot, I knock on Madame Althea's door. It swings open immediately.

"You must be Natalie," she says, those pale blue eyes sparkling, her mouth turning up in a slight smile. It's the same expression from last night, when she stood on a stage and tried to make me believe Imogen was speaking through her. I have the urge to both yell at her and run away.

"Thank you for agreeing to the interview," I say instead, stepping into her office.

I start pulling equipment out of my bag. The sooner we get this done, the sooner I can leave. I attach the camera to the tripod plate and move the pan handle, glancing around the office to find the best interview spot. Surprisingly, it's a pretty normal office. Two high-backed chairs sit in the middle of the room, a leafy green plant spills out of a brass pot in the corner, and cinnamon incense burns on the windowsill. There are bookshelves covering each wall, and an abstract painting above a minimalist desk. The only thing on the desk besides a sleek laptop and an open planner is a photo encased in a simple silver picture frame.

It's of two young women on the shoreline of a beach, their arms slung over each other's shoulders, mouths open and eyes bright, like they're in the middle of a laugh. The one on the left is definitely Madame Althea when she was younger. Those eyes are unmistakable. The other woman is a little taller but has the same dark hair, her smile so dazzling it almost radiates out of the frame.

"That's me and my sister, Marta," Madame Althea says when she sees me looking. "You wouldn't know it if you looked at us now, but we were wild in our day."

I paste on a smile. "It's a gorgeous picture." And even though I'm just here to get the interview, I can't resist poking a little. "If you posted it on Instagram, it would get so many likes."

I watch her face carefully, but she just chuckles. "I'll tell Marta you said so. She turned prudish in her old age and hates that I have this displayed. It's 'too revealing.' The next time she annoys me, I'll threaten to post it on the internet. Ha!"

My fake smile flickers into a real one for a second. It's strange seeing Madame Althea like this, like she's a regular person excited about one-upping her sister, not the mystical figure she was in the dim light of the billiards room, talking to spirits.

Madame Althea sighs in satisfaction before taking a seat in the cream-colored, high-backed chair, gesturing to the matching one across from it. "When you're ready."

I check the camera, making sure the chairs are in center frame, swallowing down my disappointment that I have to use the tripod again. "So basically, I'll ask you some questions about the Harlow, paranormal occurrences you've witnessed here, and what it feels like to communicate with the dead."

"I prefer the term *departed*," Madame Althea says, adjusting a paisley scarf on her shoulders. "I think it gives those who have passed on from this realm of existence more agency. It defines them by what they've done versus what we, the living, see them as."

"Okay. The departed." I hit Record and settle into the chair across from her. "Madame Althea," I say, making my voice clear and professional. "The Harlow Hotel has been named the most haunted hotel in the West. Do you agree with that? Or do you think it's the most haunted hotel in America?"

Althea chuckles again, her eyes crinkling at the corners. "I don't know that haunted is something you can rank. Just like you can't rank beauty or joy. I know people *try*, but it can't truly be done. If spirit energy is strong somewhere, if remnants of the past endure, then that is a haunted place. America is filled with them. The world is filled with them. And one of those places happens to be right here."

I nod. So far, so good. "Why is the spirit energy so strong at the Harlow?"

"Over a hundred years ago, the Harlow Hotel was a haven for Spiritualists and anyone who believed in life after death. They'd come from all over the country to learn from each other and commune with the spirit world. Even though they've passed on, they remember this place fondly." Madame Althea's eyes drift away from mine. "They remember the summers they spent here—the camaraderie, the crisp mountain air, the commitment to believing in things beyond this world. The excitement of exploring the mysteries of the universe."

She looks back at me. "That's why they come back."

I'm leaning forward in my chair, mesmerized by the calm conviction in her voice.

"There's an idea that ghosts haunt places where they experienced pain or tragedy or a terrible injustice," she goes on. "I believe that's true in some cases. But in my experience, it's just as often that spirits haunt the places where they were happiest."

"That's... interesting," I say. Although I don't know how well it fits into *Ghost Chasers*. Usually, the paranormal professionals on *Ghost Chasers* talk about spirits that are angry, restless, or sad. Like the miners who died in an explosion in the Coal River episode, or the Hillcrest Cemetery episode, where the team went looking for the "Woman in White," who died in a fire the night before her wedding. I've never seen an episode where they go looking for happy ghosts.

"Why do you think that is?" I ask. "If spirits don't have any unfinished business, if their souls aren't angry or tortured or out for revenge, aren't they supposed to move on?" I'd heard it enough times in movies. Once a ghost's soul is at rest, they "move on." To where, it's never really clear.

"Well, moving on isn't so easy," Madame Althea says with a sad smile. "When we lose a loved one, that loss feels immense, doesn't it? But think about what *they* lose. They lose everything. Their family and friends. Their passions and dreams. And the little things, too. They lose their favorite books and movies. They lose sunrises and the smell of the air after it rains. They lose fluffy sweaters and hugs and dancing and that feeling you get when you make someone laugh. They lose places like this."

She gestures out the window above her desk, and my eyes follow, like they're connected to her hand by a hidden string. I stare out at the mountains, vast and sweeping, the sunlight turning the green of the pines impossibly vivid.

"Wouldn't you have a difficult time moving on from all of that?"

I open my mouth, but my throat feels full of knots, because what she just said about losing sunrises and dreams and places like this is so fucking sad. I lost Imogen and that gutted me, but Imogen lost everything. Every single thing. I feel a sting in my eyes as tears threaten to spill out.

"Are you all right, dear?" Madame Althea gazes at me, her eyes full of sympathy. "Is there someone you lost?"

It's like a light flicking on, a curtain being snatched away. Madame Althea is manipulating me again. Making me emotional so I'll be more susceptible to her tricks. Making me feel desperate to talk to Imogen, so desperate I believe it can happen.

"No." I blink the tears away and smother the rage swelling inside me. *Focus on the interview. Just focus on the interview.* "Have you ever received a message from Agnes Thri—"

"Maple syrup," Madame Althea says. "Soccer. Monopoly."

I stare at her. "What?"

She smiles apologetically, motioning around herself. "They're all telling me what they miss. Egg Creams. Birdsong. Brisk walks before bed."

"The dea—departed? They're here now, talking to you?" I know it's another trick, but goose bumps are rippling up my arms, traveling all the way to my scalp.

"The sound a sugar cube makes when it dissolves in tea." Madame Althea's eyes are shut tight now, a crease forming in the space between them. "The circus. Aggie marbles. Silk sheets. Aston Martin DB4s. Kitten fur. Taking the pins out of your hair. Whiskey. Mozart's Symphony Number 29 in A Major. Celine Dion."

Madame Althea's eyes pop open. Her lips part, moving soundlessly for a moment. And then she sings.

"I'll be waiting for you. . . ." Her voice sounds soft, small. *"I'm the one who wants to love you more."*

For a second, I can only gawk at her in horror.

And then my body moves all at once, my legs straightening and my arms pushing me up off the chair so hard that it topples to the side, knocking into my tripod and bringing the whole thing crashing down.

"I'm sorry about that," Madame Althea murmurs, peering up at me with gentle, innocent eyes, seeming not to notice the mess I just made. "She's reaching out to you."

"I don't believe in that," I say forcefully, barely recognizing my own voice. I don't know how I got anything out at all. My heart is pounding in my throat, choking out all the other words I want to say. There's a video of Imogen and me singing The Song on my Instagram. How dare she. How *dare* she pull this on me again.

I try to take a breath and assess the situation. Screaming obscenities at Madame Althea won't solve anything. Neither will throwing her laptop through a window, which I really, really want to do. But that won't fix this. I just need her to stop.

"Look. I don't have money. I'm not even eighteen, so I can't pay you for a private reading anyway. But even if I could, I wouldn't. I don't need closure. I don't need to communicate with anyone. I've already grieved and worked through it. Do you understand that? I've moved on."

But I want it to sink in all the way. "I've *moved on*," I repeat.

Madame Althea blinks at me, her pale eyes tinged with sorrow. "She hasn't."

I grab my things and leave, cutting through the café, almost bumping into a metal chair as I make my way to the exit. Outside, it's hot and windless. The sun beats down on my skin, but it doesn't get rid of the goose bumps. I need to get to the dorms. I need to stop thinking about the ridiculousness of what just happened. I need to *do* something.

I pick up the pace to an actual run, and I'm sweating by the time I climb the dormitory stairs, hoping I can find Leander's room. Thankfully, I hear his voice carrying through the hallway. I follow the sound to the door at the end of the hall. When I knock, his voice cuts off abruptly.

The door yanks open and there he is, pen resting behind his left ear, a phone held up to his right. He squints at me quizzically. "Hey, Daphne?" he says, turning around. "I'll call you back later. Yeah. Love you, too."

"I'm in," I say as he turns back to me, lowering the phone to his pocket.

"What?"

"I want to help you prove Madame Althea is a fraud," I say between broken breaths. "I'll tell you what I know."

His eyebrows inch up, and he steps away from the doorframe. And then I do something unthinkable. I walk into Leander Hall's room.

chapter nine

Okay, so it isn't his *room* room. But it's his room here, and that's weird enough. It looks similar to mine except it has a blue theme—navy curtains and an aqua quilt that's smoothed over the neatly made bed, his notebook lying on top. On the desk are piles of books. I glance closer and see some titles: *Why We Believe* and *The Believing Brain* and *Spook: Science Tackles the Afterlife*.

We stand awkwardly in the small space between the bed and the desk until Leander springs into motion, pulling out the desk chair and waving at it. I sink into it, still trying to catch my breath, as he sits on the bed.

"Where do you want to start?" He opens his notebook and grabs the pen from behind his ear.

"We can start here," I say, digging my camera out of

my bag, hoping he doesn't hear the tremor in my voice. I pop open the viewer, relieved that the camera doesn't seem damaged after I knocked it to the ground. Leander shifts forward on the bed to see.

I keep glancing at his face as the footage plays. He rolls his eyes when Madame Althea starts listing all the things "the departed" say they miss about life. When she starts singing, he cringes, like he's watching a bad *American Idol* audition.

It does seem a lot cringier as I watch it back. And not nearly as unsettling as it felt when I was in her office. My breathing finally slows down. All of a sudden, I feel normal again.

It makes me think of that time freshman year when I saw *The Ring* at Penny Arcade, the single-screen theater that showed classic horror movies in October. I was sleeping over at Imogen's, and Bea was home for a rare visit. The Lucases were at some charity event for the evening, and Bea said she'd take us to see whatever movie we wanted.

Bea went all out and bought us popcorn and Twizzlers and Coke, and we all held hands as Samara crawled out of the staticky TV, lank hair plastered over her face. It was the scariest thing I'd ever seen.

Afterward, we got back into Bea's car, reliving all the best moments. One second Bea was driving us out of the parking lot, and the next, we were pitching violently to the side as a metallic crunch split the air.

I screamed my head off, utterly convinced that Samara

had crawled out of the movie screen and rammed into Bea's Subaru Outback. I'd been convinced of it all through Bea saying, "Shit, are you guys okay?" and Imogen shakily saying, "Yes." I was even convinced when we followed Bea out of the car and saw a station wagon stopped right in front of us, its headlights glowing in the dark lot.

It was only when a little old man got out of the driver's side and said, "Holy monkey balls, I thought I was hitting the brakes!" that Samara disappeared from my mind. Just like that, I was back to normal again. I looked at Imogen and we dissolved into a fit of giddy giggles. Because the world was still the same place it always was. No Samara. No monsters or demons or ghosts or slashers in scary masks. I realized then that horror movies could cast a spell over you, could make you believe, against all logic, that the supernatural was real. But the spell didn't last long.

It's the same thing with Madame Althea. She casts spells. The dim lights at the reading. The hushed quality of her voice. Her otherworldly eyes and warm demeanor and Christmas-scented office. It's all designed to make you believe, even for just a moment, in nonsensical things. But then you go back to the real world, and just like that, the spell is broken.

I stop the footage after Madame Althea finishes singing so Leander won't see me knock the camera over. Some things, he doesn't have to know.

"What the hell?" Leander says after a beat, looking disturbed.

"I know. My best friend Imogen and I used to sing that song before she died," I say, dropping eye contact to pack my camera away. "I have a video of us singing it on Instagram. Same with the 'cheese and crackers' thing. It was an inside joke, and it's also on Instagram. My account is private, but..." I look up suddenly, an idea finally dawning on me. "Maybe Madame Althea has access to the Harlow Hotel's Instagram account? I've followed them for a long time, and then once I knew I was coming here for my senior project, they followed me back."

I expect Leander to be writing this down in his notebook. I mean, isn't it pretty good evidence that Madame Althea is a fraud? But he's staring at me, a sad recognition growing in his eyes.

"Imogen Lucas," he says, and I feel the hollowness I always do when I hear her name. "I read about her in the school paper."

"Yeah." Boulder High reprinted Imogen's obituary in their first issue of the new school year, next to a waist-up shot of her playing the piano at a school concert, her hair slicked back into the chignon her mom loved so much. I saw that picture everywhere in the months after her death. Shining out on my TV screen as the Lucases made a passionate plea for parents to screen their kids for heart abnormalities. Enlarged on an easel at her funeral, next to a wreath of white roses and lilies.

Leander breathes in, like he's finally found the answer to a question that's been bothering him. "At the party, when that jerk mentioned Imogen and sang the song... *that's* why you went down the hill."

I think back to that moment—staring down the steep incline from the hull of a child's unicorn bed, Leander grabbing my elbow and looking at me like I'd lost my mind. I should feel embarrassed, but instead, I only feel satisfied that Leander called Dave a jerk. "Not my best decision. But in my defense, it was Dave's fault."

"Hell yeah it was. I would've done the same thing. Except I might have taken the karaoke machine with me."

I smile, and suddenly I don't feel as hollow anymore.

"I'm really sorry about Imogen," Leander says, looking me in the eye. "And I'm sorry I asked you about the 'cheese and crackers' thing last night. I fixate on stuff sometimes. I knew what Madame Althea said affected you, and I should have realized you wouldn't want to talk about it. I was a Dave-level jerk, and I'm sorry."

I tug at my bracelet, surprised by the sincerity of the apology. The suspicion that he was only being nice last night to get information melts away, replaced by the budding idea that Leander Hall, Mr. Truth Hurts himself, might not be that bad. "Thanks."

It's quiet for a few seconds, and my brain drifts back to why I came to Leander's room in the first place. "Why do you think Madame Althea is doing this to *me*, specifically? It's like she's targeting me, and I'm not even old enough to pay for a reading."

Leander shrugs. "She probably thinks she can use you

to get other people to pay for readings. Lots of other people. She said 'cheese and crackers' in front of a whole crowd at the reading, and she sang that song in front of the camera. Maybe she figures the *Ghost Chasers* people will see it and come do a feature on her or something."

Now I wish I had thrown Madame Althea's laptop out the window. "Okay so, I'll find the Instagram posts Madame Althea used to try to trick me. You can write about them in your article, and that'll do it, right? That'll prove she's a fraud."

Leander is already shaking his head. "I'll mention it, but there are groups of skeptics who've already outed famous mediums for using social media to trick their audiences. And you know what happens to those mediums?"

"They lose their jobs and spend the rest of their lives thinking about what assholes they are?" I say hopefully.

A corner of Leander's mouth turns up. "No. They keep their jobs. Sometimes they even get more famous. It doesn't matter."

"Why? I get wanting to believe in mediums. But if people see hard evidence that they're fake, why would they still believe?"

Leander shrugs. "People believe in irrational stuff all the time. We're kind of hardwired to believe in the supernatural. For example." He points to a worn black hoodie hanging up in the closet. "If I told you that shirt once belonged to a serial killer, would you wear it?"

"Ew, what the hell?" I recoil in my chair, inching away

from the closet. "No. Why do you have a serial killer's sweatshirt?"

Leander smiles triumphantly. "I don't. It's this experiment I read about." He gestures to the pile of books on his desk. "Almost everyone who's asked that question says no. It's because part of them believes, on some level, that objects once owned by an evil person carry some trace of that evil. That's not a logical or scientific belief. It's a supernatural one."

"That's...," I start, but I can't finish the thought because my brain is shifting, making room for this new, surreal information. I always thought of the supernatural as ghosts and demons and slashers who could get shot and stabbed and drowned and still not die. Horror-movie stuff that doesn't exist in the real world. But I guess that's not exactly true. "Fascinating," I finally finish.

"Right?" Leander says, eyes flashing with excitement.

"And it works the other way around," I say, leaning forward in the chair. "When we love a person, the stuff we associate with them feels like it carries traces of them, too." I glance at the bracelet on my wrist, the beads like perfect little hailstones, and I think of all the times I've felt glad to be wearing it, times it felt like a little piece of Imogen was with me, even though logically, I knew she wasn't.

I guess I do have a small belief in the supernatural lurking around in my head. It's surprising, but now that I've found it, I don't want it to go away. Maybe it's for the same reason that people keep believing in mediums even after seeing proof that they're frauds. "The comfort people get from believing in mediums is more important than the evidence," I say. "Logic doesn't matter when someone you love is gone. I get that. And I'd never want to take away the comfort Madame Althea gives to grieving people. But what she's doing—lying, targeting people who don't want anything to do with her 'abilities'—isn't okay."

"I couldn't have put it any better," Leander says. He's leaning forward on the bed, too, like this conversation is literally drawing us together, and I feel something I haven't felt in a long time. My chest expanding and my brain flickering in surprising directions, like the world just grew, and I have to keep up.

"Okay." I slap my hands on my thighs, suddenly energized. "So how do we expose Madame Althea as a fraud?"

"We gather all the evidence. Not just one big piece you think will blow the lid off the whole thing. But everything." Leander shifts on the bed, pulling his legs in to sit crisscross-applesauce style.

"And then we tell a story. Who is Madame Althea? Her real name, where she grew up, when she became a medium, what her family thinks of her line of work. And sure, you mention the internet tricks. You find out what she's told people in their appointments and look for similarities, patterns that might suggest she has prepared responses. But also, you make her a real person with a past, not some mysterious, mythical being. Together, all that stuff plants seeds of doubt in her abilities. I think that's the way to get through to people who believe in this stuff. You slowly, without judgment, change their minds."

I tilt my head. None of that sounded at all like his normal articles. "You're not going with your whole Truth Hurts style?"

"Someone once told me it's hard to persuade people when they feel like they're being yelled at for not knowing what I know."

Wait a minute. *I* said that. He actually listened? And changed his whole approach to the Madame Althea article because of it?

"Oh" is all I can say as a blush heats up my face. Thankfully, he's looking down at the blue quilt, casually picking at a loose thread, so he doesn't see.

"Yeah, only it's not going so great," Leander admits with a disappointed twist of his mouth. "I can't find her real name online. I put out a call on Reddit for people who wanted to share their experiences with her. I've gotten some responses, but they're mostly generic. I've looked through tons of blogs that mention sessions with her, and a few of them were interesting, maybe showing some patterns. I've reached out to the local ones to see if they'd be willing to talk to me, so that's my biggest lead at the moment."

"Okay." I nod. "We can work with that."

"Except..." Leander looks disappointed again. "I already talked to a few people earlier today and didn't get anything. It was like they knew I was trying to find dirt on her or something. They didn't want to say too much."

I sit back in the wooden desk chair, thinking of all the people who were more than happy to talk to me about *Ghost Chasers*. Then the idea hits me. "When we talk to people about Madame Althea, we can tell them it's for my *Ghost Chasers* audition."

"What?"

"People around here are all about *Ghost Chasers*. I have no trouble getting them to talk to me for that. So, if we say we're auditioning for the show, maybe we can slip in a few questions about Madame Althea, and they might be more willing to open up about what she's told them. It won't even technically be a lie, because I could use some interviews about Madame Althea in my footage."

"That's..." Leander raises his eyebrows at me. "Not a terrible idea."

"You're welcome." I cross my legs and try not to look too smug. "Who should we try first?"

"There's this one person, Frankie Funkmeier," Leander says, flipping around in his notebook. "She's a regular customer of Madame Althea's, so she might have a lot of information. She works at Six Ways to Sunday, an antiques place downtown, and she said I could swing by tomorrow morning."

"Cool. Let's do it."

"Um, thanks," Leander says as I stand up and swing my bag onto my shoulder. "For helping."

"Sure." I smile because another idea is forming in my head. "And, you know, if I ask you to do me a favor in return, like filming me as I explore certain locations to help my audition footage look better, that's cool, too, right?"

He glares at me. "I'm not doing *Ghost Chasers*."

"Of course you're not. You'd be super boring on camera. You'd be all…" I grab his pen from his hand and twirl it around my finger, doing my best pretentious Leander impression. "People *say* there are ghosts here, even though ghosts are a completely irrational belief perpetuated by existential superstitions and fear of the truth, blah, blah, blah."

"Wow. It's like looking in a mirror," he says sarcastically.

"Come on, you'll just be helping me do some of the filming in exchange for me helping you talk to people for the exposé. Totally painless. Win-win."

"Fine."

"Starting tonight. In the tunnel." I give him my most winning smile.

Leander sighs and rubs the space between his eyes.

"Meet you there at midnight." I hold out his pen, and he gets up off the bed to take it. In the small room, we're closer than probably either of us wants. It forces me to notice things—like how tall he is, how he uses a lavender-scented laundry detergent. That his usually intense brown eyes can have a soft, doe-like look to them sometimes. That despite everything, I want to step even closer to him.

I abruptly turn to the door. "See you—"

"Hold on," he interrupts. I freeze and then turn back, my heart pumping wildly for the second time today.

"I just want to make sure we're on the same page," he says, stepping into my space again. "This is important. Exposing Madame Althea as a fraud is important. If you're in, you have to be all in. You have to take it seriously. No backing out or withholding information because you get annoyed with me or something."

"Then don't annoy me," I say, because I can't resist. "Also, I wouldn't do that," I add, because it's true.

Leander's eyes roam over my face. "Okay." He holds out his hand, seemingly satisfied. "Partners."

I snort. "Partners? Can we have code names? I'll be Nantucket. You can be Leonard."

I expect a smirk, but his face stays as serious as stone. He looks pointedly at his outstretched hand. I sigh and shake it, and the whole time, Leander watches me closely, like he's daring me to make another joke. I wonder if he's this intense all the time. Like, when he browses the cereal aisle, does he stare down the boxes of Cap'n Crunch? When he's in the car, does he sit there completely stone-faced as the radio plays bop after bop? When he's about to kiss someone, does he look at them the way he's looking at me now, with complete and utter determination?

Welp. That took a turn. We let go of each other's hands at the same time, both taking a small step back, as much as the space will allow. It's then that I remember Leander on the phone earlier, telling someone named Daphne that he loved them.

I clear my throat. "Don't be late." I move to the door

for real this time. "Pardner," I add with a finger gun and a wink.

He rolls his eyes, but as I'm closing the door, I catch a smile I don't think I'm supposed to see. It sends a confusing zip of anticipation through my body, and as much as I try to put it out of my mind, I can't stop thinking about it all day.

chapter ten

"It's 12:17 AM," I say in a near whisper as I stare into the camera. "I'm in the tunnel that runs underneath the Harlow Hotel. Several employees had encounters here with Agnes Thripp, a well-known Spiritualist who died at the hotel in 1920. According to them, Agnes just wants to be heard. Tonight, we'll listen."

I turn and take several steps into the tunnel, running my hand along the rocks. Leander's footsteps crunch in the dirt behind me. "I have to say..." I lower my voice even more as I turn back around to look into the camera. "I do feel a strange energy in here. The air is vibrating with—"

Behind the camera, Leander winces like he's in physical pain.

"Dude!" I throw my hands in the air. "Stop doing that!"

"I'm sorry, but strange energy? The air is *vibrating*? Shouldn't you say something more original?"

I take in a slow breath and let it out. It's so confusing that this very afternoon, I was imagining what it would be like to kiss Leander, and now all I want to do is to throw my camera at his face. He's already wasted fifteen minutes asking annoying questions about the show. *Who's the audience for this? How obvious is it that it's fake? Like, could a third grader tell?*

"I mean, it's your audition footage." Leander holds up his non-camera hand in defense as I try to body slam him with my eyes. "If you want it to be cliché, that's on you."

I clench my teeth because he kind of, sort of, maybe has a point, which only makes me more annoyed. "You didn't even want to do this," I mutter, walking back to the tunnel entrance. "Why are you so into it all of a sudden?"

Leander's eyes darken as he follows me. "I'm not into it. But I said I'd help. This is me helping."

"Fine." I find my starting place, take a breath, and shake out my shoulders so I won't look tense on camera.

I nod to Leander and wait to see the recording light. "It's 12:22 AM, and I'm in the tunnel underneath the Harlow Hotel." I do my normal script about Agnes, but then I close my eyes and think about what it feels like, what it *really* feels like, to be standing in the tunnel. "It feels... heavy in here." I open my eyes. "Like you might run out of air. It feels like these dusty, ancient rocks are the only thing keeping you from being buried alive."

I look at Leander. "Acceptable?"

His mouth flips into a thoughtful frown. "Way better."

I shake my head but can't help feeling a little bit pleased. Because it *was* better. We film some more stuff, hitting all the creepiest parts of the tunnel, and even though Leander keeps interrupting with "notes," it doesn't bring down my mood. Because the tunnel is the perfect location, and what I have planned for later is gold. This is going to get me on the show, I can feel it.

At 12:40 AM, I call for a water break. After Leander hands me the camera and I put it carefully down on my bag, he sits on the ground, unscrewing the cap to his water bottle. I sit a respectable distance away.

"We'll film again at 12:55, pardner," I say because I know it will annoy him. And sure enough, his eyes flick up to the ceiling as he drinks.

"Why 12:55?" Leander asks, wiping his mouth with the back of his hand.

"Because the lights automatically turn off at 1:00 AM. When they do, turn on night vision mode." I hold up the camera and show him how to do it. "I'm going to pretend to hear my name being whispered. When I start looking around, swing the camera, like you're trying to find out where it's coming from. Got it?"

Leander is giving me a strange look. "Won't that look bad? You reacting to a noise that isn't there?"

"You never actually hear any creepy noises on *Ghost Chasers*. What's creepy is the idea that someone hears a noise."

"Can I ask you something?" he asks after a beat.

"Uh, sure."

"Do you believe in ghosts?"

"No." I fiddle with the cap of my water bottle.

"So, if you don't believe in ghosts, why do you want to be on *Ghost Chasers*?"

I shrug. "I don't know. I like exploring creepy locations and pretending to get all freaked out. It's fun to act scared. I do Terror in the Corn every Halloween. It's kind of like that."

"Huh." Leander nods, but his eyebrows are still wrinkled, like he's genuinely trying to understand. "So, it's the acting part? That's what you like about it?"

I stretch my legs out in front of me and drag my heel back and forth on the ground, making a groove in the dirt. "I don't know."

"There are lots of things that require acting. Why this?" He gestures around himself. "Why *Ghost Chasers*?"

"The host is incredibly hot."

Leander looks at me flatly. "Your whole senior project is based around someone else's hotness?"

"My whole life plan is based around someone else's hotness. If I get on *Ghost Chasers: Teen Investigators*, I could be on the real show in a few years." I ignore the slight edge of embarrassment poking at me as Leander widens his eyes in disbelief. But why should I be embarrassed? Not everyone has a grand calling in life.

Leander is shaking his head. "I still don't get it. Why ghost hunting? Why not try out for a play or something?"

I look up, blinking at him. It's so weird that he mentioned a play. The slim green book in the bottom corner of my cube shelf pops into my mind. *Arcadia.* How excited Imogen was for me to audition for Thomasina back in sophomore year. How excited *I* eventually got about it. How we ran lines together to prep for the audition, me firing out words about particles and physics and...

"Or is it a college thing?" Leander is saying. "Being on the show will make you stand out on applications?"

"I probably won't go to college."

"Why?"

"Oh my *God,* what's with the questions? Are you writing an article about me? 'High School Senior Has Confusing Life Goals and I Can't Let It Go'?"

Leander laughs—that gentle rumbling sound I remember from last night—and I sit up straighter, like it's a rare bird I've been lucky enough to spot twice.

"No," Leander says after he's done. "Although that's a pretty good headline." He shifts on the ground, stretching his legs out in front of him, like mine.

"Then why do you want to know?"

Leander shrugs. "Contradictions are interesting. You don't believe in ghosts, but you want to be on a show that's about looking for them. Figured I'd ask about it."

"Well, ask about something else." I want to give him an answer, I really do. But the truth is, I can't think of one. I don't know how to explain why I want to be on *Ghost Chasers*. I just do.

I don't really think Leander is going to ask me about something else, but a second later, he says, "Did you use to live in Pittsburgh?"

"What?"

"Yesterday, you called me a jagoff. I hadn't heard that one before and figured it must be regional, so I looked it up, and saw that it's commonly used in Pittsburgh."

"My mom grew up there," I say slowly, and Leander looks satisfied, like he's solved another puzzle. I can't help but smile. "So, you care more about the regional origin of the insult than the fact that I insulted you?"

Leander leans his head back on the rocks. "I've had so many insults thrown at me this past year that I'm basically immune to them now."

My smile fades as I feel a twinge of guilt laced with a surprising shot of protectiveness. I don't think Leander is outright bullied by anyone at school, but he obviously gets shit for his Truth Hurts articles. For the first time, I wonder if the backlash is truly deserved. Because underneath the pretentious writing style—underneath the football and meat lunches and promposal topics that seem specially designed to make people mad—maybe Leander is just pushing us to question if the things we eat and support and believe in are as simple as we think they are. Pushing us to find the truth, even if it hurts, even if it's buried so deeply that it's hard to see.

Isn't that what he was doing when he gave me all his "notes" tonight? They annoyed me, but they made me dig deeper and think past the easy clichés. They made me get closer to the truth of what it feels like to be in the tunnel. He did it at Dave's party, too, I realize as my mind drifts back to that night. He said I seemed miserable. I wanted to believe I was having fun, to believe that I had moved on so much that I would feel okay on the anniversary of Imogen's death, when the truth was that I didn't feel okay. I felt really fucking alone.

"I'm sorry for throwing some of those insults," I say, turning my head to stare at his profile.

He sighs. "You were right about my articles, though. They do read like I'm yelling at people." He lifts his head off the rocks, turning to look at me. "When I moved to Colorado, I wasn't in a great place...." He breaks off, looking away again.

"Why were you not in a good place?" It's strange, but it doesn't feel that weird to be asking him something so personal.

"I didn't want to leave New York." Leander waves his hand in the air, like he doesn't really want to talk about it.

"You're probably going to college, though, right? You could apply to schools in New York."

"Yeah, that's what I'm doing." I wanted that to make him feel better, but he still seems preoccupied.

"What do you want to do after college?" I ask, surprising myself by how interested I am in the answer.

"I used to want to be a journalist. I wrote for my school paper back home, too, though my articles didn't piss as many people off. But, I don't know. Maybe I'll take a bunch of random classes in college and see what sticks. I sort of hope it's something unexpected, like horticulture or puppetry or something."

I smile. Because I'm newly obsessed with the image of Leander doing a puppet show. And because even though he's Mr. Truth Hurts, his openness to the unexpected is kind of inspiring.

And there's that feeling again—the warm, bubbly one that sends a rush of heat to my face. Which is bad because I can't really be into Leander Hall, right? And that's beside the point anyway, since he already seems pretty serious with whoever Daphne is.

"It's 12:55," Leander says, holding up his phone.

I stand up quickly and brush the dirt off my jeans, bringing my head back to *Ghost Chasers* as we set up to film again. I stand in the middle of the tunnel, directly under a bright, overhead light.

"It's almost 1:00 AM," I say into the camera, using my hushed voice. "And things have been quiet so far. I hate to say this, but I'm starting to wonder if the atmosphere of the tunnel freaks people out and makes them think they see and hear things that aren't really there. I know it's easy to—" I stop abruptly and look over my shoulder before turning back to the camera. "Sorry, I thought—"

The lights go out with a sharp click. Everything plunges into total darkness right on time. "Whoa, whoa, whoa," I say frantically, scraping my sneakers against the ground.

"The lights just went out. They're totally out." I pull my flashlight from my pocket and point it at the ceiling. "I think—" I break off and spin around frantically.

"I think I heard my name. Agnes?" I project clearly. "Is that you?" I carefully twist the head of my Maglite flashlight so it turns off. I can't see anything in the dark, but I crouch down, placing the flashlight on the ground by my feet, knowing the camera will pick it all up on night vision mode. "I have this flashlight here," I say, looking around. "If you'd like to talk, just turn it on and off, okay?"

I stand up and shuffle backward a few steps, enough so that it'll be clear I'm not messing with the flashlight. "Agnes, are you here right now?"

I wait, clenching and unclenching my hands. If this doesn't work, I'll still be able to use the tunnel footage. I'll just edit this part out. But if it does...

The flashlight flicks on, and I throw my hands over my mouth to cover my smile. I make my eyes go wide and look at the camera. I can't make out Leander's expression in the dark, but I can picture it: frowning, eyebrows furrowed, trying his hardest to figure out how I did it.

I won't tell him, and it'll drive him nuts, and it'll be amazing.

"She's here," I say, pulling my hands away from my mouth. "Agnes, are you trying to tell us something?"

The flashlight keeps glaring its cold light into the tunnel. The seconds tick by, and then the flashlight flicks off.

"We want to understand what you're trying to say. Are you trying to warn us about something?" The flashlight stays off. I wait a little bit, but not too long.

"Are you trying to tell us about the afterlife?"

The light flashes on.

"Wow, okay," I whisper into the camera, stalling a little bit. "Agnes famously died at the Harlow Hotel because she wanted to prove there was an afterlife. She wanted to send a message back to the living to prove the dead could speak. This could be her message."

I clear my throat. "Agnes, is the afterlife a scary place?" I call out into the tunnel. The light stays on.

"Is it a happy place? Are you happy there?"

The light clicks off. "We hear you, Agnes. Thank you for your message. Thank you for communicating with us. Goodbye."

I hold it in for a few seconds, and then I throw my hands into the air. "Woooooo!" I scream, hearing my voice echo off the tunnel walls. That went better than I expected.

"Okay." Leander hands me the camera and turns on his own flashlight, angling it down so I can pack everything up. "How?"

"How what?" I keep my voice innocent.

"Come on, this is going to bug me."

I laugh a little, throwing my bag over my shoulder as we follow the two glowing beams lighting our path out of the tunnel. "It's payback."

The truth is, I found the trick on a Reddit ghost hunting thread. Apparently, all the ghost hunting shows use Mini Maglite flashlights because if you twist the head in just the right way, it turns on and off by itself. Something about the reflector heating and expanding, and then cooling and contracting, both of which push the metal pieces together that turn the light on and off. But it's way more fun to watch Leander be annoyed than it would be to explain it.

"Payback for what?"

I search my brain for a second, deciding what past annoyance I'll punish him for. "For grabbing me when I was about to go down the Stein Incline at Dave's party. I know I shouldn't have done it, but still. Not cool."

It's quiet for a beat. Our feet crunch across the loose dirt as our flashlight beams join in the distance, cutting a wider swath through the dark.

"I didn't grab you," Leander says.

I scoff. "Yes, you did. I was just about to get on the unicorn bed, and you grabbed my elbow."

Leander is silent again. I lift my flashlight, shining the beam at the side of his face. He looks genuinely confused. "I really didn't."

My stomach twists as I remember that moment—the icy fingers gripping my elbow, the unnerving feeling when I turned around and didn't see anyone. "But you were there," I press. "I saw you."

"I followed everyone out because I was curious about what was going to happen. But, I mean, I just stood there. You got onto the bed, and you went down. I didn't grab you."

The tunnel walls feel narrow again, and I'm relieved we're only a few feet away from the end. We step out into the night—cool, gusty, and glowing with streetlamps. Something dawns on me. "You were drunk," I say, my shoulders relaxing as I turn off my flashlight. "I'm sure your memory of events isn't the most reliable."

Leander rubs the back of his neck, his face scrunching up like he's sifting through his memory with a fine-toothed comb. "I wasn't *that* drunk. I wasn't drunk enough to grab someone and forget about doing it."

I try ignoring the shifting feeling in my belly. It doesn't work. Because I can feel the icy fingers on my elbow again—the memory of it is so strong it's a physical thing.

And then I feel a tug on my wrist.

I look down in time to see the bracelet sliding off, the beads plunking onto the pavement, one by one.

I freeze, my skin prickling as I gape at the beads rolling off in different directions.

"Natalie?" Leander's voice is far away. "What—"

"My bracelet," I say shakily, dropping to my hands and knees, gathering up every bead I can find. "Something— It broke. It...it broke." That's all there is to say, really. My bracelet broke. It felt like someone pulled it, but no one is here except for me and Leander.

He's crouching beside me, picking up beads. I saw one roll into a patch of yarrow on the side of the trail, so I crawl over there, the tiny, sharp rocks digging into my knees. The moment I see the bead, nestled in the little white flowers, I hear it again.

The deep, eerie silence. It's heavy around me, like it was the first time I stepped into the lobby. But now it's thick with anticipation, like right before a big jump scare, when the quiet is so blaring it bristles your skin as you wait for something to break the crushing weight of stillness. In a horror movie, I know what would happen. I would look over my shoulder, and Imogen would be there, wrapped in her white elk antler hoodie, her mouth Cherry Sour red.

I stare hard at the yarrow, reminding myself this is real life. But I can't get the image of her out of my head, I can't get the feel of her breath off my neck.

My heart is pounding so painfully fast I can't help it. I look over my shoulder.

And see nothing except trees, the dark outline of the mountains, and Leander kneeling on the trail under the soft glow of the lampposts. The silence is gone, my heart slows down, and a shudder passes through me.

I can't tell if it's relief or disappointment.

Leander is walking quickly toward me. I hold out my hand and he pours the beads into my palm, his eyes on my face, soft and searching. "Hey, are you—"

"I'm fine," I finish. And even though I know I am, even

though I know nothing supernatural just happened, even though I'm not cold, I start shaking and don't stop until Leander wraps his arms around me and the warmth of his body sinks into mine.

I lose myself in the comfort of it, letting my mind go blissfully blank, breathing in the slight scent of lavender on his hoodie. The pressure of his arms is strangely perfect, solid but not suffocating. I don't know how long we stay like that, but I wish it could be longer. Because as we slowly step apart, I'm starting to think again, about the strange pull on my wrist, the *click, click, click* of beads falling to the ground.

Click, click, click, clickclickclick...

It takes a second to understand that what I'm hearing isn't inside my head. It takes another to feel the small, cold stones stinging my face. And yet another to fully process that what's happening is real.

It isn't until Leander grabs my hand and starts pulling me to the dorm that I snap out of it, running alongside him to take cover on the porch, just as the hailstorm opens up, pelting the ground with frosted white stones, just like the beads I have clutched in my hand.

chapter eleven

February, four months before Imogen dies

"'When you stir your rice pudding, Septimus, the spoonful of jam spreads itself round making red trails like the picture of a meteor in my astronomical atlas. But if you stir backward, the jam will not come together again.'"

I look up from my phone, where I've downloaded the *Arcadia* audition excerpts from the Boulder Community Theater website.

"Eeeeeeeee!" Imogen squeals, her shoulders doing a little shimmy. "That was *so good*."

"You would say that if I literally barfed right in the middle of it," I say, and while that's probably true, I can't stop smiling. Imogen is so ecstatic about me auditioning for *Arcadia*, and after a couple of days reading the audition lines with her, it's starting to rub off on me. My lines are still missing something, though. I can tell they aren't totally convincing yet. But I'm getting there.

"Why do you keep downplaying?" Imogen hands me the mug of lemon water she made as soon as we got home from school, saying I needed to keep my vocal cords healthy. "You're clearly amazing at this, and when you're a famous actress being profiled by the *New York Times*, you'll talk about this as the moment when it all began."

I snort. "You are *so* into this."

"Of course I'm into it!" Imogen blinks at me earnestly. "Who wouldn't be into watching their best friend do something they're brilliant at?"

"Pshh."

Imogen grabs my shoulders and looks me in the eye. "Natalie, you're brilliant," she enunciates. Her face wants me to know she is 100 percent not kidding. Like, there's zero trace of a smile there. She gets this way sometimes. I'll be joking around, and suddenly she'll get so serious it'll throw me for a second.

"Well, *brilliant* is a strong word," I say after a pause, sipping the lemon water. It's also a word that nobody has ever used to describe me before. But I keep that part to myself because if I say it, Imogen will only get more serious and try to convince me that I am, in fact, brilliant. Her eyebrows are already wrinkling as she opens her mouth.

I hold out my hand. "I just mean I probably have to, like, read the play before I can be 'brilliant' in it."

Imogen finally smiles again. "I can help with that." She

scoots on her knees across her ivory carpet to her stuffed bookshelf, combing through the bottom shelf. Part of me can't believe I'm volunteering to read an entire play when I don't have to. Especially because I know it has lots of math and science in it. Atoms and equations and astronomical atlases. When Thomasina talks about stirring jam into pudding but not being able to stir it back out, it's apparently her discovering the basis of chaos theory.

The play does sound interesting, though. The whole past and present thing is cool, and Imogen said that sometimes, characters from the different time periods switch in and out during the same scene, brushing past each other in the hallways, like they aren't separated by hundreds of years.

And the more I say Thomasina's lines, the more I imagine myself being up onstage, in front of a crowd of people, spouting off those dazzling words. It's so outside of anything I ever imagined myself doing, but I'm super pumped about it. The audition isn't until April, and I kind of wish it was sooner. I already thrifted a professional-looking outfit for it—a satiny white button-down and pleated black skirt that falls mid-calf.

"Found it!" Imogen tosses a thin green book onto my lap. *Arcadia* is written in all caps across the cover, with illustrated flowers growing out of the letters. "Text me updates as you read. Also, I think we should stop practicing for now." She presses the space bar on her laptop, unpausing the episode of *Ghost Chasers* we were watching before deciding to practice lines. "You don't want to sound over-rehearsed."

"Okay." I run my fingers over the shiny cover as Joshua Jacobs's flashlight dances over the control room of a lighthouse. We watch *Ghost Chasers* every Friday after school, a luxury Imogen's parents allow as a way to "unwind from the week." At 6:00 PM, I'll be politely kicked out so that Imogen can have family dinner and go to bed early to be well-rested for Academic Decathlon practice on Saturday morning.

I'd planned to check out Raden's band at Java Hut tonight. But maybe I'll stay in and read *Arcadia* instead. I could break out the Swiss Miss packets and curl up in the easy chair by the front window and just dig in. It might be kind of nice. Mom would come downstairs from Bubble Bath and Book Time and totally think some *Invasion of the Body Snatchers* shit went down and I'd been replaced with a pod person. Plus, if I read the whole play, maybe my audition lines will sound more convincing.

"*Whoa, whoa,*" Joshua says on-screen. "*Something's touching me. . . .*"

Joshua feeling something touching him is the best part of any *Ghost Chasers* episode. A lot of times his shirt will lift up "by itself," exposing his abs and supporting the popular theory that even disembodied spirits are thirsty for Joshua Jacobs.

I watch as he puts his flashlight on the ground to "communicate" with the spirit of the old lighthouse keeper, but my mind keeps traveling back to Thomasina. I gesture at the laptop screen as Joshua's flashlight flicks on and off seemingly on its own. "Thomasina wouldn't believe in ghosts. She'd probably say death is like stirring jam into pudding. You can stir it in but not out. You can die, but you can't become undead."

Imogen tilts her head, digging into a bag of Spicy Honey Mustard Combos. "Maybe. But with death, what if it's not so definite?"

I expected that. When it comes to otherworldly stuff—ghosts and spirits and even God—Imogen always says "maybe" or "what if?" She still goes to church with her parents, even though she's agnostic. I've been to church with the Lucases several times on Sunday mornings after sleepovers. The Saint Thomas Aquinas Catholic Center is beautiful—the dark wooden pews and stained-glass windows grand and intimate all at once. Sometimes, when everyone would rise and sing hymns together, I'd try to get myself to believe that God was listening. But I could never quite do it. As much as I'd try—as much as I'd close my eyes and ask, "What if?"—it felt impossible to make myself believe, even when I really wanted to.

"Maybe you can't totally reverse death," Imogen says, twisting a long strand of blond hair between her fingers. "But like Thomasina says, even though the strawberry jam won't come together again no matter how much you stir it, it does keep turning the pudding pink. Maybe that's how it is after you die. You're gone, but some part of you, some essence, keeps infusing everything."

Imogen lets her hair slip between her fingers. It lands,

whisper soft, on her collarbone. "It's like when Thomasina dies in the play," she goes on. "She leaves behind these incomplete theories, which obviously she can't finish herself. But other people, over the years, pick them up and finish them. So that part of her isn't lost. Her ideas carry on, growing and changing, even after she's gone. Maybe that's what ghosts really are. The ideas you put out into the world, even the unfinished ones. The ones people pick up and think about even when you're gone."

On-screen, Joshua is listening to an EVP recording with his team. A low, moaning sound that was clearly added in postproduction rumbles through the room, making everyone gasp. Compared to what Imogen just said about ghosts, it seems laughably silly.

"So, what you're saying is . . ." I tilt my head. "When you die, you come back as ideas?"

Imogen snort-laughs. "Sort of? It's like, maybe you come back, but metaphorically. A metaphorical ghost."

"Can metaphorical ghosts still do cool shit? Can they walk through walls and bounce a rubber ball down the hallway, or are they just, like, disembodied things that people think about sometimes?"

"I'll let you know when I die and become one."

"Geez." I grab one of her Combos and throw it at her. "Morbid much?"

A sharp rap of knuckles sounds on the door. Imogen pushes the bag of Combos under her bed, and I pause *Ghost Chasers* right as the door pops open and Mrs. Lucas appears, wearing a perfectly pressed navy sheath dress. "Hi, Natalie." She gives me a thin-lipped smile, the same one I see in the Lucas Realty signs dotting front yards all over town. "Sounds like you girls are having fun."

She always says "fun" like it's an insult. Like there's something else we should be having instead.

"We are," Imogen says. "Sorry if we were too loud."

"Yeah, sorry," I repeat, trying my best to sound it. I'm always polite to Mrs. Lucas, especially because I know she's not my biggest fan. At least not anymore. When we were younger, she told me I had a "spark." I think she liked that I climbed to the top of the jungle gym and didn't let the older boys push me around and pulled Imogen out of her shell a bit. But I think she also figured that, at some point, Imogen would hit it off with someone from honors physics or piano camp and we'd naturally grow apart. It's like every time she sees me in Imogen's room, she gets confused about why it still hasn't happened.

"It's not a problem." Mrs. Lucas waves her hand in the air. "But, Immy, remember you have a Zoom with Carrie Feldman in forty-five minutes."

"I know. This is almost over." Imogen points at Joshua, frozen on-screen.

Mrs. Lucas blinks at her. "Don't you have to get ready? Do your hair?" Translation: Kick your confusing choice of a best friend out and get your hair into a chignon, stat.

Imogen sighs so quietly I'm sure I'm the only one who hears it. "Okay, I'll get ready."

"Have a good night, Natalie," Mrs. Lucas says, and shuts the door.

I grab my backpack and sneakers as Imogen pulls a brush off her dresser. "What's the Zoom about?" I ask.

Imogen shrugs, combing her hair back off her forehead. "Mrs. Nebel sent one of my essays to this student writing contest, and I guess it won. A reporter from the local paper wants to interview me about it."

"*What?* That's amazing!" I shove her lightly on the shoulder. "Why didn't you tell me?"

"I think I just got so excited about you auditioning for *Arcadia* that I forgot."

"Oh my God." Here she is, making a huge deal about me just trying out for a play when she *won a whole-ass essay contest.* But I guess she's won so many essay contests it doesn't even seem like a big deal to her anymore. Talk about brilliant.

"What's the essay about?" I unzip my backpack and tuck *Arcadia* carefully inside.

"It's a comparison of exorcism movies directed by women to ones directed by men, and how..."

As Imogen explains her essay—throwing out terms like *abject* and *binary* and *infantilization,* my brain sputtering as it tries to keep up—it hits me. *This* is what a genius sounds like. *This* is why my Thomasina lines don't sound convincing. It's not that I need more practice. The problem is, I'm not like Thomasina. At all.

How did I ever expect to pull it off? Everyone at the audition would see right through me in a second. And even if, by some random stroke of luck, I did end up getting the part, I'd have to memorize a ton of lines. I could barely memorize enough dates to pass my history exams. What had I been thinking?

"Want to run the lines again tomorrow?" Imogen asks as she starts wrapping her hair into a chignon at the nape of her neck.

"Maybe," I say, but my eyes catch on the laptop screen, on Joshua's beautiful face, and something clicks together in my brain. *That's* something I can do. Joshua Jacobs gets to travel to cool places and act all adventurous and fearless. He doesn't have any complicated lines to memorize. He doesn't have to pretend to be a genius. He just has to look good on TV. I could do that.

Imogen is holding her hair with one hand and digging through her drawer for bobby pins with the other. As she's looking down, I take *Arcadia* out of my bag and quietly slip it back onto her shelf.

Imogen straightens back up a few seconds later, blinking at her reflection in her vanity mirror. She lets go of her hair so it falls down her back. "I'm going to leave it down."

I gasp, partly for dramatic effect and partly because I'm truly shocked. "No chignon?"

"I hate chignons," Imogen says in a surprisingly loud voice, brushing her hair aggressively.

"What is *happening*?" I'm careful to keep my voice down so I won't attract Mrs. Lucas, which I'm positive would shake Imogen's newfound bravery.

"I don't know." A giddy smile edges onto her face. "But it's happening."

"Fuck yeah!" I wish I could be there when Mrs. Lucas sees, but I'll settle for text updates later. "What's next?" I stand up and heave my backpack over my shoulder. "Bungee jumping?"

Imogen laughs. "Stunt driving!"

"Hitchhiking!"

"Climbing Mount Everest!" Imogen says, throwing her hands in the air. "No wait." She lowers her arms. "I read that the path to the summit is already too crowded, so maybe not Everest." She lifts her arm into the air again defiantly. "But I'll climb something tall!"

Our laughter fills the room. Imogen would never do any of those things in a bajillion lifetimes, but I'm beyond proud that she's standing up for herself for once.

"And when I die and become a metaphorical ghost," Imogen says, tossing her brush back onto the dresser, "I *will* do cool shit."

I laugh harder because it's always funny when Imogen swears. "Like what?"

"Something so that you'll know it's me." Her smile fades. She's doing that thing again, the one where she gets suddenly serious out of nowhere.

"I'll need you to know it's me."

chapter twelve

Eight days until the Spirit Ball

I skirt around a snowplow as I trek along Elkhorn Avenue, where everyone is taking pictures of the three-foot piles of hail lining the curb. "What season is it?" a news reporter says into a giant camera. "An unusually strong hailstorm last night has turned downtown Estes Park into a winter wonderland. . . ."

I walk faster because I'm meeting Leander at Six Ways to Sunday so we can interview Frankie Funkmeier, but it's taking forever to weave through the people milling around outside the ice cream parlors and mountain gear stores and pubs, commenting excitedly on the hail.

"It came out of nowhere!"

"I've never seen it hail like that before!"

I sidestep a group of kids trying to sled down a

particularly big pile, stifling a yawn. I didn't sleep well. Again. After the bracelet and Leander's hug and the surprise hailstorm, I lay in bed for a long time, staring at the loose beads on my desk as absurd, irrational questions ran through my brain.

I spot Leander standing outside Sunday's, his tall figure leaning against the stone facade, scanning the shops across the street. When he sees me, he pushes off the wall, eyes unsubtly searching my face. "Hey. You okay?"

I feel a fresh wave of embarrassment that I needed a pity hug last night. That I was so shaken I couldn't even explain myself, so after the hailstorm died down, I just mumbled something about being tired and went up to my room.

"I'm okay." I look Leander in the eye so he'll believe it. "I'm sorry I was so weird last night."

"You weren't—"

"My bracelet broke. Imogen gave it to me a long time ago, so when it broke suddenly, it got to me. And then the hailstorm threw me because Imogen loves...loved hailstorms."

Leander opens his mouth, but I can't stop.

"And I mean, was I a little freaked out when it broke? Yes. Do I have an easy explanation for what *caused* the bracelet to suddenly snap? No, but it's not like the elastic was going to last forever. Was it weird that it happened when I wasn't even touching it? Sure, but it doesn't mean I think Imogen somehow did it from beyond the grave.

Was it even weirder that a hailstorm happened right after? Yeah, but I'm not a meteorologist...."

I trail off when I realize I'm cycling through all the irrational questions that kept me awake last night and Leander is looking at me like he's not buying the idea that I'm okay. I expect him to take a step back, to say he doesn't need me to help him with his exposé anymore, but instead he reaches into his back pocket and pulls out a small spool of elastic string.

"I thought you might want to fix it. The bracelet," he says, handing it to me.

I stare at the tiny roll of string in my palm, totally thrown. "Where did you get this?"

"I figured one of the jewelry stores around here might have some."

My mouth hangs open. I'm sure it's not the best look, but I can't help it because I'm picturing Leander coming downtown early to look for elastic string to help me fix my bracelet. Maybe he feels bad for me or maybe he's just a surprisingly thoughtful person or maybe...

I think about the hug again. It might have started because of pity, but it was a really, really good hug. The kind where you could still feel the imprint of the other person's body afterward, the kind I spent a fair amount of time thinking about last night despite everything else that happened.

I blink up at Leander. Are we...? Is this...? The questions break down before I can fully articulate them because two days ago, Leander and I pretty much hated each other.

Things have changed, I know that. I just don't know how much they've changed. Or what Leander thinks about it. Or what I think about it, really. And of course, there's also Daphne. A dull ache that feels a lot like jealousy spreads through my chest.

"Thank you," I rush to say when the quiet between us stretches out a beat too long.

"You're welcome." Leander puts his hands in the pockets of his sweatshirt. "Anyway, about what you were saying, I know you don't believe Imogen was responsible for breaking your bracelet or causing the hailstorm. But still, she had a connection to those things, so it makes sense that you'd be thrown." He shrugs, still keeping careful eyes on me. "If you don't feel like talking to Frankie today, I can do it and tell you what she says."

I stand up straighter. I don't want him to treat me with kid gloves just because I had a bad night. I'm okay. My bracelet breaking was a coincidence. So was the hailstorm. I'm fine. "No, I'm going in there, too. We're pardners, remember?" I do my best cowboy impression and chuck him on the arm.

Leander looks me dead in the eye, and I wonder if he's going to push back, tell me he doesn't think it's a good idea. But all he says is, "When I'm old, and my grandchildren ask me what my biggest regret in life is, I'll say it was telling Natalie Nakada that we were partners."

I laugh, my shoulders relaxing. "Your future grandchildren sound intense." I turn and pull open the glass door to

Sunday's, the smell of old things hitting me square in the face. "Like, come on, kids. Why don't you go play outside instead of asking your dorky grandpa about his regrets?"

"You're presupposing that I'll be a dorky grandpa, which you can't know for sure." Leander follows me inside, looking around at the packed store, where every inch is filled with stuff—shawls, beaded lamps, leather-bound books, clocks, phonographs, and stacks and stacks of maps. There are even maps hanging on the ceiling.

"I *can* know because you're in high school and just said 'presupposing.' Studies show that's the highest indicator of one day becoming a dorky grandpa. The second highest indicator is falling asleep to *The Golden Girls*."

"Yikes, I guess I'm pretty much destined to be a dorky grandpa. Might as well embrace it now. Get some suspenders. Start calling everyone 'sonny.'"

I laugh again, feeling lighter than I have since last night. We should be going up to the counter at the far end of the store and asking for Frankie. But instead, we're lingering by the shelves and display cases, poking at random things.

"What makes a grandparent dorky, though?" Leander says after a pause, flipping the page of a photo album filled with vintage postcards. "Aren't all grandparents a little bit dorky by default because the things they found cool when they were young now seem dorky to the rest of the world? Or maybe you can age out of dorkiness. Like, once you live to be a certain age, people think of you as 'eccentric' instead."

"Oh my God." I smile and shake my head because Leander is now genuinely pondering our joke conversation. It reminds me of Imogen, the way she'd sometimes treat completely hypothetical situations as real.

"Climbing Mount Everest!" I remember her shouting that one day in her room. *"No wait, I read that the path to the summit is already too crowded, so maybe not Everest. But I'll climb something tall!"*

She was so amped, a seemingly small thing like refusing to wear her hair in a chignon made her feel like she could be immensely brave. I wish she'd had more of those moments.

"You don't think grandparent dorkiness is an important issue?" Leander asks, fake-offended.

I smirk, but I'm suddenly wondering what Imogen would think about Leander. Imagining an alternate junior year where Imogen read Leander's Truth Hurts articles. *I feel bad for him,* she probably would have said. *Everyone hates him, but his points aren't wrong.*

Before I can stop myself, I imagine telling her about the hug last night, about him buying me elastic string. *He hugged you and bought you a present?* she'd say, eyes going puppy-dog soft. *Do you want to kiss him?*

I focus back on Leander. "There's a slight possibility you could be an eccentric grandpa rather than a dorky one. Okay?"

"Thank you." We're both smiling now, Leander leaning against a glass display case, me fidgeting with my hair.

We really should get to interviewing Frankie instead of loitering in the front, doing what can only be described as obnoxious flirting.

Leander straightens up suddenly, like he just had the same thought. "I'll ask for Frankie," he says, heading toward the back.

I follow him through the stuffed shelves to where a white woman in her sixties with chin-length, bright silver hair glances at us from behind the counter. "Are you the kids who want to talk to me about Madame Althea?"

"Yes. I'm Natalie," I say in my most professional voice. "And this is Leander. Thank you for agreeing to talk to us. I don't know if Leander mentioned it, but we're filming our audition for *Ghost Chasers: Teen Investigators,* and wondered if you'd be willing to talk about any and all paranormal encounters you've had at the Harlow Hotel."

Frankie's face lights up. "I love *Ghost Chasers*! That Joshua Jacobs is the prettiest man on TV."

"Right?" I say enthusiastically, glancing at Leander, because here's proof I'm not the only one who appreciates Joshua's hotness. He shakes his head, flicking his eyes to the ceiling.

Frankie's blue eyes sparkle as she moves boxes off a few chairs and scoots them forward. "Come on back and settle in, because I've got some stories to tell."

We set up as quickly as we can, with Leander behind the camera and me sitting across from Frankie. When I start the interview, it's clear she wasn't lying about the stories. She tells one about a champagne cork flying out of a bottle all by itself at the Harlow's bar and restaurant. About a low, maniacal laugh that rumbled through the lobby one night. About Agnes Thripp breaking one of the hummingbird feeders when someone hadn't filled it up correctly.

I can use a lot of it for my audition footage, plus Frankie seems thoroughly at ease with us now, which hopefully means she'll tell us something useful about Madame Althea.

"Thank you again, Frankie," I say, because she insisted I call her that. "We're also interested in ghosts that communicate through mediums. You're a client of Madame Althea's, right?"

"Yup." Frankie nods. "I've known Madame Althea since I moved here in my forties. I go see her about once a month."

"Would you be willing to share any details about your experiences with her? We're not filming it for the audition footage," I explain as Leander lowers the camera. "But we might write about it as part of our senior project, as long as you're okay with that." I'm not telling the whole truth, but I want to be as close as possible.

"We wouldn't use any real names," Leander adds.

Frankie shrugs. "Sure, I don't mind sharing. What do you want to know?"

"What first brought you to see Madame Althea?" Leander asks.

"I wanted to contact my mother."

"Did Madame Althea contact her?" Leander asks.

"Mm-hmm. It took a little while, but then she said she was there and asked if I wanted to say anything. I said, ask her if she forgives me. She'll know what for."

Frankie smooths out a crease in her black pants. "For context—and I didn't tell Madame Althea any of this—but my mother owned a restaurant in Mississippi that was her whole heart and soul. I was her only child, and the understanding was that I'd take it up once she was gone. I was in my thirties when she died, and I tried it for a few years. Hated it. It just wasn't in me. So, I sold it, moved here, and opened up this place. I knew my mother would have been devastated, but... I had to live my own life. Anyway, I asked Madame Althea if Mom forgave me."

I nod, knowing what's coming. *Yes, of course she forgives you,* Madame Althea would say. *You made the right choice.*

Frankie lets out a sharp laugh. "She said, 'I'm so sorry. She's saying no. She says she'll never forgive you.' "

It takes me a second. "Wait... what?" I glance at Leander to see if he's as confused as I am, but he's only looking intently at Frankie.

"That's how I knew Madame Althea was the real deal," Frankie says, beaming. "My mother was the pettiest person on God's green earth. It was her way or the highway my whole life. She would have rather I'd been unhappy and running the restaurant than happy and doing anything else. It's just the way she was."

Frankie shrugs, like she came to that conclusion a long

time ago. "That's my little test, see? When I moved here, I went to see a few different mediums and asked them to ask my mother if she forgave me. And they'd all smile at me and say, *Oh, of course she does. She wants you to be happy.*" Frankie scoffs. "Bullshitters. All of them. Madame Althea was the only one who knew."

It's quiet for a moment, an unsettling feeling twisting through me until I remember what Leander said about mediums using the internet to research clients. "Have you ever talked about your mother online? Like, in a blog or on social media?" I ask, trying not to sound too suspicious.

"Never had social media." Frankie shakes her head. "My niece tried to get me to do it, but the way I see it, social media is like a casino. You spend all your time there, getting more and more anxious and depressed, but you can't walk away because it does everything it can to keep you there. I don't need another casino in my life. And no, I've never talked about my mother online. I wrote a review of Madame Althea on the local supernatural blog, but I didn't disclose what we talk about in our sessions."

My brain is buzzing with questions, but I can't ask any of them. I can't just turn to Leander and say, *Please explain to me how Madame Althea knew about Frankie's mom.* Anyway, there has to be some explanation I'm not seeing right now.

My fingers drift absently to my wrist, and it's not until I feel bare skin that I remember my bracelet isn't there anymore.

"You said you go to see Madame Althea about once a month," Leander says. "Do you mind if I ask who you contact in those sessions?"

"I talk to my grandmother sometimes, and we contact my spirit guides. They aren't related to me, but they give me advice. I'll admit, though, I call up Mommy dearest a lot. I guess I want her to keep knowing that I'm happy I went my own way, even if she doesn't understand. Maybe, against all odds, she'll see it my way one day."

We thank Frankie for her time and leave Six Ways to Sunday, wandering west down Elkhorn Avenue. I inhale a deep breath of vanilla-scented air, the smell wafting out of the dozen ice cream parlors on every block.

"What did you make of that?" Leander asks as we sidestep a sandwich board outside the Beef Jerky Outlet. His voice is calm, but he's twirling his pen around his fingers, which I know now is a nervous twitch.

"Frankie's story about Madame Althea was convincing," I say, brushing some hail spillover back onto the curb with my shoe. "I mean, if I had a terrible, dead mother who Madame Althea knew was terrible, especially when no other mediums did, maybe I'd believe in her, too."

Leander nods, but he doesn't say anything, so I turn on my rational brain, pushing aside Madame Althea's mystique and examining the facts under a microscope.

"But obviously...I don't believe in Madame Althea. Do you think she deduced it somehow? Like, maybe there was something about Frankie's body language or tone of voice that made Madame Althea sense that her mother was awful? So she took a calculated risk?"

Leander tilts his head, working his mouth from side to side. "Maybe." We pass Chet's Old-Fashioned Candy, zigzagging through a pack of kids watching the antique taffy puller in the window.

"I guess there are a lot of people who have complicated relationships with their dead relatives," Leander says distractedly, blinking up at the sky.

"And all Madame Althea knew about Frankie's relationship with her mother was that she was asking her for forgiveness," I add. "Like, Frankie didn't ask how she was doing on the other side or anything else about her, just if she forgave her. Maybe Madame Althea assumed they didn't have a great relationship, and that the chances were high that her mom's answer would be no?"

"And if that rings true to Frankie," Leander chimes in, "especially when every other medium is saying something else, then that's a way to stand out from the competition and get a customer for life."

But now I'm thinking of Dan Callahan at the reading. He asked his mother for forgiveness, too, and Madame Althea's answer was the opposite of what she had said to Frankie.

That unsettling feeling from before is back, and I recognize it now as a faint twinge of doubt. Because Madame Althea gets things right a lot. Doesn't taking calculated risks mean you get it wrong sometimes?

"Wait...," I say, letting some of the doubt spill over. "Telling someone that their dead mother doesn't forgive them is a pretty big risk. Madame Althea would have to be really, really sure. Wouldn't it be better to make up something about how Frankie's mom had changed on the other side and was ready to forgive? Wouldn't it make more sense that Madame Althea would try to make Frankie happy? At peace?"

"Maybe," Leander says, his eyebrows wrinkling as he bites his lip. "But maybe being at peace doesn't bring people back for more appointments."

"What do you mean?"

Leander fidgets with the zipper of his hoodie. "Maybe it's like what Frankie said about social media and casinos. They don't necessarily make people feel good, but they hook them, keep them coming back. Because the point isn't to make people happy, it's to make money."

He breaks off, still fiddling with his zipper. "Maybe it's the same with Madame Althea. Maybe she sometimes says things to make people happy and at peace. But if she thinks a client has money, maybe she says whatever she thinks will keep them coming back for private readings. And maybe it's the negative stuff that keeps people hooked. Like, they want to keep seeking the approval of whoever they're contacting, or at least they enjoy the disapproval."

It's an interesting argument, but it seems far-fetched. "Wouldn't we need a lot more evidence to prove that? I mean, the stuff with Frankie, that's just one person's story."

"It's not just one person's story," Leander says as we skirt around a crowd outside a pub.

"Who else's story is it?"

"My mom's."

And before I can say "explain yourself," Leander pivots and starts walking back from where we came.

chapter thirteen

"Whoa, whoa," I say, jogging to catch up to Leander. "What do you mean your mom? She knows Madame Althea?"

Leander keeps walking, like he didn't even hear me.

I cup my hands around my mouth. "Earth to Leander," I project, knowing I'm being annoying, but so is he. "You can't just drop a bomb like that and then walk away."

"Sorry." Leander shakes his head like he's coming out of a trance. "I just... I'm trying to think, and I can't..." He gestures around him to the street crowded with tourists and kids and noise.

We're almost at the end of downtown. I can see the familiar brown and green building on the corner—the Estes Park Public Library. My eyes catch on it, imagining the tiny outdoor reading spot behind the building, shaded by blue spruces, where Imogen and I would talk for hours. Oasis.

It feels a little wrong to take someone else there, because it's our place, mine and Imogen's. But I need to know what Leander is talking about. I take a breath and tell him to follow me, leading him past the library sign, decorated with a furry cartoon bear. We duck behind the building to the cool, secluded spot.

It's the same as I remember. The blue-green of the spruces, the spicy-fresh smell of them. The small bench of slightly warped wood and the smooth, round boulder sitting across from it. It all looks untouched, like no one has been here since me and Imogen last year.

"Wow," Leander whispers. He looks around, brushing his finger against a prickly spruce needle.

It's bizarre. Leander being here is bizarre. But I push that away. I push everything away. The place is full of memories, just like the rest of this town. That's all.

"It's a good talking spot," I say, gesturing to the bench. "Hint, hint." I smile to show I'm not pushing anything, remembering how kind Leander was to me last night when I was freaking out. Remembering the spool of elastic string tucked into my camera bag.

Leander takes a seat on the boulder, stretching his legs out in front of him. "My mom's a decent person," he says a few seconds later.

"Okay." I sit across from him on the warped wood bench.

"She just...She makes terrible decisions sometimes. A

lot of times. She puts her trust in people who don't deserve to be trusted, and then she believes them about everything. She—" He pauses, taking a breath. "Once, there was this psychic who came up to her as she was coming out of a Whole Foods, and he told her he knew exactly what path her life was supposed to take."

Leander rubs the space between his eyes. "My mom comes from a rich family, so people know she has money. That's why he targeted her. Anyway, long story short, she lost over fifty thousand dollars buying sessions and other useless shit from this guy before she realized he was exploiting her."

"Geez," I breathe out.

"Yeah. And the worst part was, we *told* her it was bullshit. We told her and she still believed."

"Who's we?"

"Me and Daphne. My little sister."

I breathe in. Daphne. His little sister. "Oh." I nod rapidly as my brain almost skitters off in an entirely new direction. But I focus again because what Leander is telling me is important.

"I was thirteen when it happened," he says. "Daphne was nine. Mom rebuilt afterward, got over it. She even apologized to us, saying she should have listened. We thought, okay. That's over. Thank God. But then, two years later, she came to Estes Park on a trip with some friends, and I guess she heard people talking about Madame Althea. So she went to see if she could contact my dad."

"Your..." I squint at him. "Your dad?"

"He died when I was seven. Car accident."

"Oh my God." My heart stutters in my chest, the ground shifting out from under me. "That's...awful. I'm so sorry." I don't know what else to say, but Leander is already nodding.

"It sounds weird to say this, but I didn't know him very well. He didn't have a relationship with me or Daphne. Not a real one. He worked, and then he came home and went to his home office to work more. The only thing I remember about him is that he yelled a lot—about us being too loud, about how we needed to get out of this 'overcrowded, dirt-encrusted city,' about my mom not wearing her hair right."

I must look confused because Leander says, "He liked it down, parted in the middle, in waves. Honestly, after he died, things were better. Everyone was more relaxed. Mom especially, after she grieved for a while. She wore her hair in a ponytail and smiled all the time. She was happy. And I was relieved. I used to feel guilty about that, but therapy helped."

I let the revelation sit around us in the quiet shade of Oasis, picturing Leander in an office like Dr. Salamando's, working through his loss. I wonder what it's like to feel relief when someone is gone instead of sharp, slicing grief. It had to still be hard, just in a different way. "Why did your mom want to contact him again after so long?"

Leander's face turns grim. "I asked her the same thing when she called me from Estes and told me she was going. She said that he was a difficult person, but that they'd had a whole life together, even before us, and it was hard to just say goodbye to that forever. Which is fair. And if that had been it, if she'd just asked Madame Althea how he was doing on the other side and left it at that, it would have been fine. But she didn't." His mouth twists to the side. "And it wasn't."

"What happened?"

Leander sighs. "Mom wanted to know if he approved of the way she was raising us. It was one of the questions she asked Madame Althea. And apparently, 'Dad' had some suggestions."

My eyes widen. "Oh."

"Yeah. She wouldn't tell us what they were exactly, but it was pretty obvious, because all of a sudden, she was second-guessing everything. Was she too lenient with us? Was the city a bad influence? And no matter what Daphne and I said, she kept making appointments with Madame Althea. She'd do them over Zoom once a week. And afterward, she'd be all distracted and weird."

Leander takes a breath. "And then she started wearing her hair down, parted in the middle, in waves." His shoulders twitch ever so slightly in an almost suppressed shudder. "She hadn't worn it that way since he died, and then suddenly, she's walking around the house, looking and acting like this person I hadn't seen since I was seven. Like she was possessed. It was creepy."

It *is* creepy. I'm leaning forward on the bench, my fingers clutching the bottom of my shirt, like I'm listening to a ghost story. I guess, in a way, I am. Ghost stories are full of creepy men coming back from the dead. They just usually came back by way of a haunted cemetery or a séance, not Zoom.

"Anyway, this all went on for a few months. And then, one day, after a session with Madame Althea, Mom was acting all excited. Daphne and I had no idea what was going on, but then we sat down to eat dinner, and she told us we were moving to Colorado. She said that we needed to be closer to nature, have a house and a yard. She said we needed to get out of this overcrowded, dirt-encrusted city."

I scrunch my eyes shut, feeling an echo of the discomfort Leander and Daphne must have felt that night. I can picture how the scene would play out in a horror movie. Dim lighting at the dinner table throwing shadows over everyone. Leander's mom with her wavy hair, smiling so wide she looks like a Stepford Wife. Eerie strings coming in whenever she parrots things her dead husband used to say. In real life, it wouldn't have had the lights, the music, the effects. But I bet it was just as unsettling.

"So that's why you moved to Boulder," I say quietly.

"Yeah." Leander shifts on the rock. "It made no sense. Mom loved the city. We all did. Our lives are there. And then, we're moving to some random place that just happens to be close to Estes Park and Madame Althea?"

A wave of sympathy rolls through me. His whole life was uprooted. No wonder he wants to take Madame Althea down. "So, you think Madame Althea was pulling the same thing with your mom that she did with Frankie?"

"Maybe. I think she must have gotten the sense from Mom that our dad was controlling and critical. So, she said controlling, critical things, which made my mom feel insecure and like she wanted to please him, like she did when he was alive. And then Mom wanted to keep pleasing him, keep coming back." Leander looks at me, determination etched into his face. "But I can help this time. Mom reads every single one of my articles. She says they make her proud, that they make her wish she could tell the truth even when it hurts. Maybe if it gets through to her, she'll go back to being herself again. Move back to New York."

My stomach thuds at the idea of Leander leaving. But I shrug it away, because now that I know exactly what Madame Althea did to Leander's family, I feel even more resolved to expose her. Leander is right. What she does is dangerous.

"I really am going to help you prove she's a fraud," I say, leaning forward on the bench. "You can trust me on that."

Leander smiles for the first time since Frankie's interview. "Thank you." His eyes linger on mine for a second before darting down to the grass. "I just hope it works. I want to help Mom, but I'm also doing it for Daphne. She just finished eighth grade, and she misses her old friends, her old mom. Her old life. The day before I left to come here, Daph's best friend from home texted her a picture of the Wonder Wheel in Coney Island, and Daph just, like, started full-on sobbing. I had no idea what to do."

A surge of sadness for Daphne hits me in the chest. And then something dawns on me. "Is that why you came to Dave's party?"

Leander picks absently at some grass, collecting the blades in his hand. "Yeah. There's only so much of your little sister's crushed spirits you can take before you need more alcohol than the mini bottles of wine Mom brought home from book club six months ago and forgot about. I only live a block away from Dave's and heard the noise. Figured it was worth a shot."

Dave's party seems like forever ago, even though it's only been four days. It's hard to believe how different Leander seems to me now. How sad I am that he might be leaving. How much I want to squeeze next to him on the boulder, just so we can be closer.

"Anyway," Leander says, still looking at the grass. "I finally found a therapist here, so that's helping, at least."

I blink at him. "You still go to therapy?"

"Yeah," he says, eyes sliding over to mine. "You?"

"I did. For a while, after Imogen died." I picture Dr. Salamando's office—the soft cream couch, her cobalt-blue tub chair. The huge, bright windows that showered the room in light and made everything seem like it might be okay.

"Not anymore?" Leander asks.

"No. I mean, I've moved on. So, no."

Leander's eyebrows wrinkle. "I'm not questioning it or anything, but I know that for me, moving on is kind of a recurring thing. Like sometimes, even now, my dad comes back in weird ways, and I have to move on all over again."

I straighten up on the bench. "He...comes back?"

"Like, at Dave's, when you said it felt like my articles were yelling at everyone. My dad's whole thing was yelling. I didn't use to write like that, but I guess I was mad and taking it out on everyone. I didn't realize that's what I was doing until you said it. And then, I don't know, it was like my dad was haunting me, turning me into this angry, ranting person. Obviously, I didn't actually believe that. But for a second, it felt true."

"I can see that," I say slowly. "The stuff your dad said, the way he acted, those things don't just disappear because he died. They live on. They're in your head. It makes sense that he haunts you sometimes."

Leander nods, his eyes turning unfocused as he stares over my shoulder. He stays that way for a few seconds, like he's in a trance. A slow breeze drifts into Oasis, carrying a faint smell of butterscotch.

"He's a metaphorical ghost," he finally says.

I go still. "What?"

It's cool in the shade of Oasis, but sweat is prickling the

back of my neck. Because that's the second time Leander has essentially quoted something Imogen said. And like the first time, in the lobby, I feel the same surreal sensation. That it's really Imogen's voice speaking to me.

"You know, not like a literal ghost, but more like memories haunting you?" Leander looks at me questioningly.

"No, I... I get it. It's just..." I don't know how to finish the sentence because her voice is still echoing in my head.

And when I die and become a metaphorical ghost, I will *do cool shit. Something so that you'll know it's me.*

"You okay?" Leander is peering at me from the boulder, eyes sharpening with concern.

I breathe like Dr. Salamando taught me, but when I whoosh the air out, I still feel unsettled. Which is frustrating, because it's just a coincidence that Leander said what Imogen said. I don't know why I'm freaking out. I'm breathing out again when the silence comes back, moving gently across the grass.

And it's like she's here again. Sliding in next to me on the bench, looking at me with the slightly exasperated expression that means I'm not understanding something fast enough.

I close my eyes. It's the memories, that's all. The memories are sitting here with me. It's metaphorical, not real.

"Natalie?" Leander is leaning forward on the boulder, like he's about to stand up.

"Sorry, I just... Imogen and I used to come here a lot. She found this place." That's all I mean to say, but then my mouth is opening by itself, the words spilling out before my brain can catch up.

"She was always finding stuff. Like this ponderosa pine on the Starlight Trail we named Agnes Tree. It has a hole in the trunk way up high. . . ." I tell him about the hummingbird, about how I climbed the tree every summer after we found it but there was never anything else up there. The words are coming fast, like I'm not in control of them. "And last summer, she wanted me to climb it again, but I didn't. I knew there was nothing up there, so I didn't climb it, and then she . . . and then . . ."

I'm shivering now, the old mixture of guilt and loss roiling around inside me, only getting worse as I picture her face. Eyes wide as she begged me to climb the tree, dorky headlamp slightly askew.

Surprise tears spill out of my eyes. I thought I'd gotten past this. I thought I'd moved on. A frantic, panicky feeling fizzles through me, and then instead of feeling like Imogen is on the bench beside me, Leander is actually there, putting his hand over mine.

I squeeze, hard. Because I want to feel the solid, warm realness of his skin. I want him to wrap his arms around me like he did outside the tunnel and bring me back to reality. I want to smell the lavender on his hoodie and feel the perfect pressure of his arms.

We look up at the same time from our clasped hands. Leander stares at me, his eyes radiating with their familiar intensity and also something completely new—a kind of warmth that does fluttering things to my stomach. I move closer to him on the bench, running my hands up his arms. And then I brush my lips against his.

It goes gently at first, a swarm of soft kisses that turn deeper, until his arms are fully wrapped around my waist and mine are in his hair, the warmth from his body heating me up, making my face flush.

When we break apart, the silence and memories and metaphors are gone. Suddenly, everything feels very tangible. The smooth softness of Leander's hair on my fingers. The gust of his breath on my cheeks. The stunned look in his eyes that I'm sure is mirrored in mine. Because I've never kissed anyone like that. Ever.

With Raden it was always fun, but this felt different. Deeper. Like a part of me I didn't know about is fully awake now, alert and wanting more. But I have no idea how to put any of that into words or if I should or what Leander is thinking, and as I draw my hands back from his hair and he lets go of my waist, an awkwardness springs up between us so thick it's like a solid mass.

"I didn't mean to—I mean, I didn't *plan* on..." Leander waves his hand between us.

"No, um, me neither." I comb my fingers through my hair.

"I just, I didn't mean to take advantage or anything," Leander says, his face getting even pinker. "You were obviously going through something...."

"No, no, no," I rush to assure him, and now the highly unpleasant thought that pity had something to do with why Leander kissed me back runs through my mind. "It's fine. I'm fine. This..." Now it's my turn to wave a hand between us. "This was all fine."

Leander's eyebrows wrinkle. "Fine...," he repeats, almost like a question.

And God, I didn't mean to say the kiss was fine. It was amazing. But there's no way I can say that now when we're about ten seconds from spontaneously combusting from awkwardness. We need to regroup. Refocus.

"We should talk about our game plan with Madame Althea," I say, a little too loudly.

"Yeah. Yes." Leander nods, smoothing out his hoodie. "Um, we should follow up on the angle that Madame Althea tells people negative stuff so they keep coming back. Hard to prove, but compelling if we have enough stories that fit."

"Cool, cool." I still sound a little out of breath, and my heart rate is going berserk.

"Dr. B said the Harlow's showing an outdoor movie tomorrow night in the courtyard, and she'll be there. Maybe we can see if she knows anything."

"Great."

"Good." Leander stands up at the same time as I do, and we bump into each other like complete idiots. This is not good.

Leander walks out of Oasis first, and when I'm sure he's gone, I let out a huge breath, my head falling into my hands. I've been through multiple tornadoes of emotion in the past half hour, and I feel dizzy and depleted.

Did I really just kiss Leander and then tell him it was "fine"?

Before I can replay the moment in excruciating detail, another slow wind creeps into Oasis, rustling the spruces. And I swear I hear Imogen snort-laugh, clear as the air around me.

chapter fourteen

Summer after sixth grade, four years before Imogen dies

"There's probably nothing up there," I say as we stare up at the dark hollow in the trunk of the ponderosa pine, craning our necks back as far as they'll go.

"There *has* to be." Imogen pushes her glasses farther up her nose. "In a story, that's exactly where you'd find the missing diary or the key to the old chest or whatever ancient object you need to finally learn what the ghost's whole deal is and put their soul to rest!" She puts her hands up like *duh*!

I laugh, a giddy lightness swirling through me. It's already been the best summer ever. Imogen never thought we'd convince her parents to give up two whole weeks to come to Estes Park, let alone rent the cabin right next door to mine and Mom's. But we did, and now we're running around the trails unsupervised, and it's the best thing ever.

"Why a ghost?" I ask.

"Why not?" Imogen is still blinking up at the small, dark hole in the trunk that, from down here, seems miles away. She hasn't taken her eyes off it since she spotted it five minutes ago, as we meandered down the Starlight Trail. Her eyes have their familiar faraway look, but she looks different than she usually does. It takes me a second to realize it's because her usually paper-white skin has turned a sandy gold in the mountain sun.

"What do you think is in there?" I ask.

"I don't know. It could be anything." Imogen drums her fingers on her thighs, and I know she probably wants to go back to her cabin immediately, so she can write this story down in her notebook. But instead, she digs her fingers into the bark and lets out a frustrated groan. "I wish I knew what was up there for real!"

"Again, probably nothing," I say. "Right?"

Imogen shakes her head. "No, there's something, I can feel it. I wish heights wasn't my number-five fear."

A few months ago, our English teacher had us list out our fears as a writing exercise. Most people had a few things on the list, but Imogen's list filled an entire page, front and back. "Heights" was right above "skiing accident" and right below "a bat biting me in my sleep."

"I'll look," I say, glancing at the boulder sitting a couple of feet away from the tree. If I stand on top of it, I could reach the first crooked branch easily.

Imogen gasps. "Oh my God, no. I didn't mean we should actually look. It's way too high."

"It's just a tree." I'm already stepping onto the boulder. "Tell me if you see a park ranger." I put my knee on the low branch, lean my hands against the trunk for balance, and push up.

"I hate this so much," Imogen moans, dancing from one foot to the other.

"It's fine," I call down. "It's actually way easier than I thought."

The branches aren't the thickest, but they're sturdy, and even have a little spring to them as I push off each one and onto the next. It's a strange feeling, almost like the tree wants me to climb it. I'll make sure to tell Imogen that when I'm down so she can put the detail into her story.

As I keep climbing, sweat coating my neck, the branches guiding me with their subtle spring, anticipation whirls through me. But I remind myself there's probably nothing in the hollow.

I look down at miniature Imogen, her head cranked all the way back. "Don't look *down*!" she yells wildly.

"Don't look *up*!" I yell back. I watch as her hands fly up to cover her eyes.

Another minute and I'm right underneath the hollow. It's bigger up close and not as round as it looked from the ground. It's more of a twisted oval shape, like a mouth stretched open, right in the middle of saying something.

There's probably nothing, there's probably nothing, I repeat as I lift my hand up and reach inside. My fingers brush over gritty dirt, dry leaves, knotty sticks, and then something cold and hard and smooth. I scream from the surprise. Then Imogen screams. I grasp whatever it is and pull it out.

It's glittering and green. A crystal hummingbird smudged with dirt, but still sparkling. As I turn it in the sun, I see it has lots of colors in it. An emerald-green body, sky-blue wings, a blood-red neck. I can't stop staring at it. I still can't quite believe there was really something in the hollow, even though it's right here in my hand. I look down at Imogen, who is bouncing up and down.

How did she know?

"What is it, *what is it?*" she squeals. I stash the hummingbird in my pocket and climb back down the tree. As soon as I touch the ground, I pull it out to show her.

"I almost peed!" I say giddily, handing the hummingbird to Imogen, whose eyes are triple their normal size behind her glasses. She turns it over in her hands.

"A hummingbird," she whispers, looking at it in wonder.

"I really didn't think anything was up there," I whisper back. I don't know why we're whispering. It just feels right. "How did you know?"

Imogen shrugs, not taking her eyes off the bird. "I just did." We sit down on the boulder next to the tree, hip to hip. We stay like that, passing the hummingbird back and forth, until the sun sinks down, throwing its pinkish light between the crooked branches.

"It's the missing message from Agnes Thripp," Imogen declares.

"Who?"

"Didn't you read the *Ghosts of the Harlow Hotel* pamphlet?" Imogen asks, slightly scandalized.

"No." We'd convinced our parents to wander around the Harlow Hotel the other day because we heard it was haunted. My mom liked all the old portraits, and Imogen's parents thought it had historical value. Imogen and I loved its spooky vibe.

"Agnes Thripp was the only person to have died at the hotel," Imogen says, telling me the whole story about Agnes getting pneumonia and not taking her medication, promising her friend that she'd send a message back to prove the afterlife existed.

"Cynthia supposedly never got a message from Agnes, which some people took as proof that there is no afterlife," Imogen goes on. "But there are other possible explanations. Maybe Agnes tried to send her a message. Maybe she left her favorite hummingbird figurine in the tree for Cynthia to find. Maybe Agnes tried to lead Cynthia to it, but Cynthia didn't understand the message. Agnes was a brand-new ghost then, so she was still learning how to communicate. Agnes kept trying to reach out to Cynthia, to anyone, but as the century passed, the tree grew taller and taller until the hollow was so high up that no one found it. Until us."

I smile, a sparkling shot of excitement flurrying around in my chest. Imogen sees stories everywhere. It makes the world feel different. It's like she sees this magical potential in all things, no matter how ordinary they are. Like, instead of this tree being a random tree in a place full of a gazillion trees, it's the key to a mystery. A ghost mystery.

"What does she want us to do with it?" I ask, whispering again.

"We'll have to keep coming back to find out. We're part of the story now. Agnes sent her message from the afterlife, but no one heard it. But then, years and years later, two girls walked along this same trail. One girl believed and the other girl was brave, and they found Agnes's bird. And they promised to return to the tree every year to see what other messages she sends."

Imogen looks at me, holding her pinkie in the air. "They promised to always be brave and believe."

I grasp her pinkie in mine, but then I hesitate. "What if we never find anything up there again?"

"We will," Imogen says, handing me the hummingbird.

"Okay...," I say uncertainly, passing the bird from hand to hand. It's surprisingly heavy for being this small.

"You didn't think anything would be in there this time," Imogen says, like she can hear my doubts.

"True."

"But something was."

"Yeah, but..."

"I know you don't believe in ghosts."

"No."

Imogen is quiet as I turn the hummingbird over in my hands, watching its beak glint in the sun.

"But I do," she finally says as a gust of wind blows in. It picks up her words, spinning them around us before carrying them off to some distant place.

chapter fifteen

Seven days until the Spirit Ball

Trying to edit Frankie's interview footage is impossible. Ever since Oasis yesterday, my brain has been a disaster, and whenever I try to focus, it flitters off in completely unproductive directions. Imogen and Agnes Tree and metaphorical ghosts and Leander's mouth on mine.

I haven't seen him since we kissed, and I can't tell if I'm thankful or disappointed. Regardless, we're supposed to meet at 9:00 PM tonight to catch Dr. B at the outdoor movie and see if we can find anything else out about Madame Althea. As I walk to the Harlow's front courtyard, I can't help wondering what it'll be like to see him. Because as much as our secret project to expose Madame Althea has brought Leander and me closer, and as earth-stopping as that kiss was, do I really believe we could be an actual thing?

I've never had an actual thing before. It's always been sort-of things, like with Raden. Light and fun and shallow in a good way. I don't know how to do anything more. And even if I did, Leander has one foot out of Colorado already, so it wouldn't matter. Plus, wouldn't Leander want to be in a relationship with someone more like him—someone brainy and serious and all that?

I blink up at the black sky and try to clear my head, to calm the restless energy that's been zipping through my body ever since the kiss. As I turn into the courtyard, I see lantern lights dotting the yard, people setting up lawn chairs and shaking out blankets, buying hot chocolate and striped bags of kettle corn from a red popcorn wagon. The whole setup is so charming, I wish I could spread out a blanket and watch *Psycho* with everyone else. The jumbo movie screen is set up so its back faces the surrounding wooded trails—a patch of white against the murky darkness.

I keep my eyes away from the small gap in the trees marking the Starlight Trail and remind myself that I'm not here to watch a movie. I'm here to find out more about Madame Althea.

"Hello, Natalie." I spin around to find Madame Althea's pale blue eyes staring back at me.

"Oh . . . hi." My body goes on high alert, but I resist the urge to take a step back.

"It's a beautiful evening," she breathes, her voice as soft and cool as the air. "I was wondering if you'd like to take a quick walk around the grounds."

"Okay," I say slowly. I should be glad to have an opportunity to talk to her and maybe get some information. But my stomach twists as we step away from the movie crowd. I remind myself that there's no audience, no camera to perform in front of this time, so there's no reason for her to try anything again.

We're heading toward the wooded trails, our pace slow and meandering. "I wanted to apologize for yesterday," Madame Althea starts, clasping her hands behind her back. "When a spirit is insistent, I do whatever I can to make them heard. But I think about the departed so much that sometimes I forget to think about the living. I shouldn't have pushed you."

You shouldn't have snooped on my Instagram, more like. But I plaster a pleasant smile on my face. "It's okay."

"How is your *Ghost Chasers* project coming along?" Madame Althea asks, looking at me with kindly interest.

"It's great." I push aside the fact that I haven't been able to focus on editing it today. "Everyone here loves the show, so it's easy to get interviews."

"I can see why they're fans." Madame Althea nods as we pass by the empty mini golf course, a paint-chipped windmill spinning slowly in the breeze. "That Joshua Jacobs is a handsome son of a bitch."

I huff out a surprised laugh and then feel guilty. Because I shouldn't be laughing with the person who's trying to exploit my best friend's death.

Madame Althea turns her wide, innocent eyes to me. "Don't you think so?"

"Oh, of course," I say, trying to sound natural. "It's my main reason for auditioning for the show."

She smiles slyly. "Well, when you meet him, tell him he has a fan at the Harlow Hotel. You could slip him a picture of me, too," she says, winking. I think of the picture on her desk of her and her sister, Marta. And it strikes me that maybe I should learn more about her sister. Leander said he wanted to get the full story of Madame Althea and her life, even the things that don't seem important, because you never know what might help people see beyond her mystique.

"Maybe the picture on your desk," I say, taking a shot. "Though your sister probably wouldn't be too happy about that."

Madame Althea laughs. "No, certainly not. It's a shame, too, because it commemorates such a wonderful time. We'd gone to California to celebrate my twenty-first birthday."

"Oh, cool. That sounds fun."

"It was. Although a particularly stubborn spirit who'd died during the Gold Rush kept pestering me. Wouldn't stop yammering. But I didn't let it ruin my stay."

"Could, um, could Marta hear the spirit, too?"

Madame Althea laughs again, her eyes lighting up. "No, she said I was full of it. She wasn't a believer back then."

My brain starts buzzing. Marta didn't believe her own sister could really speak to the dead. Did she have proof of that? But Madame Althea said Marta didn't believe "back then," so did she change her mind at some point? What made her believe?

"We were nearly arrested when we were there," Madame Althea goes on, the sly smile coming back. "Disorderly conduct."

"You never told me you had a criminal record," a familiar voice behind us says. Dr. B is strolling up, raising a playful eyebrow at Madame Althea.

"*Almost* had a criminal record," Madame Althea corrects. "Marta sweet-talked our way out of it. Always had the gift of persuasion, that one."

Dr. B smiles and tucks her hair behind her ears. "How is Marta?"

"Oh, same old." Madame Althea waves her hand in the air. "Thinks she can tell me what to do because she had the wisdom to be born three years before me." There's genuine annoyance mixed with genuine fondness in her voice, a combination I remember hearing when Imogen talked about Bea.

"Oh, wait...," I say, racking my brain for a way to find out Marta's last name. "I actually met a Marta here the other day. I forget her last name, but I think it started with an *R*? Was that your sister?" I'm inwardly squirming, hoping Madame Althea won't realize I'm using the same technique she used at the reading.

"Hoffman, right?" Dr. B jumps in, looking at Madame Althea for confirmation. "After she married the professor?"

"That's right." Madame Althea's mouth turns down at the corners. "Hoffman. Never thought he was good enough for her, but there you go."

"Oh, I guess it wasn't her, then," I say casually. Inside, I'm jumping up and down. Marta Hoffman. Marta Hoffman! I got her name! I don't know how much it'll help, but I got it. My chest balloons with something that feels a lot like pride.

Until I look up and realize we're walking straight toward the Starlight Trail. I can see the small wooden sign.

"I better get back so my kids don't eat all the popcorn before the movie starts," Dr. B says, looking back toward the courtyard. "Have a good night." I watch her walk away, trying not to think about the fact that I'm alone with Madame Althea again.

"Are you staying for the movie?" I ask, sidestepping away from the trailhead.

"No, Morris is expecting me," Madame Althea says. "My dog. And I'm afraid I've never been a *Psycho* fan."

"Oh. Why not?"

Madame Althea shrugs her shoulders elegantly. "It suggests that hearing the voices of the departed makes you insane and murderous."

"Right." That's kind of the whole twist. You think it's the mother of the mild-mannered innkeeper Norman Bates who stabs Marion Crane in the famous shower scene. But it's actually Norman himself, driven mad by the vicious, imagined voice of his dead mother.

"I know it's only a movie," Madame Althea says. "But stories like that contribute to the belief that hearing the voices of the departed is a bad thing. When the departed reach out to the living, the most common reaction people have is fear or disbelief. They feel like they're losing their minds. And if they tell anyone about it, they're laughed at. So they push it away. They decide not to believe."

She's looking at me so intensely she's barely blinking. "I can't help but think that if hearing from the departed was more normalized, people would be more open to listen."

A strange chill runs through my body as Madame Althea suddenly cocks her head toward the Starlight Trail sign, her eyelids fluttering closed.

I hold my breath. There's no way she's pulling this again. My rational brain tells me to walk away right now. Away from the fake medium, away from the Starlight Trail. But I stay.

When Madame Althea opens her eyes, they're clouded with uncertainty. "I'm sorry. I'm doing it again."

I can't move. Despite my brain yelling at me to get out of there, to find Leander, I can't move. "What?" I ask, the word slipping out as a whisper.

"It's mountain dark." Madame Althea's eyes drift back to the trail. "She says to wear a headlamp when you go in."

I'm speed-walking back to the courtyard, my heart pounding as the frantic pulse of *Psycho*'s opening credits fill the air. I let out a relieved breath when I see Leander standing at the back of the movie crowd. He'll see through Madame Althea's latest trick. He'll know how she did it. When he sees me weaving through the blankets and chairs, he smiles. But it fades when he takes in my face up close.

"I have good news and bad news and...weird news," I say, trying to catch my breath.

"Tell me everything. Here." Leander hands me a bag of popcorn and I sit down beside him. It takes me a second to register that he's laid a blanket out on the grass. The aqua quilt from his dorm room. He brought it with him and got popcorn, like we're here to watch the movie. Like it's a date.

The thought spins around in my head until I remember I have so many things to tell him. We're far enough away from the rest of the crowd, so I launch in. Madame Althea's apology, her thirsting over Joshua Jacobs, her sister and how I found out her name is Marta Hoffman because she married a Professor Hoffman, who Madame Althea thinks isn't good enough for her. And finally, what Madame Althea said at the edge of the Starlight Trail.

It's mountain dark. She says to wear a headlamp when you go in.

"'Mountain dark' was Imogen's phrase," I explain, keeping my voice as level as possible. "And she always made me wear a headlamp even though I never wanted to. There's nothing about any of that on my social media. And there were no other people or cameras around when Madame Althea said it."

"Okay," Leander says, forehead creased as he takes it all in. "Let's go through it, thing by thing."

His voice is calm and steady, and I instantly feel reassured. He's going to do what he does. Find the truth underneath all the bullshit.

Leander picks up his phone and taps around on it, tilting his head as he squints at the screen. I lean forward and see a close-up of Joshua Jacobs's face from Google Images.

"He's all right, I guess," Leander declares.

I stare at him. "*That's* what you're starting with?" I try to keep my face stern, but my mouth is spreading into a smile.

"I had to know." Leander puts his phone down on the blanket, his expression softening when he sees me smile. I get the feeling he did this whole thing just to make me feel better, and now my heart is pumping for an altogether different reason.

"Okay, the next thing," he says, all business. "Madame Althea's sister, Marta Hoffman, didn't believe Madame Althea could really talk to the dead."

"At first. She said she wasn't a believer 'back then,' so it sounds like that changed."

"Right. But still, at one point, Marta Hoffman thought her own sister was lying. If we find out why, that could be useful. Maybe if we can find Marta or Professor Hoffman, they'd be willing to talk to us. But most importantly, you used Madame Althea's own trick against her to find out her sister's last name. That was some all-around impressive detective work." He chucks me on the shoulder. "Pardner."

The glow of admiration in his eyes, the inside joke, the light touch that's sending sparks through my body shove everything else clean out of my brain for a moment.

"Then there's the headlamp thing," Leander says after a beat.

I immediately focus again. "Yeah?"

Leander opens his mouth, then closes it and sighs. "I thought something would come to me, but it didn't. I guess I can't explain that one."

It takes a few seconds for that to sink in. Leander has been debunking Madame Althea's tricks left and right since we got here. But he can't explain this one.

"Maybe it'll make sense to us later," he says, unfazed. "I'll see if I can find anything about Marta Hoffman online."

He picks up his phone again. I should be looking up Marta Hoffman, too. But my thoughts are veering off in an entirely different direction. Because the things I can't explain are adding up. The elbow grab, my bracelet breaking, both Leander and Madame Althea saying things that Imogen used to say. The strange silence that seems to be following me around.

I close my eyes and try to slow my brain down, but the questions I've kept a tight lid on since Frankie's interview burst out.

What if Madame Althea doesn't have access to my Instagram? What if she knew all that stuff—cheese and crackers and The Song and mountain dark—all on her own? What if she's telling the truth, and Imogen is really out there, trying to contact me?

It's sounds so ridiculous when I lay it out like that. Too unbelievable to even think about. But I can't stop.

"I've never seen this," Leander says, and I realize he's stopped looking at his phone and is staring at the movie screen instead.

I jump at the distraction, pushing the absurd questions out of my head. "You've never seen *Psycho*? It's a classic. The first slasher movie."

"Really?" Leander looks doubtful. "I thought slasher movies had a higher body count."

"A lot do. But it all started with the *Psycho* shower scene." I imitate the screechy violins and slash a knife through the air.

Leander chuckles as he watches me.

"And in most slasher movies," I go on, because I don't want to think about Madame Althea again. And because I want Leander to keep looking at me the way he is right now—eyes bright, smile big and goofy and unrestrained. "The killer is practically invincible. Like, he can keep coming back even after he's been shot or stabbed or thrown out of multiple windows."

I think of all the scenes I've seen like that. Michael Myers sitting up after Jamie Lee Curtis stabbed him with the knitting needle. Jason Voorhees opening his eyes after he's anchored to the bottom of the lake. The fisherman crashing through Julie James's shower door after he supposedly drowned. It's the biggest horror movie cliché of all, the monster coming back when you think it's gone.

"I guess horror movies aren't known for their realism," Leander says.

"Nope." In real life, when someone dies, they're dead. They don't come back and grab elbows and pull on bracelets and speak through mediums. They don't tell their best friend to wear a headlamp in the woods, even though they always used to....

"So, what's your favorite horror movie?" Leander asks, once again pulling me out of a ridiculous thought spiral.

"*Evil Dead II*. It's pure chaos. You think you're going to get a quiet, chill moment but then a window shatters or a mounted deer head starts laughing or the main character cuts off his possessed hand and replaces it with a chainsaw."

"That sounds..." Leander is looking off into the distance, like he's trying to find the right word. "Disgusting."

"Oh, it is."

Leander laughs again, and for one beautiful moment, it feels like I'm just at an outdoor movie with a boy I kissed, and there are no mediums or exposés or strange, lingering doubts.

"So, are you and Raden Suzuki together?" Leander says out of nowhere.

"What?"

Leander shrugs, his face unreadable. "Just curious."

"No. I mean, we sometimes...in the past, we've..." I can't bring myself to say anything more specific in front of Leander. Not because I'm embarrassed but because I suddenly need him to know that Raden and I were never a serious thing. "But we're not together. We never were."

"Oh?" I still can't read his face, and it's driving me insane.

"We're mostly just friends. He hasn't even seen *Evil Dead II*," I add because I'm losing all verbal communication skills.

"So that's a prerequisite?" Leander asks, a corner of his mouth tipping up, his tone breezy. "For being your boyfriend?"

Is he joking around? Is he seriously asking? I laugh because I don't know what else to do. I wish I could see into his brain. I wish he could tell me how Madame Althea knew about mountain dark and headlamps.

My gaze floats back to the Starlight Trail in the distance, all my questions about Madame Althea and Imogen mixing in with my confusion about Leander, causing a strange, shifting feeling to churn inside me, like all the things I once believed have been tossed up into the air and haven't fallen back into place yet.

"Mother! Oh God, what..."

I glance at the screen. I was so wrapped up in everything else that the famous shower scene came and went, and now Norman is finding Marion's body. He slowly starts the whole cleaning-up business, which I always thought went on for way too long. But Imogen said it was that way on purpose because the audience needs time to process the shock of the fact that Marion isn't the main character after all. They need time to accept the shift in reality.

Movies can do that. They can get you to accept a

surprising twist if they give enough cues that say you're supposed to. Marion isn't the main character after all. Bruce Willis was dead all along. Jason's not the killer, his mother is.

But it doesn't work that way in real life. In real life, a few strange, unexplainable things happening can't make me believe that the ghost of my best friend is haunting me. Flirting and a kiss, no matter how amazing it was, can't make me believe that Leander Hall wants to be my boyfriend.

But…

A movement from somewhere behind the movie screen makes me glance into the woods again. There's a girl standing at the edge of the Starlight Trail, her white sweatshirt glowing against the dark backdrop of trees. She's staring at me.

After a second, she angles her head back in the direction of the woods, turns, and disappears into the dark.

chapter sixteen

It's not Imogen. That would be impossible, so it's not her. It only looks like her—the height, the build, the white sweatshirt. It's not her.

But all of a sudden, I'm on my feet.

"Natalie." Leander is standing, too, staring at me. He glances out to where I've been looking, and I get the feeling it's not the first time he's done that, or the first time he's said my name.

"I should get some shots of the woods real quick." I grab my camera bag off the blanket and sling it over my shoulder. "Be right back."

I skirt around the lawn chairs and blankets, hurrying toward the Starlight Trail, not really sure what I'm doing. I just know I have to follow her. Not Imogen. Obviously.

Whoever it is. Maybe the girl I saw was nodding to someone else in the crowd. Maybe she's meeting someone on the trail. Maybe...

I try to unzip my bag, but my hands are shaking, and my legs slow down when I'm a few paces away from the trailhead. Then I stop completely, and I just stand there, staring down the dark. The only sound I'm aware of is my heartbeat hammering in my chest.

"Don't you want me to film?" Leander says, slightly out of breath as he comes up next to me.

"Oh." I blink down the trail again. It would be impossible to explain why I'm really going into the woods. "Thanks." I take the camera out of the bag and hand it to Leander, willing my hands to be steady.

"Just follow me," I say, once he lifts the camera to his face.

I take a breath and step onto the trail, walking quickly, the dirt and rocks scraping under my feet. It takes several paces for the darkness to settle around me like a fog, the camera light only tearing a small slash of brightness into the surrounding black.

I pull my headlamp from my bag and snap it around my forehead, trying my hardest not to think about Madame Althea, not to think about anything except figuring out exactly what I saw. I turn around to offer Leander my Maglite, but he waves his hand and points at the camera, signaling it's enough light for him. We keep going.

The spicy scent of sage fills my nostrils, and in the light

from my headlamp, I spot Harvey the Aspen, his black-scar smile looking big and silly as always. Patches of yarrow line the trail like Barbie bouquets, nodding gently in the wind. It's quiet. So quiet, like Leander and I are the only ones on the—

A white sleeve flashes in the corner of my eye, up ahead. Someone is there, moving quickly down the trail. I gulp in so much air my throat goes dry. "Oh my God, did you see that?" I snap my head back to Leander, whose eyes are on the viewfinder.

"Did you *see* that?" I repeat when he doesn't answer. Leander startles and looks up, eyebrows knitting in confusion. *Do I talk?* he mouths. And then I realize he thinks I'm faking it for the camera again.

I whirl around and speed-walk down the trail, keeping my eyes up, trusting my feet to avoid tripping on roots and rocks and— There it is again! A sliver of white behind a branch, completely still for a second before disappearing, like it was waiting for me to catch up.

I'm running now, Leander's footsteps growing fainter behind me. My brain says to slow down, but my body is moving on its own. Going deeper and deeper down the trail, following the flashes. Every time I think they're gone, that maybe I just imagined them, I see one again—a glimmer at the edge of a boulder, a streak through the leaves.

Everything else goes away except those flashes, drawing me down the trail. Until a memory springs up. Me in Madame Althea's office. I can see it as clearly as if it was playing on the outdoor movie screen.

"She's reaching out to you."

"I don't believe in that.... I don't need closure. I don't need to communicate with anyone. I've already grieved and worked through it. Do you understand that? I've moved on. I've moved on."

"She hasn't."

When she said those words in her office, they enraged me. But now, it's not anger coursing through my body. It's something else.

It's hope. Foolish, irrational hope.

And then I see her.

Not a flash of something. *Her.* Imogen. Standing up ahead, by Agnes Tree, half beside and half behind the trunk, her hood pulled up over her head.

I run faster than I ever have in my life. I'm still several feet away when she steps behind the trunk, and when I reach the tree, putting my hand out to touch the rough bark, circling all the way around, she's gone. Frustration boils through my body. I look up at the familiar branches, the dark hollow carved high into the trunk.

Aren't you going to climb it? Imogen says, her voice sharp and close, like she breathed it into my ear.

It's not a memory of her voice, it's *her voice.* The way I used to hear it in the weeks after she died. Like it's real.

I snatch my hand away, almost tripping over my feet as I shuffle back. What the fuck? What the *fuck* just happened?

I stand there, heaving breaths in and out, staring at Agnes Tree like it could give me answers. I can't move. It's like the roots have wrapped around my feet and nestled back down into the ground. I'm vaguely aware that Leander has caught up to me. That he's standing very still a few feet away. That he hasn't said anything in a weirdly long time.

I finally turn to him and realize he's still filming. "Okay," I say, my voice hoarse. "You can stop now."

Leander lowers the camera, his eyes studying me. "I think I got most of it. You were going so fast, and I didn't want to trip and break the camera. But it should come out okay."

I blink at him. He didn't see anything. I can tell by his voice, his expression. He didn't see anything on the trail.

Leander steps closer, peering into my face. "Natalie, are you sure you're okay?"

"I'm fine," I say automatically, but I can't help glancing at Agnes Tree again. The idea of seeing Imogen here a moment ago seems so unbelievable now. But I did. Didn't I? Didn't I see *something* at least?

"I just got into it, I guess. The filming," I say when I realize Leander is still watching me.

"Yeah. You were…really convincing." Leander flicks his eyes to Agnes Tree and then back to me, a slow realization spreading across his face. "Is this…This is the tree, isn't it? The one where you and Imogen found the hummingbird."

His expression shifts from surprised to sympathetic to worried.

I nod, because I don't trust myself to speak right now. And before Leander can say anything else, my eyes catch on the camera he's still holding. It would have proof. It would show the flashes, the girl. Imogen. Or it wouldn't. Either way, I'll *know*. I'll know if what I saw out here was real or all in my head.

I practically lunge forward and grab the camera.

"Whoa." Leander startles, letting go.

"Sorry." I tell myself to calm down. "I'm just excited to edit this. The deadline is coming up, so I want to get it done tonight." I pack the camera carefully into my bag, turning so Leander doesn't see that my hands are still shaking.

"Okay..." Leander looks like he wants to ask me a million more questions. To my everlasting relief, he doesn't. He only turns and matches my quick pace back up the trail.

But he watches me the whole way. Quick, sidelong glances.

When we pass the edge of the trees and step out into the Harlow's courtyard, *Psycho* is still playing, the blankets and lawn chairs and popcorn wagon still glowing in the light from the screen. It's so surreal that everything out here is completely normal when back there in the woods...

I suppress a shudder as I take off my headlamp and turn to Leander. "Would you mind if I just head up to my room so I can get started on this?"

"Oh. Yeah, no problem." He's still holding in all the questions he wants to ask me, I can tell. I feel awful about it, but I wouldn't know how to answer them anyway.

"Okay. See you tomorrow." But before I can turn away, Leander takes my hand, lacing his fingers through mine. His eyes roam over my face, and it looks like he's deciding what to say. "I know we've only really known each other for a few days." He bends his knees so he's eye to eye with me. "But I hope you know you can trust me. You can tell me anything, and I'll listen."

I squeeze his hand, just like I did in Oasis, and I wish I could tell him everything, and he would somehow make it all make sense. But what would I say? That I might have seen the ghost of Imogen on the trail tonight? How would he make that make sense?

"I know," I say, and I'm surprised at how much I mean it. I trust him. I know he'll listen. I just can't tell him about this. Not yet. Not until I know what I saw.

Leander squeezes my hand one more time before letting go.

As I walk back to the dorm, I can still feel the impression of his fingers, the warmth radiating out from them. It feels like something that, under any other circumstances, I would have turned over in my head for a while, right alongside the kiss.

But there's the camera bumping against my hip, which I'll connect to my laptop as soon as I get to my room, and then I'll watch the footage, and…

Maybe there will be nothing. No flashes. No girl who looks like Imogen by Agnes Tree. I have to prepare myself for that. If there is nothing, then that means I got tricked by the woods. It happens to a lot of people. Haven't I read somewhere that over half of Americans believe in ghosts? And that a fair amount of those people believe they've actually seen one? It's probably easy to trick people into seeing things in a dark place next to a haunted hotel.

But if there *is* something in the footage, if I see on my laptop what I saw out there, then that means...

I can't think about what it means. I can't even speculate about it until I play it back. I hurry up the stairs to my room, my heart thrashing around in my chest like a wild animal. My hands are shaking again, but I manage to plug in the USB cord. My desk chair creaks as I plunk onto it, and the footage lights up my screen.

I'm walking into the woods—tinted a sickly greenish-gray from the night vision. I'm going fast, my hands balled into fists at my sides. The only sounds are our quick, rhythmic footsteps on the trail. It strikes me how different this looks from an episode of *Ghost Chasers*. It's scarier. Because I'm not saying anything. I don't look like a host, investigating a haunted place. I look like a girl in the woods at night, digging a headlamp out of her bag with trembling hands.

"*Did you see that?*" I say frantically on camera, the night vision turning my eyeballs into glowing green orbs. I slam my finger into the space bar and go back, looking all over the screen.

At nothing. There's nothing there. I pause and go back, pause and go back, but all I see are the greenish woods.

Something squirms in my stomach, taking on weight until it's like my whole body is sinking. There's nothing there. But I have to keep going. I push the space bar and watch the woods shake to life again, staring at the screen as the footage gets bumpier and blurrier, as I get smaller and more distant and—

I pause again, going back a few seconds, and suck in a gulp of air. *There.* By the boulder. A long, white blur that looks like an arm. I hit Play and sit up straighter in the chair, hardly blinking as I watch myself hurry down the trail. My heart pumps as Agnes Tree comes into the frame. My hands fly to my mouth. I stop breathing.

Because I see it. A body, or half of one, peering out and then stepping back behind the trunk.

It's *there.* Blurry and quick, but clearly there. I go back and replay it again. Then again, and again, and again, my face so close to the screen I can feel the warmth from it. Every time, I see the same thing. A body in Imogen's sweatshirt, with Imogen's hair, looking at me and then disappearing.

Was it another trick? Shadows? My headlamp hitting the surface of the tree in just such a way?

But that's *twice* now that I've seen her. Out in the woods and now here, on this footage from my camera. And while there are a lot of things that can lie to you—people and memories and even your own eyes—cameras aren't supposed to. I close my eyes to clear my head for a second, but the figure behind the tree flashes inside my eyelids, lighting up the dark.

I don't believe in ghosts.

But I do. Imogen's voice, for the second time that night, speaks sharply in my head.

chapter seventeen

Six days until the Spirit Ball

It's 8:30 AM. Half an hour before Leander and I are supposed to meet Dr. B in the billiards room to update her on our projects. But I couldn't stay in my room any longer, watching the trail footage, so I gathered my stuff and came down to Jitter Beans to get a jumbo muffin. After ten minutes, I haven't taken a single bite.

I'm too busy staring at Madame Althea's office door, contemplating the dark slit underneath with a vague sense of disappointment. She isn't inside.

I should be glad about that. I shouldn't want to show her the footage I've now seen hundreds of times. I know what she'd say anyway. That Imogen is reaching out to me. She'd say it even though I told her I don't believe in ghosts.

But I do. Imogen's voice sounds in my head again, like it has since last night.

I've been here before. Last summer, I heard Imogen's voice in my head all the time. It faded after a while, especially after therapy. In a way, it feels like I'm right back to where I started. But it also feels different because last summer, I was sure Imogen was gone. This summer, I don't know.

Since last night, I've felt split in two. One part of me is interpreting everything that's happened so far like I'm a character in a horror movie.

Come on, that part keeps yelling. *Madame Althea? The bracelet? Leander talking about metaphorical ghosts? Seeing Imogen's literal ghost? It's so obvious something supernatural is happening! Don't be an idiot!*

But then there's the actual me, the one who lives in reality. *Dude! Ghosts. Aren't. Real. If they were, there'd be proof of it by now! Don't be an idiot!*

The back and forth is exhausting. I know I should try to focus on *Ghost Chasers* and the meeting with Dr. B. But my arm stretches to my laptop so I can stare at the blurry figure behind Agnes Tree again.

"Hey."

I jerk my arm back as Leander walks up to my chair, looking down at me with the same concerned expression as last night. Warmth blooms on my palm as I remember his hand there, the gentle squeeze before letting go. And suddenly I'm also remembering a whole host of things the blurry figure on my laptop blocked out last night. Leander asking me about Raden. The whole "is watching *Evil Dead II* a prerequisite for being your boyfriend" thing. And now my face feels warm, too.

"How's it going?" Leander asks, twirling his pen around his finger.

"Okay," I say, hoping I sound normal. "I didn't sleep great."

"Me neither." Leander sits in the chair across from mine. There's a heaviness around his eyelids, and his hair is messier than usual. It still looks good, of course, but—

"What was your reason?" Leander asks before any words get around to coming out of my mouth.

"I was just really in my head, missing Imogen," I say, wanting to tell him as close to the truth as I can right now. "What about you?"

"I was in my head, too. About . . . a lot of stuff." His eyes flick to the floor as he shifts on his chair. "But I think telling you about my mom yesterday dug up a lot of memories. I kept getting these flashes of my dad, stuff I hadn't thought about in ages. The metaphorical ghost strikes again."

"I'm sorry," I say, and I mean it. But at least he knows for sure that his ghost isn't real. At least his ghost is safely in his head, not possibly peering out from behind a tree.

"Anyway, eventually, I just got up and tried to work on the article. I figured it's the best chance I have at getting things to go back to normal." He runs a hand roughly through his hair. "But it's a mess. We have my mom's story, we have Frankie's story, and we have whatever it is she's trying to do to you. And that's good, but it's not enough. We need something that ties them together, shows who Madame Althea is and why she might be doing this. But we haven't found that yet."

Maybe we haven't found it because she's for real, Horror Movie Me says.

Or maybe it's because we're just two high school kids and we've only had four days, Reality Me says back.

"We didn't get a chance to talk to Dr. B last night, but she might know something," Leander goes on, sounding hopeful.

"Yeah. Maybe."

Leander is looking at me like he wants to ask if I'm okay again. He opens his mouth, but luckily, my phone alarm goes off. It's time to meet Dr. B in the billiards room. We both stand up slowly, gathering our things. I remind myself to put everything else on hold and finally focus on *Ghost Chasers.* This is the first time I'll be showing my footage to anyone else, and even though I'm not finished, I need to pay attention to everything Dr. B says so I can make it better.

As we climb the stairs to the lobby, Leander starts planning our strategy for asking Dr. B about Madame Althea. "Let's do our project reports first, and then I'll ask her something about how modern-day mediums are viewed differently than the ones in the past, and from there I'll try to get her talking about Madame Althea."

"Sounds good," I say, but I can't help feeling like we aren't going to find anything to prove she's a fraud.

And I realize that part of me doesn't even want to.

As Leander presents what he's learned so far about Agnes Thripp, it becomes clear that while he was secretly trying to expose Madame Althea and helping me with *Ghost Chasers*, he was also doing a ton of real research for his fake project. He knows everything about Agnes, including that her love of hummingbirds probably came from her mother, who was an amateur ornithologist. A week ago, that would have been more proof of what an insufferable know-it-all he was. But now it strikes me as both funny and oddly touching, like he did right by Agnes.

Like Imogen would approve.

Dr. B clearly approves, too. "Wonderful work, Leander," she says when he finishes. "A thorough overview of how Agnes Thripp's life and death connect to shifting attitudes toward Spiritualism. My only suggestion would be to end with how you think this research is valuable to the present day."

Leander closes his notebook and stares thoughtfully at the ceiling. "I think Agnes Thripp's life and death show how one story can be interpreted in opposite ways, depending on your beliefs. To skeptics, Agnes is a cautionary tale, proof that believing uncritically in the afterlife can lead to death. To believers, she's a hero, stopping at nothing to prove that the world is bigger than we understand. I think it shows that finding the truth can seem impossible, but that doesn't mean it doesn't exist. We should always keep searching for it, because the truth matters. It always matters."

I stare at Leander, whose voice is bursting with conviction, and suddenly feel totally out of my depth. Compared to what he said, my project must sound so flimsy. A tremor of nerves runs through me. Because with everything else going on, I completely forgot about the fact that I have to present at an academic conference on Saturday.

I'm wondering if there's a way to bail on the presentation while still getting credit for my senior project when I remember that day in Imogen's room again—when I decided not to audition for *Arcadia*. When Imogen told me about her award-winning essay, making me realize that the idea of *me* pretending to be a genius was ridiculous.

It's been in my head for the past couple of days, floating in and out. I don't like thinking about it. It led to the first and only fight Imogen and I ever had. But it keeps coming back, annoying and persistent.

And then it's my turn.

I take a breath, set up my laptop so it faces Dr. B, and press Play. A night shot of the Harlow's exterior appears on-screen, its windows glowing brightly in the dark, as Madame Althea's voice says, *"If spirit energy is strong somewhere, if remnants of the past endure, then that is a haunted place. America is filled with them. The world is filled with them. And one of those places happens to be right here."*

The footage segues into my intro filmed in the lobby, followed by my interview with Silas, and finally the tunnel scene where I "contact" Agnes Thripp with the flashlight. I've left out most of my interview with Madame Althea and the footage from the woods. They didn't fit the *Ghost Chasers* structure.

When it's over, I glance at Dr. B. "Well, that was fun," she says, leaning back in her chair with a thoughtful expression. "But I wonder if there's anything more that you've experienced here?"

My heartbeat stutters. "What?"

"I just mean," Dr. B goes on, circling her hand in the air. "For the presentation, you could add some insight you've gained as to why people are so fascinated with haunted places like the Harlow. Connect it to that bigger question."

"Honestly, I don't think *Ghost Chasers* is that deep. It's mostly about, like, exploring a creepy location at night and pretending a ghost touched you."

Dr. B squints at me. "Natalie, can I ask you something? Why do you want to be on *Ghost Chasers*?"

Leander leans in, waiting for my answer. But I don't have one because that stubborn memory is still running through my head—deciding not to audition for *Arcadia* because I could never play Thomasina convincingly. Deciding I *could* audition for *Ghost Chasers*, because it doesn't involve memorizing lines or pretending to be smart.

The fight Imogen and I had after, which we got over but never really talked about.

"I don't know," I say finally, looking at the floor.

"Well. It's something to think about." Dr. B gives me a gentle smile that has a touch of disappointment in it.

It's quiet for a moment, and I have a surprising urge to apologize to Imogen for not auditioning, even though I still can't explain why it made her so mad.

And then a question pops out of my mouth that I didn't intend to ask. "Dr. B, do you believe in ghosts?"

Dr. B looks a little thrown but covers it up quickly. "No," she says simply. "I don't. I've worked here for years and have heard the stories and have even been spooked a time or two, but no, I don't believe in ghosts."

I nod. It's the answer I expected, but I still feel some part of me deflate. Until Imogen's voice sounds in my ear again.

But I do!

"So..." My mouth keeps moving, faster than my brain can catch up. "Does that mean you believe Madame Althea is a fraud? She says she talks to the dead, but you don't believe ghosts are real, so..."

Leander is staring at me, and I try to apologize with my eyes because this is totally not how we planned to ask Dr. B about Madame Althea. It just came out.

Dr. B looks back and forth between Leander and me, and I'm not sure if I'm imagining it, but I think I see a flicker of suspicion there. "Are you two incorporating Madame Althea into your projects in some way?"

A few awkward seconds tick by, and I wonder if I've

ruined Leander's chances of learning anything useful from Dr. B.

"We've just been talking about how mediums handle skepticism regarding their abilities," Leander says, sounding calm, but he's twirling his pen around his finger, so I know he isn't. "It's not directly related to our projects, but we were curious."

Dr. B chews on the end of her pen, considering us. "Well, what do you think about Madame Althea's abilities?"

"I think it's interesting how beliefs about her abilities can change," I jump in, trying to save this. "Like, Madame Althea told me that her sister Marta wasn't a believer at first but then changed her mind."

Dr. B seems intrigued, so I go for it, hoping I can find out how to contact Marta Hoffman and maybe make up for the fact that I almost exposed Leander's plan. "It would be interesting to talk to someone like Marta about why she went from skeptic to believer," I say.

Dr. B raises an eyebrow. "That might be difficult, considering Marta Hoffman died twenty years ago."

My mouth drops open. "But Madame Althea said...," I start, racking my brain for all the things Madame Althea said about her sister.

I'll tell Marta you said so. She turned prudish in her old age and hates that I have this displayed.

The next time she annoys me, I'll threaten to post it on the internet.

She thinks she can tell me what to do because she had the wisdom to be born three years before me.

"Madame Althea still talks to her," I say as the truth sinks in. "She hears her voice from the other side. Or I mean"—I catch myself—"she believes she does."

Dr. B nods. "She's talked to her sister for a long time. We've all gotten to know Marta around here."

An excited little shiver runs up my back, but my brain is telling me to be cautious.

"To go back to your question, though," Dr. B says, looking at me. "About if I believe Madame Althea is a fraud? The answer is no. I don't believe she can speak with the dead. But I believe that she believes she can. Fraud suggests intentionally fooling people, and I don't think she's doing that."

Horror Movie Me jumps on that answer. Because if Dr. B is right, and Madame Althea really believes she can talk to the dead, then she didn't do all that stuff to me to get exposure and make more money. Cheese and crackers. The Song. *It's mountain dark. She says to wear a headlamp when you go in....* She said all of that because she believed she was really speaking to Imogen. And why would she believe that if it wasn't true?

"But that's just my opinion." Dr. B stands up, checking her watch. "There are other people who know Madame Althea better than I do." She starts packing up her messenger bag, eyeing us like she's deciding something.

"One of those people is Professor Hoffman, Marta's husband," she finally says. Leander sits up straighter, on high alert. "He's known Madame Althea since she was a teenager. He's a history professor at the University of Colorado, which is only forty-five minutes away from here. If you're both interested in the question of mediums and skeptics, I'll tell him you want to visit during his office hours tomorrow. I mean, if you want to extend your research beyond your proposed projects, that's a win for education, right?"

"We'd love to see Professor Hoffman," Leander jumps in.

"I'll email and let him know you're coming." Dr. B gives us a brisk nod and turns out of the room. I wonder how mad Leander is at me for botching this whole thing.

"I'm sorry I messed that up," I say as we pack up our stuff.

"Are you kidding?" Excitement flows through his voice. "That was a breakthrough. Tomorrow, we get to talk to someone who knew Madame Althea before she was a professional medium. Professor Hoffman knows something important, I can feel it. This is going to help us find the truth."

I nod absently as we wander into the lobby. I'm glad Leander isn't angry. But I can't be as excited as he is to see Professor Hoffman tomorrow. Which feels a little bit like a betrayal. Leander and I are supposed to be partners. It's supposed to be us on one side and Madame Althea on the other, but now I feel like I'm in the middle somewhere. Like I've started to switch sides without telling him.

"Anyway..." Leander brushes his hand down my arm,

and my body feels the way it always does when he touches me—warm and sparkly and secure. "I'm still here if, you know. If you want to talk about anything."

A stab of guilt cuts through me as I blink into his clear, earnest eyes, and I wish I could tell him everything. But I know he'll look for a rational explanation. That's what he does. And I'm starting to wonder if there is a rational explanation for this.

"I'm fine. Really."

"Okay." Leander's eyes dart away from mine, a small, sad smile on his lips.

chapter eighteen

April of sophomore year, two months before Imogen dies

"You didn't go?" Imogen stares at me in disbelief. A Safeway bag full of snacks hangs limply at her side, and the wide smile on her face when she burst into my room to ask how the audition went is gone.

"Nah," I say from my bed, where I'm reading the results of my latest internet quiz. It's what I've been doing the entire Saturday morning instead of going to the audition. I now know I have a green aura and that Milwaukee is my ideal city and that if I was an Arby's menu item, I'd be the Bacon Beef 'N Cheddar.

"Why?" Imogen asks, still frozen in place by my bedroom door.

"I had to find out what niche tortilla chip flavor I am."

For the first time ever, Imogen doesn't laugh at my joke.

She doesn't even smile. She crosses the room, the springs on my bed creaking as she sits down on the edge and drops the Safeway bag on the floor. "Why really?"

"I just..." I shut my laptop and lean my head back against my headboard. "Memorizing all those lines about physics and equations isn't really me."

Imogen opens her mouth but closes it again, shaking her head a little. "Are you serious?"

"Yeah. Anyway, are we doing the *Evil Dead* marathon or what?" The plan had been for Imogen to come over after the audition with snacks, and then we'd binge the *Evil Dead* series, all three movies. It had been a while since we'd seen them, and it felt like the right time. Imogen had been pumped, but now she's just sitting there with a pinched look on her face.

"I guess," she says quietly.

I squint at her, noticing the way she's keeping her eyes steadily on my carpet. "Are you mad at me?" Imogen has never been mad at me before. Annoyed or frustrated, sure. But never mad.

Imogen sighs. "I don't want to pull the whole 'I'm not mad, I'm disappointed' thing because I hate it when Mom does that, but there it is. I'm not mad, I'm disappointed."

"Why? Because I didn't go to the audition?"

"Yeah. You were really good, and more importantly, you *wanted* to go, I could tell!"

"It's really not a big deal."

"It *is*, though. You wanted to do it, and you didn't. Why?"

I shrug. "I didn't think I could play Thomasina convincingly, okay? She's this genius, and I'm..." I wave at myself.

Imogen imitates my gesture. "What does *that* mean?" I'm startled by the sharpness of her voice. It's so out of character that I'm temporarily speechless. But she keeps looking at me, waiting for an answer.

"What's with you today?" I blurt out. "Why are you so mad?"

"I'm mad because you probably would have gotten the part, and I think you would have loved it, and now you missed out on that for no reason!"

"Imogen, I'm telling you, it's not a big deal." I try to sound convincing, but a glimmer of disappointment creeps into my voice. I clear my throat, my eyes drifting to the back of my closet, where I stuffed the satiny white button-down and pleated black skirt I'd gotten for the audition.

"Plus, it would have looked awesome on college applications," Imogen goes on.

I huff out a laugh. The college stuff again. "So, that's what this is about. Imogen, I'm not you."

Her eyebrows wrinkle in confusion. "What does that mean?"

"It means that you're supposed to go to an Ivy and write horror movie screenplays one day and do, like, awesome, important, world-changing things."

"And what about you?"

"I'm not."

Imogen gasps, rearing back a little like I just slapped her across the face. "What do you mean you're not?"

"I mean we're different. We're meant to do different things. And that's okay."

Imogen looks at me for so long I start to feel like the specimens we study under microscopes in biology. "Do you want to know what I think?" she finally says. "I think you're the bravest person I've ever met. And that's why I didn't see it for so long—even you get scared sometimes. That's why you didn't audition. You were scared you weren't smart enough to be in *Arcadia*, which isn't true at all. So, you didn't go."

I sit there with my mouth open, trying to process. It's like in a horror movie, when the slasher is finally unmasked and you start going back through everything that happened to see if it all adds up. I'm trying to understand what Imogen is saying, but my brain feels tangled and messy tired, and I want to return to what I know for sure.

"Look," I say, keeping my voice steady. "I'm not smart the way you are, and that's just a fact."

"Natalie, you're brilliant!" She says it just like she did when we were practicing *Arcadia* lines. Like she really, truly believes it.

"And that's okay!" I barrel on, ignoring her. "Not everyone has to be that smart." I sit up on my knees, trying to get my point across. "Remember when we found the hummingbird in Agnes Tree? How did we do that? You were smart, and I was brave. You made up a story, and I climbed the tree. I wouldn't have climbed the tree if you hadn't made up the story, and the story wouldn't have been finished if I hadn't climbed the tree. See? The world needs both kinds of people."

Imogen is shaking her head. "But that was one situation. It doesn't mean we can't change or that I can't be brave and you can't be smart!"

"I mean, I guess," I say, remembering back to the time in her room when she spouted off all those totally hypothetical brave things she was going to do, the things she'd never do in real life—climbing Mount Everest and stunt driving and hitchhiking. "But it doesn't mean that you'll climb Mount Everest and I'll get my PhD in physics."

"You might! I might! Again, I wouldn't climb Everest because it's unethical, but I could climb something tall!"

I laugh a little because the whole thing is so ridiculous.

But Imogen stays serious, not taking her eyes away from mine. "It could happen! It's possible!"

I want to believe her. I want to believe that Imogen and I have the potential to do anything and everything in the whole goddamn world. I want to believe that one day, we'll do something that will surprise the hell out of each other and ourselves. But...

"I just don't believe it," I say quietly.

"Well, I do," Imogen says briskly. She digs her copy of *Arcadia* out of the Safeway bag and tosses it on my bed. "You should really read it this time."

It stays there through the whole *Evil Dead* marathon, as we eat chips and candy and watch Bruce Campbell disembowel demons, and the weirdness between us slowly melts away.

After Imogen leaves, I stuff *Arcadia* into the bottom of my cube shelf, knowing I'll probably never touch it again.

chapter nineteen

Five days until the Spirit Ball

When we get to the University of Colorado, Leander parks in a visitor's spot and we walk down a winding path in the direction of Professor Hoffman's office in Aster Hall. The path runs alongside a reedy pond and is dotted with people lounging in hammocks, reading or typing or talking to another person squished in there with them.

Leander checks the time and zooms in on the map on his phone, still super pumped about meeting with Professor Hoffman. The whole way here, he was planning questions and follow-ups, drumming his fingers on the steering wheel. And the guilt that's been swirling inside me since yesterday balloons because I'm too preoccupied by other things to care about Professor Hoffman. The blurry figure in the woods and the fact that Madame Althea has never been wrong once and what Imogen said to me during our fight—that I was scared to audition for *Arcadia*, that I didn't believe I could pull it off, so I didn't even try.

"Natalie?" Leander glances at me, and I realize he asked a question I was too distracted to hear.

"Sorry, what?"

"We have some time before Professor Hoffman's office hours. Is there anything you want to see?"

"Um, I don't think so," I say, coming back to the present. Because despite everything else, I'm still Leander's partner. I promised I wouldn't back out of helping him with the exposé. We're here to talk to Professor Hoffman, and I need to focus on that. Or at least, I need to stop weirding Leander out so *he* can focus on that.

"There are a lot of people around for summer," I observe. I watch a girl on a skateboard roll past, her electric-blue hair flying backward in the breeze, the wheels of the skateboard bumping rhythmically on the sidewalk cracks, like a beating heart.

"Lots of people take summer classes," Leander says.

I'm wondering what class skateboard girl is going to when my eyes catch on an intricate chalk drawing covering five squares of sidewalk. It's mesmerizingly elaborate, full of shapes, letters, and numbers, like a secret message. I stop to stare at it. "This is amazing."

Leander leans forward, tilting his head. "It looks like a code."

"What do you think it means?"

Leander lifts his shoulders, still staring at the drawing. There's such an otherworldly look to it that it's hard to imagine some student out here, putting so much care into the lines and letters, knowing it will eventually be snuffed out by bike tires, people's shoes, the rain.

"I think it's aliens," I say. "And if we crack the code, we'll find out when they're coming to harvest our brains."

Leander laughs. "I think it's an ad. And if we crack the code, we'll get a half-priced pizza."

"So boring."

"What's boring about cheap pizza?"

"Touché." We smile at each other, holding it for a moment before Leander's eyes search my face, like he wishes I would tell him what's really on my mind. I look away and we move on down the sidewalk, eventually taking a right and crossing toward the center of campus. I glance around at the buildings, the pale red of the sandstones giving off a watercolor look. More students are meandering, sipping smoothies, listening to music, talking.

As we weave our way between them, I find myself smiling again. The energy of campus—vibrant and alive—is seeping into me. It's a relief, to be away from Estes Park, to get out of my head a little. Plus, Leander is walking close to me, and his arm brushes against mine now and then, and it's impossible not to smile when it happens.

"Do you think you'll apply to any colleges outside of New York?" I ask, because even though I have no idea what me and Leander are, I have the immediate urge to know how far away he's going to be next summer.

Leander runs his finger along the side of a sandstone building. "I wasn't planning on it at first, but…I don't know. There are a lot of things to consider." There's a pause, enough to make me wonder about what those things are. "Plus, I don't know if Mom and Daphne will still be in Colorado or not. I want to go back to New York, but I don't want to abandon Daph."

I nod. I know that Leander and Daphne are close. I'm an only child, so I don't know anything about sibling dynamics. Imogen had Bea, but she was more like a cool aunt, jetting in and out, taking us to movies and buying us treats.

"So, what's it like having a little sister?" I ask.

"Loud," Leander says, and I laugh. "And now that she's going into high school, she's taking the summer to find a 'signature scent' that defines her 'as an individual,' so I've sniffed more perfumes than I ever thought I would."

I'm laughing again, and picturing Leander sniffing bottle after bottle of perfume, and hoping there aren't actual hearts in my eyes. I realize that the box in my head reserved for things that don't make me want to stab Leander Hall is now more like a large, sprawling house, with new additions and wings being built all the time.

"Will Daphne be at Boulder High next year?" I ask. "I mean, if you haven't moved back to New York already."

There's a pang in my stomach, along with the familiar feeling of being left behind.

"Yeah. She'll be at Boulder High. If we're still here," Leander says after a beat, and then it's quiet as we climb the stairs to a main quad.

"You never told me why you might not go to college," Leander says, breaking the silence.

"Oh. It just always seemed like Imogen's thing, not mine."

"Why?"

"She was so smart. Like, valedictorian, genius smart. It made sense for her to go."

Leander blinks at me like he's genuinely confused. "But you're smart, too."

I start to shrug it away but can't help thinking it's the kind of thing Imogen would say. What she did say, in various ways, all the time.

Natalie, you're brilliant!

Your purpose is not *hunting fake ghosts with a hot guy.*

You were scared you weren't smart enough to be in Arcadia, *which isn't true at all.*

It feels like a shadow is lifting, like I'm seeing something clearly for the first time. How scared I've been to believe in myself sometimes. I feel the truth behind Imogen's words, but it's hard to let go of the feeling that I'm not cut out for college or intellectual plays. It's hard to say goodbye to old beliefs, even when new ones come along that make you question them.

We pass the enormous student union building and see

another chalk drawing next to a curving bike path. We stop again to look, the same mysterious lines, shapes, and numbers winking up at us.

"You must hate not knowing what these things mean for real," I say, snapping a picture of the drawing. Then my eyes catch on the spiky Flatirons in the distance. I've seen these peaks every day of my life, but they look extra beautiful here, encircling the watercolor-red buildings of campus. I take another picture, realizing this is kind of a perfect spot. There's a cute little café called the Laughing Goat behind us, with outdoor tables facing a walkway where you could people watch or listen to music or just stare at the mountains.

I glance at Leander when he doesn't answer and see that he's absorbed in something on his phone.

"Wait, *are* you going to find out what these mean for real? You're looking up information so you can write an article about them, aren't you?"

"Nope," Leander says simply. "I was looking up this." He hands me his phone and I stare at the screen. It's a course listing for a University of Colorado class called Horror Film. I quickly read the description: "An investigation into the horror film genre and its cultural relevance. Films include: *Night of the Living Dead, The Blair Witch Project,* and *Evil Dead II.*"

My eyes widen. "You can study *Evil Dead II* in college?"

"Looks like it."

"That would be... awesome?" And just like that, I'm

picturing myself here, in this perfect spot, staring at the mountains and then going to horror film class to discuss something I love with a room full of people.

The familiar doubt creeps in. Maybe I won't have anything interesting to say, and maybe everyone will know I'm not cut out to be here, and maybe I can't even get into this school in the first place. But I close my eyes and call up Imogen's voice, telling me I can do it.

It could happen! It's possible!

My grades aren't that bad, and if I write a good essay, maybe it *is* possible?

I'm smiling as a cautious bit of hope sprouts inside me, and when I look at Leander, he's smiling, too.

"Well, you should write an article about these drawings because I really want to know what the deal is," I say, feeling giddy as I hand his phone back and we walk on toward Aster.

"Maybe I will."

"'Alien Mystery or Pizza Conspiracy: Exposing the Truth of the University of Colorado's Chalk Drawings.'" There's your headline."

Leander laughs, throwing his head back. "Natalie, you're brilliant."

I stop short. Because that's not just something Imogen would say. It's something she said. Leander echoed Imogen for the *third* time. And for the third time, it's like she's here, speaking to me, pleading with me to believe. And I want to believe, I really do. I want to tell her everything. Leander and college and the horror film class and everything that's happened this past week, this past year. I want to tell her that she was right about why I didn't audition for the play. I want to tell her I'm sorry.

I want it so much it feels like it's possible, like the force of my wanting is so strong it can reach out into the universe and make unimaginable things true. And then I see her.

Standing at the top of the library stairs, her white hoodie luminous in the sun. The same figure that waved from the Starlight Trail. That disappeared behind Agnes Tree.

Imogen, Horror Movie Me whispers. And for once, Reality Me stays silent.

She's moving now. Darting down the stairs with flip-book speed, her head tilted down, not weaving in between people like everyone else. She moves in a perfectly straight line.

"I think that's Aster," Leander is saying, pointing at the building to the left of the library. But I'm tracking the girl in the white hoodie, cutting across the quad in the opposite direction, toward a cream-colored building with tall, arched windows.

"I'll meet you there," I say, taking a step away.

"Wait, what?"

"I'll explain later, I just...I have to see something. Go to Professor Hoffman's office, and I'll be there in a minute, I swear." I take off in a run toward the cream-colored building, where the girl is hurrying up the stairs, hearing Leander call my name.

I reach the bottom of the stairs a few seconds after she disappears into the door. I climb as fast as I can, swinging the door open and looking around wildly. I breathe out in relief when I see her at the end of the hallway, her back to me, head still tilted down.

When I take a step toward her, she straightens up and turns the corner. I pick up the pace and turn the corner, too, but all I see is an empty hallway. There's an open door at the far end, and I practically sprint there, my body moving automatically now, like it did in the woods. I stop short at the threshold when I see the room is full of people. A circle of students sit around a large table covered in backpacks and books.

It's a class. And no one is wearing a white hoodie. And the books scattered around the table have a familiar green cover.

"*Arcadia* is a play that looks backward and forward, to the past and to the present and to the future, sometimes all in the same scene," the professor says from the head of the table.

I can't take my eyes off the bright green books on the table. The same book that's sitting on the bottom of my shelf at home.

"Seriously?" I whisper as my heart pounds erratically.

A few people at the table are shooting baffled glances at me, but I don't care. I don't care all the way through the hall and out of the building and down the stairs. I don't care because a brand-new feeling is surging through me. It's beautiful and bright and dizzying, like a hummingbird's wings.

Imogen isn't gone.

chapter twenty

"Sorry," I gasp out, catching my breath after running up to the second floor of Aster and spotting Leander pacing at the far end of a long hallway.

"What was that?" Despite the distance, he's right in front of me in less than three strides, eyes wide with confusion.

I'm going to tell him. That I saw Imogen. Twice. That once she led me to Agnes Tree, and this time she led me to a random classroom that just happened to be discussing *Arcadia*. It's not a coincidence. He would have to see that. He would have to see that Madame Althea has been telling the truth, that Imogen really has been reaching out to me.

I open my mouth, but a door swings open right next to us, and a man I can only assume is Professor Hoffman steps out. "If it isn't the two young skeptics, out to find the truth," he says in a booming, German-accented voice.

We both just stare at him for a second, and then Leander sticks out his hand and puts his game face on, which is only slightly more serious than his regular face. He introduces us and then we're stepping into Professor Hoffman's office.

There are books everywhere. Fancy, leather-bound hardbacks lining floor-to-ceiling shelves. Beat-up paperbacks stacked on every surface and sticking out of every crevice. They all surround a large, polished desk. The whole thing strikes me as exactly what I thought a professor's office would look like, except more chaotic.

Professor Hoffman gestures for us to sit in the two low-backed chairs facing the desk while he plunks down in the desk chair. "Dr. Bobincheck told me you were coming. I hope you don't mind if I finish my lunch while we talk. I'm at the good part." He toasts us with his spoon before dipping it into a single-serving chocolate pudding cup. There's something funny about seeing Professor Hoffman—in his grand, book-filled office—scarf down a pudding cup like he's an elementary schooler.

It's the kind of detail that Imogen would have loved. The thought lingers in my mind, but instead of making me feel lonely, it only makes me smile. Because maybe I can tell her about it. Because Imogen isn't gone.

"We're writing an article about Madame Althea that raises doubts about her abilities," Leander says, because we decided on the way here to be honest with Professor Hoffman about what we're doing. We don't want to lie to someone who knows Madame Althea so well, and if it gets back to Dr. B, we'll just have to take our chances that she won't be too angry.

"Dr. B told us Madame Althea was your sister-in-law," Leander goes on, coming across as ultra-professional, except for the glances he shoots in my direction every once in a while, charged with confusion and concern. "We wondered if you knew anything about her that might be useful to us?"

Professor Hoffman nods while wiping his mouth with a napkin. "I know a lot of things about Anna."

"Her name is Anna?" Leander asks.

"Anna Christine Moore." Leander writes it down in his notebook, but I can barely pay attention. Because Imogen isn't gone.

"Do you know where she was born?" Leander asks, his voice sounding far away. "And any details about her early life, including when she became a medium?"

"She was born in Madison, Wisconsin, in 1969. She grew up Catholic and was an altar girl at Saint Vincent Pallotti Parish. Her mother was a schoolteacher, and her father was a car salesman. She was a bright, brilliant person. Gifted well beyond her years. She excelled in English and history in school. Hated science and math. She once got in trouble for writing poems about the periodic table of elements in the margins of her chemistry textbook,"

Professor Hoffman says with a fond smile. "Epic odes to moscovium and astatine."

Leander's pen scribbles across the page as I picture Madame Althea as a teenager in a classroom, getting in trouble in the nerdiest way possible. I want to tell Imogen about that, too.

Professor Hoffman's chair squeaks as he leans back. "The first time Anna claimed to speak to the dead was when she was about fourteen years old. I was eighteen and already dating Marta, so I was around the house a lot." His eyes go soft. "My family had just immigrated the year before, and Marta had taken an interest in me, the new kid in school with the funny accent. Lucky for me, she always fancied the unusual. She was so kind to me. Anna was, too. We had a lot of fun together. Their father called us the Three Musketeers, but Anna took issue with that, saying she was a pacifist, and changed it to the Three Ambassadors. She was like that. Quick-witted. Not afraid to stand up for her beliefs.

"Anyway." Professor Hoffman waves a hand in the air, like he's pushing the memories away. "When Anna was fourteen, her neighbor from across the street died. Mrs. Franklin. She was in her eighties, and her health had been declining for some time. One day after school, Anna started telling everyone that Mrs. Franklin talked to her at night. Nothing ominous or even that important. She just chatted. Told her about the other side."

Now I'm fully paying attention, picturing a young

Madame Althea in her bedroom, talking to a ghost. It's like the story Imogen told me about Maggie and Kate Fox, communicating with the ghost of a peddler in their farmhouse hundreds of years ago.

"We all thought it was part of a story. Anna wanted to be a writer one day, after all. We thought she was trying material out on us. But she insisted and insisted. Eventually, her parents told her to stop making up morbid things, so she only talked about it with us—Marta and me. Marta wanted to go along with it. She said that Anna was always imaginative, and that this was just a phase."

Professor Hoffman sighs. "But it wasn't in me, back then, to go along with things. So, I told her about my grandfather. I said, 'Anna, my grandfather died back in Germany six months ago,' which was true. I said, 'I didn't get a chance to say goodbye. Could you tell him?' Anna closed her eyes and leaned her head to the side, like she was listening to something I couldn't hear."

It's the same thing she does now. I latch on to that detail. It doesn't prove anything, but it seems important somehow.

"Anna opened her eyes and said that he was there with us," Professor Hoffman goes on. "She said he's saying something about music and records. Then she looked at me, with this glowing, confident smile that I'll never forget. 'He wants you to have his records,' she said to me."

Professor Hoffman shrugs, a sheepish expression on his face. "Well, there I had her. My grandfather was a very practical-minded man. He thought music was a waste of time. He didn't even own any records. I told her that, and I had a bit of fun with it after. Teasing her, telling her she should contact the spirit of Jack the Ripper to finally solve the mystery. She did not appreciate this."

Leander is nodding as he writes, and I know he's glad to be getting this story. Madame Althea's future brother-in-law tricking her into revealing she's a fraud would fit nicely into the article. But it doesn't change my mind. Madame Althea had just started to hear the voices of the dead when Professor Hoffman tricked her. She was probably still learning. Of course she would make mistakes.

"Anna soured toward me after that," Professor Hoffman says, scratching at his chin. "She felt like I was making fun of her, which, at the time, I was. I didn't think she'd take it as seriously as she did, but she felt betrayed. I apologized, but she never warmed up to me again. The Three Ambassadors split up. As far as I knew then, Anna stopped saying she was talking to the dead. Of course, I saw her at family gatherings, and she was cordial to me, but we didn't have any one-on-one conversations. Until after Marta died."

Professor Hoffman shifts in his chair, like whatever comes next is hard for him to talk about. "I got a letter from Anna a few weeks after Marta's funeral. She asked if I remembered Mrs. Franklin. She confessed that she had been making things up all those years ago, about talking to Mrs. Franklin's ghost."

The air in the room goes thick. Leander's pen stops moving across the page. "She admitted she made it up?" he asks, a cautious note of hope in his voice. I'm barely breathing.

Professor Hoffman opens his bottom desk drawer, pulls out a folded piece of paper, and hands it to Leander, who quickly opens it as I lean in. And there, after a paragraph of commiseration over the death of Marta, is Madame Althea's confession in neat, careful script:

> *Do you remember the whole business about Mrs. Franklin talking to me at night? I made it up. I was scared of death, and I wanted proof that life didn't just end. So, I created a fiction. I'm sorry I got angry with you for exposing it. I'm sorry for the rift it caused between us. I'm sorry I lost the chance to get to know you as a brother.*

Beside me, Leander's eyes are wide. I read the words again, like there has to be something else to them. But it's right in front of me. *I made it up*. My mouth goes slack as confusion spirals around in my stomach, but before I have the chance to think, Professor Hoffman is talking again.

"I was touched when I got that letter. So imagine my surprise when a month later, she sent a new one." He takes another piece of paper out of his drawer, and Leander and I pore over a fresh set of words.

Dear Alexander,

I know this will sound strange to you, especially after my last letter. But I'm asking you, with all my heart, to believe me. Marta is communicating with me. I know what you're thinking. I can even imagine your face as it is right now, distorted by the frowning mouth of skepticism. But will you open your mind, even if it's only for the time it takes to read this letter? Will you do that for me, Alexander? For me, and for Marta?

It started about a month ago. I saw her, just a flash of her, passing across my back patio. I didn't know then that she had died, so I thought she'd come for a surprise visit. I went out to look for her, but I saw nothing. I thought it was a trick of the light.

But I saw her several times over the next week. Just flashes again, standing over the stove in my kitchen, outside the grocery store, by the hammock in my backyard. I didn't want to believe it at first, but it was so clearly her. She was reaching out to me, and I wanted to speak to her, but I didn't know how. So I went to see a woman—a friend of a friend who called herself a medium. I know your frown is deepening now, your eyebrows getting so wrinkled they might never smooth out again. But this woman taught me how to listen. She taught me how to hear things beyond the world we encounter every day. And, Alexander, I heard. I heard Marta.

Just like I heard Mrs. Franklin all those years ago. I know I told you that I made it up. I thought I had. When you have so many people telling you that something is impossible, you start believing it. So I believed that I imagined it, but I know now that I didn't. I heard her, just as I hear Marta now.

Marta told me she was okay. She has told me so many things. Our connection is very strong, and I speak with her every day. The medium has become my mentor, and with her guidance, I have begun to hear other voices of the departed. Marta is encouraging me to listen to them as well, and I am beginning to wonder if I could give this gift to others who are grieving—the ability to communicate with loved ones on the other side.

But the real reason I'm writing is that Marta has a message for you. She knows you won't believe it right away. She understands, as I do, that beliefs don't change all at once. That is why I didn't come to see you in person to tell you this. It would be too much to take in. You'd have dismissed it even more than you're dismissing it now.

Beliefs aren't like the winds, changing course, quick and effortless. Beliefs are like houses—it takes time and patience and many small pieces fitting together to create a new one to live in. I hope this letter will serve as one piece.

But, the message: Marta says that you were right about Helen. She always thought you were right, but she kept disagreeing because she liked to hear you argue. I don't know what she means, but she wants me to tell you.

She has much more to say, of course. I hope that, with time, more and more pieces will fit into place for you. If that happens, come and see me, and we'll be the Three Ambassadors once more.

Yours, always, Anna

I stare at the page long after I've finished reading the words, so many thoughts rushing through my head it's impossible to grasp on to any of them. Leander turns to look at me. We hold eye contact for a moment, and I want to know what he makes of it all, but his expression is unreadable.

"I cried when I read that letter," Professor Hoffman admits quietly. "For the memories it brought up about Marta. And for Anna, the brilliant girl I knew, lost to grief and delusions." He lets out a long sigh. "I never did go to see her."

He clears his throat and moves some papers around on his desk, and it's only then that I realize he's emotional. He's hiding it well, but I know what it's like to have tears in your throat, to try to swallow them down until you can talk again without your voice quivering and giving everything away.

"I'm so sorry for your loss, Professor," I say, my heart leaping out to him. "And I'm sorry to bring it all up again."

"Oh, don't be sorry." Professor Hoffman waves his hand in the air again. "It's inevitable, isn't it? When you've lost someone who was so essential in your life, reminders of them are everywhere. Sometimes it's like when you catch the scent of freshly baked bread in the air. You inhale, and it's lovely, and then it's gone. Other times, it's like a knife to the gut. It knocks you down for a while. I don't believe that Marta is communicating with Anna. But, I suppose in a symbolic way, I see and hear and feel Marta's ghost everywhere."

I find myself gripping the smooth arms of the chair. *Maybe it's not symbolic!* I want to yell. *Maybe it's really Marta, and you're not listening!*

"Anyway." Professor Hoffman checks his watch. "I hope the letters are helpful for your project."

"They are," Leander says, handing the letters back. "Incredibly helpful. We can't thank you enough. Could I..." He hesitates, but then pushes on. "I wondered if I could take a picture of them. I won't put them directly in the article. I won't even mention them if you don't want me to. But there's someone I'd like to show them to. Someone it might help save from being lost to grief and delusions."

I barely hear Professor Hoffman's reply, and hardly register when Leander carefully positions the letters on a cleared space of the desk and snaps pictures. I'm too busy re-reading Madame Althea's words in my head.

Marta told me she was okay. She has told me so many things. Our connection is very strong, and I speak with her every day.

"I have class in ten minutes," Professor Hoffman says, tucking the letters back away in his drawer, his voice lighter now. "But there's a final part of the story I want to tell you. About a year after Anna sent me the second letter, I went to visit my grandmother in Germany, the one who was married to the grandfather I'd tricked Anna with all those years ago. It was a wonderful visit, and at the end of it, she took me into the attic where she'd boxed up some things my late grandfather wanted to leave to his grandchildren. There was a box marked for me."

Professor Hoffman folds his hands in front of him on the desk. "It was full of records."

I gasp. And I think about the Fox sisters again. The bones they found in the Fox sisters' bedroom wall.

The final, eerie "what if?" Imogen's voice whispers.

Professor Hoffman smiles at me. "I had the same reaction. Apparently, my grandfather started enjoying music and collecting records in the later part of his life. I don't know what surprised me more. That Anna was right all those years ago or that my grandfather had changed so much from the man I once knew. I think about both things quite often. When I think about my grandfather, I marvel at the idea that you can never fully know a person, and you can never know when they might shock you. When I think about Anna..."

Professor Hoffman pauses. "I'm positive it was a coincidence," he says after a while. "But I will admit that every so often, when the house feels particularly empty, I listen to my grandfather's records and think, *What if? What if Marta is out there somewhere? What if Anna isn't lost?* I never get further than asking the questions, but sometimes, it helps."

It's time for Professor Hoffman's class, so we thank him for talking to us. Then Leander and I walk out of Aster, back across campus, and to the car, quiet the whole way.

chapter twenty-one

Leander carefully rounds a curve on our way back up the mountain to Estes Park, my ears popping as the air gets thinner. We've been quiet for so long, ever since we walked out of Aster and Leander asked me why I ran away and I said, "I can't explain it right now."

I'm going to tell him. It's just impossible to know how when my brain is busy fitting all the small pieces into place. Imogen grabbed my elbow at Dave's party to stop me from going down the Stein Incline. Imogen was responsible for the eerie silences. She spoke through Madame Althea and Leander. She led me to Agnes Tree and the college class discussing *Arcadia*. She broke my bracelet and snort-laughed after I kissed Leander and maybe even made it hail. And it was all to get my attention. To tell me she was here and make me believe it.

I believe it now. But I can't keep chasing Imogen around corners only for her to disappear. I want more than that. I want to know how she is, *where* she is, if she's okay. I want to know so many things. Which is why as soon as we get back to the Harlow, I'm going to find Madame Althea.

I glance at Leander, his eyes focused on the road, jaw tight. When I told him I couldn't explain why I ran away, he didn't push. He just nodded and kept quiet. Not in the silent treatment way, more like the "I'm giving you space even though it's super frustrating" way.

I turn back to the window. I can't spring it on him while he's driving up a winding highway. Not only is it a lot to take in, but what does it mean about Leander's dad? Is he here, too? A small shudder passes through me. I have to do this gradually.

"What did you think of the letters?" I say as we pass a quaint roadside diner, its bright red sign advertising famous fruit pies and cherry cider.

Leander's eyes dart to mine quickly before settling back on the road. "I think that Anna admitted she was a fraud. She said she made up hearing voices of the dead. In writing."

"Yeah, but then she said she really did hear them."

"Right," Leander says slowly. "But I think it's pretty easy to see why. She said she wanted proof that life didn't just end, so she made up hearing Mrs. Franklin's voice. I can only imagine how much she wanted that proof after her sister died. I assume her grief made her believe again." He shrugs. "It seems pretty obvious, doesn't it?"

It's what I expected him to say, but it still bristles. I stare at the winding road in front of us.

"I mean, am I missing something?" Leander asks.

"I'm just thinking about something Madame Althea said at the outdoor movie," I start, hoping I can slowly bring him around. "She said that when someone hears a voice from the other side, they usually think they're losing their minds, and if they tell people about it, they're laughed at. So they end up pushing it away. They convince themselves that they don't believe. I think she was talking about what happened to her when she was fourteen. How no one believed her about Mrs. Franklin, so she ended up not believing, either."

"Okay..." Leander squints over the steering wheel, clearly confused about why I'm bringing this up.

"But then her sister died, and her grief was more powerful than her doubts. So instead of denying it, she believed. And then she started communicating with Marta."

"You mean she started believing she was communicating with Marta."

The highway ends and we join the slow-moving traffic downtown, only a few minutes away from the Harlow.

"I *mean* that there's more than one way to interpret why she said two different things in the letters. I mean that her grief didn't necessarily make her delusional. Maybe her grief helped her believe what was right there in front of her."

Leander shakes his head a little. "Sorry, I'm…I'm not following."

"I just think…" My mouth stays open, but I can't get anything out. I see the Harlow up ahead, and the idea of being so close to Madame Althea, to Imogen, is so intense I can hardly breathe.

"I don't mean to be insensitive about the letters," Leander says. "I'm sorry if I was. I know Madame Althea was hurting when she wrote them and still is." He sighs and clenches the wheel. "I don't even think she's just doing this for profit anymore. Part of me thinks she really, truly believes. But that doesn't change the fact that what she's doing is dangerous. That it can hurt people."

We turn into the parking lot, and I stare at the Harlow's white facade and red roof. It still seems bigger than I remember, even though I just saw it a few hours ago. As we climb the steps, we have to weave through more people than usual—returning hikers and people heading out to dinner downtown.

When we step into the lobby, my body is ready to run downstairs and knock on Madame Althea's door, but I hold back. Because I need to tell Leander first. It would feel wrong not to. I touch his arm. "Hey, could we talk—" But Leander is frozen in place, staring at a woman standing by the fireplace, examining the photo of Agnes.

"Mom?" Leander's eyes go wide.

The woman spins around and rushes over. "Hi!" she says a little breathlessly. "I know this is a surprise. I decided to drive up for my weekly appointment with Madame Althea instead of doing it over Zoom—I was just sick of staring at a screen, you know?—and then I thought I'd see if I could catch you. Dr. Bobincheck told me you'd be back soon, so I waited. But I hope I'm not cramping your style? That's probably not something people say anymore, but oh well." She says all of that seemingly in one breath, and then turns to me, holding out her hand. "I'm Gwen, Leander's mom."

"Natalie," I say, shaking her hand. The warmth of her smile makes me smile, too, even though beside me, Leander has become a ball of fidgety discomfort.

"Mom—" Leander starts, but Gwen is already going again.

"I thought so. Leander isn't very wordy in his text responses, but I've heard about you. A little bit, anyway." Despite everything bottled up inside me, my smile grows, and I raise my eyebrows at Leander, enjoying seeing him flustered.

"This place really is spectacular, isn't it?" Gwen says, looking around. "The energy here is amazing. No wonder the psychics chose this spot all those years ago."

"It was Spiritualists, Mom."

"Spiritualists, that's right." Gwen snaps her fingers. "I always get the terminology wrong. But luckily, Leander is always there to correct me." She laughs, the cheerful sound lighting up the dim lobby. "That sounds sarcastic, but I actually mean it. I really do appreciate it, honey." She gives his arm a squeeze. "Sorry, I'm prattling your ears off. I tend to do that after an appointment because I'm so invigorated. Madame Althea is incredible. I always feel like a new person after an appointment. I went ahead and paid her for the whole year."

Leander flinches. "I'm not here to do my senior project," he says sharply, and Gwen's smile falters. "I mean, I am, but the main reason I'm here is to prove Madame Althea is a fraud."

For the first time since we walked into the lobby, Gwen is speechless. She looks back and forth between us. "What?" Her eyebrows wrinkle, and for a moment she looks like Leander when he's trying to figure something out. "Why?"

"Because it's the truth. Because you're being tricked again. I hate it, and Daphne hates it, and we need it to stop." Leander takes a breath, like he's going to soften his approach, but then he just launches in again. "You changed after you started going to see Madame Althea, whose real name is Anna Moore, by the way. You think you're communicating with Dad, but you're not. None of it is real. I'm writing an article about it, but here..."

He brings out his phone and taps on it for a second before handing it to his mom, who still looks stunned. "These are letters that Madame Althea wrote. Please read them."

Gwen's eyes scan the screen, her mouth moving a little as she reads. Leander bends his neck from side to side, like he's trying to let out the tension. It's rubbing off on me, and the whole time Gwen is reading, I'm wondering if she's going to interpret the letters the way Leander did or the way I did. If she's going to believe or not believe.

When Gwen finishes, she looks up at Leander, her expression carefully blank. "What do you think this proves, Leander?"

"That Madame Althea isn't communicating with the dead. That Dad isn't out there, telling you what to do again."

Gwen hands Leander his phone back with a tired sigh. "Madame Althea and I don't talk about your dad."

Leander blinks rapidly. "What?"

"When I first went to see her, I did ask about him. But Madame Althea said he didn't have much to say. She said he'd finally found some peace and just wanted to be left alone. Now, I know you don't believe in that kind of thing, but that's exactly what he would have said, isn't it?"

Leander doesn't answer. "Isn't it?" Gwen presses, her chin slightly raised.

"It's something a lot of people would say," Leander mutters.

"Including him," Gwen goes on, unfazed. "So, anyway, I was already there, and I couldn't think of any other people on the other side I particularly wanted to chat with, so we talked about other things. I think she could see that I was at a bit of a crossroads. So, she taught me how to reach out to my spirit guides for advice. I think of them as wise, understanding women who are looking out for me."

Frankie had mentioned talking to her spirit guides, too. She said they helped her, gave her advice. A knot in my stomach is loosening now that I know Gwen isn't communicating with Leander's dad. That he's not back, controlling her again.

"But..." Leander scrunches his eyes closed and shakes his head, like he's trying to wake up from a dream. "What about the hairstyle? The move? Those were all things *he* wanted, not you. We were happy in New York."

"Oh, honey," Gwen says, her voice softening. She squeezes Leander's arm again, her silvery rings catching the light. "I wasn't happy in New York. Too many memories there, and a lot of those memories were difficult ones. I felt the weight of them every day. I could tell that you felt them sometimes, too, just being in the home your father kept such tight control over."

Leander's stoic expression flickers, like he's going back in time, wading through the memories again.

"And even though your dad was a difficult person, I know it was hard for all of us when he died, in different ways. I'd been feeling for a long time that we needed a change, but I was too scared to make it. I told myself I'd stick it out for you and Daph, at least until you were both out of school, but I could feel myself going through a crisis. You kids are growing up, but you still need me. I'm all you've got, and you need me to be the best version of myself. I felt like I couldn't be that there." Gwen's voice wobbles a little, but she keeps her chin up, her eyes focused directly on Leander.

His face softens. "Mom," he says gently.

"And then I came to that conference here, and I traveled all around Colorado, and I just fell in love with it. Boulder, especially. The mountains, the sunny winters, the open space. I wanted this to be our place. Our fresh start."

Gwen takes a breath and runs her fingers through her hair, the wavy strands bouncing back into place. "As for the hair," she says, a whisper of a smile coming onto her face. "I'm getting older, and I don't know if you've heard, but that's hard for some people. It's not completely unusual for someone my age to try and recapture their younger look. I remember it's how your father liked me to wear it," she says quietly. "But that's not why I do it."

The revelation hangs in the air around us. Guests mill around the lobby, flowing in and out of the doors, but the three of us stand perfectly still.

"Was it your spirit guides who told you to move or was that you?" Leander finally asks, his voice strained.

"It was me, honey. I made the decision. I know I should have been more transparent with you, and for that, I'm sorry. But I'm not sorry for having sessions with Madame Althea. She really does help. It's difficult to be a single parent going through a midlife crisis."

"Then why don't you see a therapist? Or talk to me and Daph?"

"I can't put my problems on you two." Gwen shakes her head resolutely. "And, I don't know why I don't see a therapist. Maybe I should. It's just that with Madame Althea, things feel easy. Like I'm talking to a friend. I know you generally don't have to pay your friends," she says, with a slight wrinkle of her brow. "But I'm lucky enough to have the money."

Leander shoves his phone back into his pocket. "The letters don't change your mind at all, then?"

"No, honey. I'm sorry if that disappoints you."

"It—" Leander starts, but he ends on a sigh. "I..." He trails off again. It breaks my heart because I know how bewildering it is when your beliefs get blown up. And this one is major. His mom wasn't tricked into upending their lives. She did it on her own. I have no idea if knowing that truth makes things better or worse for Leander right now. Either way, I want to wrap my arms around him like he did for me after my bracelet broke. I want him to hold on to me while the world shifts beneath him.

But before I can do anything, Leander takes a step back, says something that sounds like "sorry," and walks out the front doors.

chapter twenty-two

I know where Leander went. And as I pass the Estes Park library sign and turn down the small walkway that leads to Oasis, I do my best to send Imogen a message. I tell her that I'll talk to her soon. I just have to make sure Leander is okay first. I know she'll understand.

When I duck into the shade of Oasis, Leander is lying on the bench, his head resting on the wooden arm. It reminds me of how he looked at Dave's party, lounging in that Adirondack chair. I don't need to ask him why he's here this time. I already know.

"Hey," I say gently.

"Hey," he answers, sitting up. His voice is calm, which surprises me. I expected angry or defeated or just plain sad. But he doesn't look like any of those things. He's even smiling a little.

"Are you okay?" I sit beside him on the bench. Our arms are touching even though there's plenty of space on either side. It makes me remember, in full technicolor detail, what happened on this bench the last time we were here, and I immediately feel flushed.

"I'm okay. Sorry I got all dramatic back there. I just needed a place to think, and I knew you'd find me here."

"A cowgirl always knows where to find her pardner," I say, nudging him. Leander huffs out a laugh, and then we sit for a moment in silence. It's not the heavy, overwhelming silence that's been following me around. It's peaceful and warm and light, leaving room for the faint noise of cars and tourists in the distance. Birds chirping. Leander's breathing, the whisper of my skin brushing against his.

"But really, you're okay?" I ask.

"Yeah." He drums his fingers on the arm of the bench. "It's just...the truth hurts, I guess."

"And the truth is?" I say carefully.

"That my mom started acting weird, so I basically made up a whole story about how a medium was using the ghost of my dead father to control her. Instead of, I don't know, asking her what was going on. Or even just considering other possibilities."

"I see why you did it, though. She told you she was going to see Madame Althea to ask about your dad. And then she started acting the way you remember her acting when your dad was alive. I get why you made that connection."

Leander sighs and pinches the bridge of his nose. "I just assumed that Madame Althea was the problem, and she wasn't. And then I got so invested in the idea of her being the problem that I convinced myself it was true. I should have known that the truth is never that simple. I write a whole column about it." He shakes his head in disbelief. "And now I don't know how to feel about my mom's appointments with her."

"Maybe they really do help her."

"Maybe." Leander still sounds unsure. "I guess talking with Madame Althea could be good for her. But, I don't know. I still wish she'd see a therapist."

"Maybe she will when she's ready. Maybe what she's doing with Madame Althea will get her there, like one small piece that helps her see that she needs help." I shift on the bench, bringing both knees up and turning so I'm fully facing Leander. "It's like what Madame Althea said in her letter about how people have to come to new beliefs slowly, like building a house. Maybe your mom will get more comfortable talking about her feelings with Madame Althea, and that will make her more comfortable going to see a therapist."

Leander tilts his head, considering. "That's a good point."

"I liked that part of the letter." I watch his face

carefully, wondering if his feelings about Madame Althea have changed now that he knows she didn't manipulate his mom into moving.

"I did, too," Leander says, staring at the grass. Then he takes a breath like he's gearing up for something big. "She was right about how beliefs change bit by bit. Little things start to happen, but you deny them because they don't fit with what you think is true. But then those things keep happening and they get bigger and bigger until it's impossible to ignore them anymore. You have to admit that it's real."

He turns to face me, his eyes diving into mine. For one wild moment, I wonder if he's about to say he believes in Madame Althea, too. But then he takes my hand in his.

"You have to admit that you're way less sad than you thought you'd be about not moving back to New York. You have to admit it's because you're really into a person you've only known for a week. And that she's fascinating and you want to kiss her all the time and hang out with her and watch horror movies, which is weird because you don't even like those. And that you're going to have to be more likable at school next year so that she doesn't take any shit if she agrees to date you, which you really hope she will."

I can't say anything for a second because I'm smiling so much. I expect the doubts to creep in—that I've never actually dated anyone before, and maybe I can't do it. That Leander is too smart for me and will eventually leave me behind. But miraculously, they stay quiet. It would be hard to hear them anyway, over the exhilaration thrumming in my chest. Over the explosion of wonder at how much the world has changed since coming to the Harlow Hotel.

"I really hope you're not talking about someone else," I say, so giddy my teeth are almost chattering. "That would be such a dick move."

Leander's mouth flicks up. "Nope. Talking about you."

I throw my arms around his shoulders and practically launch myself onto his lap. "Then who cares if I get shit for dating you. Because if I get shit for dating a person who's smart and kind and cares about the truth, then I'll throw that shit right back in their faces."

Leander circles his arms around my waist. "That's the most romantic thing I've ever heard."

I barely get a laugh out before I'm kissing him, once again, in the cool shade of Oasis. It's just as amazing as the first time, and as the gentle breeze swirls around us, shaking the spruces, Oasis feels like it's our place, too, Leander's and mine. And it doesn't even feel like a betrayal. I don't think Imogen will mind sharing.

We stay cuddled up together on the bench for a long time after, Leander's arm wrapped tightly around my shoulders, my head resting against his chest. It's so comfortable I almost forget about everything else. About what I have to tell him. Almost.

A nervous tremor shoots through me. I'm scared that he won't believe me. I'm scared that he'll think I'm imagining it, that my grief has made me delusional. But I'm stronger than those fears now. I think about what he said, about how much he likes me, about how I could trust him.

I sit up, turning to face him again. "I have to tell you something."

"Okay." Leander sits up straighter, too, smoothing out his shirt where it had bunched up.

"It's big. So I need you to open your mind. As far as it will go."

"All right. Mind opened."

"Even further."

He runs his hand down my arm. "Hey, it's open. I meant what I said before. You can tell me anything. You can trust me."

"Okay." I gulp in a huge breath. "What if...I mean, I know it sounds unbelievable. But what if Madame Althea is for real? What if she really can do what she says she can do?"

"Talk to the dead?"

"Yeah."

Leander leans in, like he's waiting for the punch line. When I only stare at him, he shakes his head a little. "Wait, what?"

"I think she's for real," I say firmly, not taking my eyes away from his.

Leander blinks at me, like he can't even process it. But of course he's surprised. I haven't told him everything yet.

"We never actually figured out how she accessed my Instagram," I start. "She could have used the Harlow account, but that's just speculation. And even if she had seen my account, we don't know how she knew about 'mountain dark' and that Imogen was always telling me to wear a headlamp in the woods."

"Yeah, but..." Leander's eyes are darting wildly across my face, like he's desperately searching for some sign that I'm kidding.

"And it's not just Madame Althea," I keep going. "It's Imogen. She's been reaching out to me all this time. She's the one who grabbed my elbow at Dave's party. And she broke my bracelet outside the tunnel because she was trying to show me it was really her. And then I *saw* her. In the woods during *Psycho*. That's why I went in. I saw her, and I followed her, and she led me to Agnes Tree."

"Okay...," Leander says slowly, and I swear his face is going pale. But I have to keep going.

"And then I saw her again at the University of Colorado. That's why I was late to meet with Professor Hoffman. She led me to this classroom where they were discussing *Arcadia*, which is this play she wanted me to audition for." I wait for some kind of reaction. A gasp or at least a look of surprise. But Leander just keeps staring at me with the same worried look.

"I *saw* her!" I repeat.

"Okay, okay," Leander says gently, holding both hands up to calm me down.

I feel myself shriveling up, like the dried spruce needles littering the ground. "You don't believe me."

"No, I mean... I just... It's a lot." He runs a hand back and forth through his hair a few times. "It's a lot to take in. But it's almost like... Remember when I told you it feels like my dad comes back in weird ways sometimes?"

"Yes..." I don't like the careful tone of his voice, like he's about to explain that I'm wrong in the nicest way possible.

"Could something like that be happening? I mean, you're back here, in a place that's full of memories of Imogen, and it *feels* like she's back?"

"No." I shake my head. "I would know if it was all just metaphorical, and it's not. She's reaching out. She's trying to talk to me. She—" I break off suddenly because I remember the footage from the woods. Imogen peeking out from behind Agnes Tree. "I have proof."

I grab his hand and pull him off the bench. I keep the pace quick as we walk back to the Harlow, Leander shooting worried glances at me the whole time. But he'll see the footage. He'll believe me then.

When we get to my dorm room, I practically dive for my laptop on the desk, pulling up the footage of the woods.

"Natalie, can we just—"

"Watch," I say once it's all set. I pull out my desk chair and Leander warily sinks into it as I press Play. I stare over his shoulder as the night-vision woods come to life. It's the shakiest part because I'm running, and Leander is trying to keep up.

"Watch the tree." I point to Agnes Tree on the right

side of the screen. I've seen it so many times I know exactly when...

"Whoa," Leander says, leaning forward sharply to stare at the spot where Imogen disappeared behind the tree.

"See?" I'm so excited I almost start jumping up and down.

"Go back," he murmurs, squinting at the screen as I scroll back on the progress bar and hit Play again. He glares at the screen in disbelief. Then he does the same thing I did the first night I saw it, rewinding again and again, inching closer to the screen each time. Finally, he looks at me. "It could be anything."

Now it's my turn to wonder if he's kidding. "Are you serious?"

"There's something there." Leander points at the screen. "But it could be anything."

"Like what?" I snap.

"A branch. A cobweb. A camera malfunction. I don't know. It's blurry and dark and—"

"I saw your face!" I yell, my disappointment spilling over. "When you saw it for the first time, you were freaked out. And now you're explaining it away even though I *told* you all these other things that happened. Why can't you just admit that it could be her?"

"Because..." Leander breaks off, his voice wavering, like he's begging me to be rational. "Listen, I know it feels real—"

"You think I'm imagining it," I say, feeling myself closing

up, and all I want to do is run out of the room and find Madame Althea. "You think I'm being tricked."

"No! I don't—" Leander stands up and puts his hands on my shoulders, looking directly into my eyes. "I think that memories and metaphorical ghosts are real, powerful things. I think they affect us in mind-boggling ways sometimes. But—"

"Imogen hasn't only been speaking through Madame Althea," I say, because I want him to believe me so desperately. Because maybe he felt Imogen's presence, too, he just didn't know it. "She's spoken through *you* a few times."

His hands squeeze my shoulders. "What?"

I rattle off the times he's echoed something Imogen said, word for word.

There are other possible explanations.

Metaphorical ghost.

Natalie, you're brilliant.

Leander doesn't take his eyes off mine the whole time I'm talking. When I'm done, he pulls his hands away from my shoulders. "Natalie . . . that was me. *I* said those things. They came from my brain. *I* think you're brilliant. . . ."

I see the moment his frustration turns to wariness. "Wait, this whole time we were hanging out, were you just waiting for me to say things that proved Imogen was back? Was I just part of your evidence?"

"No." I step closer to him, and he doesn't move away. "You weren't. You were your own separate, amazing thing."

I pause to link my hand in his. "And I know you don't believe in ghosts and mediums. I just…I thought you'd believe *me*."

I look up at him, hoping against everything that he'll finally see. But his face is falling, and it's like he can hardly look at me anymore. "I'm sorry, Natalie."

"Me too." I slip my hand out of his.

And then I'm out the door and down the stairs and cutting through the tunnel to Madame Althea's office.

chapter twenty-three

My knuckles sting as I knock on the smooth wood of Madame Althea's door, hoping with everything I have that she'll answer. A few seconds later, it opens, and I'm staring into Madame Althea's pale blue eyes.

"Hello, Natalie," she says, not looking at all surprised to see me.

"I know I'm too young to make an appointment," I say, struggling to get it out after running all the way to her office. "I don't even have the money for one. But I could pay you later. I—"

"Natalie." Madame Althea's voice hushes me instantly. "Why did you come?" The question is tinged with hope.

I take a steadying breath. "You told me that my best

friend was trying to reach out to me. I wasn't ready to listen then, but I am now."

Madame Althea's face breaks into a smile as she moves away from the door. "Please, come in."

I step into her cinnamon-scented office, glancing at the framed picture of Madame Althea and Marta on her desk as an overwhelming wave of anticipation washes over me.

"I'm glad you're here," Madame Althea says, sinking down into the cream armchair and gesturing to the one across from it, like she did when I came to interview her. "She's wanted to talk to you for a long time. It'll be a weight off my shoulders to let her do that."

I lean forward. "Okay. I'm ready."

Madame Althea closes her eyes, like I knew she would. I watch as her forehead wrinkles every once in a while before smoothing out again. She breathes in through her nose a few times and then opens her eyes. "She's here."

And it's so strange, but I feel another presence in the room. Quiet as a blink, the rustle of a white sweatshirt sleeve, a hand passing through dark blond hair.

"Would you like to say anything to her, Natalie?" Madame Althea speaks softly.

"Is she okay?" My voice is barely a whisper.

Madame Althea tilts her head to listen. "Yes. She says she misses you. She misses a lot of things. But she's okay. She's happy and at peace. She finally knows that what's on the other side is nothing to be afraid of."

Tears of relief leak out of my eyes. It's like something

inside me had been bleeding since Imogen died, an open wound I bandaged over and ignored even as it oozed and festered and hurt. A wound that heals as soon as I hear those words. I thought I'd moved on before, but I realize now that I'd been deluding myself. Because how could I have truly moved on without knowing that?

I sniffle, and I don't even care. Madame Althea's eyes are misting over a little, too. "Thank you," I say. I've never meant it more in my life.

Madame Althea nods kindly, wiping the corners of her eyes with her sleeve. "Is there anything else?"

"Yes." There's so much. An infinite number of things I want to say, an eternity of questions I want to ask. But one thing rises to the surface.

"I'm sorry for not climbing Agnes Tree," I say, my voice thick. "I wish I could go back and do it. It was our tradition, and I wish we could have done it one last time. I'm sorry I broke our promise to always be brave and believe."

I wait as Madame Althea listens.

"She says you don't have to apologize for that. You two shared so many amazing memories together, especially here in Estes Park, and she wants you to focus on those."

I smile, relieved, but part of me is waiting for more. Waiting to truly hear Imogen in Madame Althea's words. I'm happy that Imogen forgives me, and it makes sense that she would. But I want that moment. That moment where Imogen jumps out and says, *It's me! I'm here!*

"Can you ask her what we found in Agnes Tree the first summer we were here?"

I rub my clammy palms against my jeans as Madame Althea leans her head to the side again, her eyes fluttering closed. When she opens them, they're clear and knowing.

"It wasn't a feather, was it?"

It works like a sharply honed knife. I don't even know it's sliced me open until the blood starts draining and I'm numb and nauseous.

I'm waiting for Madame Althea to laugh, to say, *Just kidding, Imogen says it's a hummingbird, of course.* A crystal hummingbird with an emerald-green body and sky-blue wings that she kept in her dollhouse. But Madame Althea is looking at me expectantly, and now the room feels different. Empty. The shift sends me reeling, and my brain grasps for something to hold on to. I saw Imogen. Behind Agnes Tree. On campus. But the image of her wavers now, shaken loose by shock and doubt and something I'd wrestled into a hole and buried. The truth.

Imogen is gone.

Reality Me is shouting, trying to pierce the terrible numbness that's swept over me. *You've known she was gone for a year! You moved on, remember?*

But I can barely hear because I've been cut open and hollowed out, like the taxidermied mountain goat in the lobby. And all the things I used as proof that Imogen wasn't gone suddenly seem just as fake. A random drunk person grabbed my elbow at Dave's party and then slunk back into the crowd. My bracelet broke because I'd been messing with it so much lately. I saw Imogen in the woods and on campus because my grief made me delusional.

"Natalie, are you all right?" Madame Althea's face is threaded with concern. I can't look at her yet, so my eyes drift to the picture on her desk. Madame Althea laughing with her sister on the beach. The sister who died twenty years ago. The sister who Madame Althea never let go of, even after her death.

When I do finally look into her impossibly light eyes, I don't see cruelty there. Or greed. I just see loneliness. The same loneliness that's wrapped itself around me. In her case, it's masked with hope and belief, but it's still there underneath. I can tell because I see it in my own face when I look in the mirror sometimes, even when I'm telling myself I'm fine.

I feel an instant, devastating connection with her. We're just two people who haven't moved on.

I wiggle my fingers and clear my throat, trying to get my body to work again because I need to leave. I need to be anywhere but here.

"Yes," I say, when I remember I haven't answered her question yet. Because if Madame Althea really does believe she hears the voices of the dead, I won't play a part in shattering that. I won't take her sister away again.

I hold it together until I'm outside, in the front courtyard of the Harlow Hotel. I gulp down the cool air and stare at the familiar pine-covered mountains and the silver-gray ones beyond as tears stream down my face. Then the panic sets in, spasming in my chest, shortening my breaths, making my hands shake. I glance behind me at the Harlow, its shining white facade and crimson roof towering over me, larger than life.

What happened to me here? Why did I believe Imogen was back? I close my eyes and try to call up her voice again, even though I know it's just a memory. But I can't. It's other voices I hear now.

Professor Hoffman. *I suppose in a symbolic way, I see and hear and feel Marta's ghost everywhere.*

Leander. *Memories and metaphorical ghosts are real, powerful things. I think they affect us in mind-boggling ways sometimes.*

I was tricked. Fully and completely tricked. By a haunted hotel, by Madame Althea, by my own fucking head.

I should feel gullible, foolish. But I'm still too numb to feel anything beyond emptiness. I sit down hard on the gravel. I don't even realize I've gotten my phone out to call Mom until I hear her trying-hard-not-to-panic voice on the other end. Until I hear myself croak out that she needs to come and get me.

When I'm too hollowed out to cry anymore, dusk is falling. And when the thick silence comes and wraps itself around me, like I knew it would, I let it sink into my skin.

I understand what it is now. Loneliness. The kind that only happens when the person who knew you the best is gone. When the memories and the jokes and the pieces of yourself that only she knew—only she believed in—are gone, too.

Imogen is gone. She's been gone for a year.

But it feels like just now, outside the Harlow Hotel, in the vastness of Estes Park, she died all over again.

chapter twenty-four

Mom can tell I don't want to talk about it. To her credit, she doesn't make me right away. I know she will when we get home. But for now, we spiral down the mountain in silence. The radio won't pick up service until we hit Lyons, so there isn't anything to distract me. Just the dull throb in my head from all the crying, and the silence that's still holding on tight.

When my phone gets service again, it lights up with a text from Leander.

I'm sorry. I hope you're okay.

I stare at the message, trying to remind myself that I will be okay. To remember that over the past week, I've laughed and kissed and felt genuinely happy. But I can't. In my head, I know it happened. I know I haven't always felt this bad, which logically means I won't feel this way forever. But I can't make myself believe. I can't make myself believe that I won't feel this lonely for the rest of my life.

It isn't until we get home, and I've eaten an entire sleeve of Girl Scout Thin Mints, and Mom plunks a steaming mug of tea in front of me on the kitchen table, that she says, "Okay, what happened?"

I tell her all of it because I want to get it over with, going through it as factually and robotically as I can so I won't start crying again. Madame Althea's "messages" from Imogen; Leander and I teaming up to expose her as a fraud; the eerie, shapeless silence that seemed to be following me; seeing "Imogen" in the woods and on campus. When I get to that part, Mom's eyes widen. They go back to normal a second later, but I saw it. She's freaked out. Of course she is. I told her I saw a ghost.

"But Madame Althea didn't know what Imogen and I found in Agnes Tree. And that was when I knew Imogen wasn't trying to reach out to me. And then I called you." I take a long sip of green tea but barely taste it.

"Oh, honey," Mom says, the tears freely flowing down her face. "You thought she was back, and then you lost her again. No wonder you needed to get away. I'm so glad you called me." Her chair scrapes against the floor as she stands up to wrap her arms around me, pressing my cheek into the soft fabric of her T-shirt.

The longer she holds me, the more I feel the pressure of tears building up in my already aching head. I don't want to cry again. I'm tired of crying. I search for some other emotion to latch on to and only come up with frustration.

"There are still some things I can't explain, and I hate that I'm still thinking about them."

"Like what?" Mom asks, still holding on, rubbing my back in soothing circles.

"Like the class discussing *Arcadia*. Madame Althea knowing about 'mountain dark' and telling me to wear a headlamp."

Mom goes still for a second and then pulls back a little, her eyes cautious. "I don't know about *Arcadia*. But, does Madame Althea have dark hair and light blue eyes?"

"Yeah," I say slowly.

Mom breathes in. "I think I met her a few years ago when we were all at the Harlow for that Spiritualists and Skeptics exhibit. You and Imogen were laughing about something, and Madame Althea came up to me and said she loved seeing the two of you come to the Harlow, year after year. She said there was nothing in the world better than a best friend."

My mind is spinning now, trying to remember seeing Madame Althea at the Harlow all those summers with Imogen. But I can't. I would have sworn the first time I saw her was at the reading. "So are you saying, maybe she overheard Imogen and me at some point?" I ask. "Talking about mountain dark and headlamps?"

"I honestly don't know," Mom says. "I just remembered it."

The frustration boils over because the tears I thought

were gone are dripping down my face. Because it's true. There is nothing in the world better than a best friend.

"I'm so stupid," I whisper. Imogen died a year ago. Why did I have to go and believe in ridiculous things? Why did I make myself feel this way again?

"You're not." Mom hugs me tighter. "And you know I don't like that word."

"Then I'm losing my mind."

"You're not."

"Then I'm..." I close my eyes, digging deep for the truth, like Leander always pushes me to do. I try to delve beneath the easy answers, even if it hurts, and then I'm thinking of the outdoor movie night. Leander and I were talking about slasher movies, and how unrealistic it is when the killer dies in some spectacular way but then keeps coming back to life, again and again. But maybe it's not unrealistic at all. People don't come back, but feelings do. Memories do. Pain does. Even when you think you've moved on from them, you haven't. They'll always be lurking in the shadows, waiting for you. Over and over and over again, slashing you open like it's the very first time.

"I'm scared," I whisper.

Mom brushes my hair behind my ears, bending down so her face is level with mine. "And you need help. I'm calling Dr. Salamando."

I don't argue. In my room later, after Mom stops plying me with cookies and tea, I open my suitcase. My rumpled clothes are infused with the smell of Estes Park—smoke and pine and crispness. I throw them all into the laundry hamper and close the lid.

In the quiet of my room, the pine scent still hanging in the air, I take my phone out of my sweatshirt pocket and read Leander's text again. **I'm sorry. I hope you're okay.**

It sounds like a goodbye. I didn't realize I could feel any lonelier, but I do. It's not that I blame him. Why would he still want to be my boyfriend after everything I said today? Yelling at him for not believing me, telling him Imogen was speaking through him. The worry and then confusion and then hurt on his face...

I scrunch my eyes closed like that will wipe the memory from my head. I want to text him back, tell him I'm sorry, too, but I don't know if he'll want to hear it. If he'll want to hear from me. And I couldn't stand another goodbye right now.

I stare at Leander's message, telling myself that I'm okay. I try to think of how I felt earlier today on the University of Colorado campus with Leander, picturing myself going there, like it could really happen. How I felt in Oasis, when Leander told me he liked me, and I accepted it without questions or doubts. That giddy, sparkling, expanding feeling—like anything was possible—was coursing through me only hours ago.

But that was when Imogen was back. When I believed she was back. Now that she's really gone, the feeling is gone, too.

I take a breath. I try as hard as I can to feel it again.

But nothing happens.

chapter twenty-five

Four days until the Spirit Ball

Being back in Dr. Salamando's office feels like bad déjà vu. Like going back in time to the worst point of my life. The cream couch is still soft, Dr. Salamando's tub chair is still cobalt blue, and the big windows still let in tons of afternoon sun. The room gives off an airily cheerful vibe, a magazine-spread peacefulness that clashes with the pit of sadness that reopened in me yesterday.

As I finish rehashing everything that happened in Estes Park, Dr. Salamando is looking at me in the way I remember—attentively, nodding a lot but never giving anything away about what she thinks. I go all the way up to yesterday in the kitchen with Mom, to how slasher movies aren't so unrealistic after all because when the pain of loss comes back, it guts you without mercy, even when you think it's gone.

"Is it useful to you, to think about what happened over the past week in terms of horror movies?" Dr. Salamando asks.

"No. It's the opposite of useful. It's what got me here."

"Let's think about that." Dr. Salamando rests her chin on her hand. "Is what got you here your willingness to believe in horror movie logic, in the idea that Imogen's ghost was still present? Or was it being back in a place that was full of memories of her?"

The second one obviously makes more sense. It's what Leander told me after I showed him my footage of "Imogen" in the woods, which I know now could have been a light reflection or a cobweb or a camera malfunction, like he said.

And instantly, just like any time I think of Leander, I'm hit with a wave of missing him. His laugh, his know-it-allness, his nervous pen twirling, the way his jokes always snuck up and surprised me.

I hope he's okay. I hope he talked to his mom more. I hope they all talked—him and his mom and Daphne. But I don't know because I haven't responded to any of his texts.

He sent one this morning before my appointment. **I was looking for you, and Dr. B told me you went home?** I felt too embarrassed to confirm that my mom had to come get me. That she had to email Dr. B to tell her why I had to leave the Harlow early. She didn't go into the details, and Dr. B was super understanding, saying I could still get partial credit for the senior project work I did there, and

I could make up the rest another way. I thought I'd feel relieved that I don't have to present at the Conference for the Paranormal, but part of me feels a slight pull of regret. I'm bailing again, like I did with the *Arcadia* audition. And I definitely regret not being able to go to the Spirit Ball. But I don't think I'd have much fun anyway.

A few minutes after that text, Leander sent another. **Are you okay?** And I couldn't reply to that one, either. Because I don't know the answer.

"I was fine before I went to the Harlow," I say, bringing myself back to Dr. Salamando's office. "So, I didn't think that going back there would push me all the way back *here*." I wave my hand around the office. "Back to the beginning again."

"What did fine look like to you?" Dr. Salamando asks.

"It looked like..." I pause, remembering Dave's party and how I tricked myself into believing I was having fun. "I think maybe I was fine sometimes, and other times I wasn't," I say slowly, trying my best to find the truth. "But I didn't want to admit that I wasn't fine because I wanted to be strong, and I didn't want to go back to feeling like I did right after Imogen died. So I tried to pretend I was always fine, even when I wasn't."

Dr. Salamando nods. "Did you try to pretend you were fine at the Harlow Hotel?"

"Yes." I remember all the times I suppressed how I was feeling because I wanted to believe I'd moved on. "But I think the memories and feelings got so big that I couldn't pretend I was fine anymore."

"That would make sense, considering how significant the Harlow Hotel and Estes Park were to your friendship with Imogen."

I lean forward a little on the couch. "So then, why didn't I just realize what was happening? Why did I see Imogen's literal ghost? Why did I start believing in a medium?"

Dr. Salamando is quiet for a moment. "Grief is a powerful thing," she says after a while. "I've found that it doesn't always make sense."

I sigh, pressing my fingers into the couch cushion. "But you said the only way out is through. I thought I went through, but clearly, I haven't. Am I never going to get out? Every time I see something that reminds me of Imogen, am I going to wonder if she's trying to communicate with me? Every time I see someone who looks like her, am I going to think it's her ghost? Am I going to be like the final girl in a horror movie who thinks she's all done with the trauma but then oops, they make it a franchise and she has to be traumatized all over again?"

Dr. Salamando smiles, her eyes crinkling at the corners in a familiar way, and I feel a slight lift in the heaviness hanging around us. It reminds me that not all the conversations we've had in this room were sad. We laughed sometimes, too. About Imogen, about me, about the absurdity of life.

Dr. Salamando leans back in her chair as her smile turns thoughtful. "When I said the only way out is through, I didn't mean you get through the grief and then you'll never miss Imogen again. I meant that when your feelings of grief become so powerful that they start to feel overwhelming, you shouldn't ignore it. You should face that moment of crisis. It doesn't mean you'll never have another. Although in my experience, it does get easier with time."

I nod, trying to work through it all. "I think... my grief became so powerful when I was at the Harlow that it started to overwhelm me. But I was too scared to face it. So instead, I started explaining what was happening to me in other ways. My bracelet didn't break because I was messing with it, it broke because Imogen was trying to tell me she was there. That eerie silence didn't keep enveloping me because I felt lonely in this place that used to be ours, it was more proof that she was there. I didn't metaphorically see Imogen because Estes Park is filled with memories of her, I saw her literal ghost."

I take a breath, and I think I'm all talked out, but it keeps coming. "You know what else I realized?" I say, remembering last night in my room, how I tried to feel the way Imogen used to make me feel but couldn't. "I don't just miss Imogen. I miss the way she saw the world. She always saw these big, magical possibilities in everything. Including me. She always believed I was smarter and more capable than I ever felt I was. I miss the way she saw me. I miss the version of me she believed I was."

Dr. Salamando is looking at me intensely. "You said something last year that stuck with me. You said you missed the person you were with Imogen. You couldn't describe that person then, and I'm wondering if you have any more insight now?"

I think back to last winter, sitting on the same couch, trying to describe the person I was with Imogen. Laughing hysterically at cheesy inside jokes. Getting excited about stuff I never thought I'd be into, like watching a six-hour version of *Pride and Prejudice* or auditioning for a play.

And before I can think of an answer, new memories are flashing up. Leander and me calling each other "pardner." Leander and me getting excited talking about serial killers' sweaters and supernatural beliefs. Me walking around a college campus and fantasizing about going there.

On top of the fresh pang of missing Leander, a new idea is forming. I used to think that the person I was with Imogen died when she did. But maybe that's not true. I know I won't ever be the same after her loss. But certain things have come back—in bits and pieces and flashes.

"I'd describe her as someone who doesn't limit herself," I say. "Who believes that anything is possible."

Dr. Salamando is leaning forward in her chair now, too. "I don't think you have to let go of that person."

"But I didn't always believe I was that person, even when Imogen was alive."

Dr. Salamando shrugs. "I don't think that matters. You don't have to let go of the way Imogen saw the world or the way she saw you, just because she's gone. You can see yourself the way Imogen did. As limitless and bursting with possibilities. It might take some practice. But that idea of you isn't gone. She gave it to you. It's part of you now."

As Dr. Salamando's words reverberate in my head, I feel a subtle, strange shift in the air, like I did in Madame Althea's office. Like a new presence just came into the room. But this time, it doesn't feel like a ghost. Not a literal one, anyway. This time, it feels like some long-buried part of me is coming back to life.

chapter twenty-six

Two days until the Spirit Ball

Despite all the thoughts swimming around in my head from therapy, for the next couple of nights, I sleep better than I have in a long time. When I wake up on Thursday, the glare of the sun through my blinds tells me it's practically afternoon. I feel weirdly energized as I grab my phone off the nightstand and bring up Leander's text.

Are you okay?

I stare at the words for a long time as my stomach dips. I have no idea how he feels about me right now or what he thinks about us or if there even is an us anymore. But I finally know how to answer his question.

I will be okay.

The three dots appear immediately, like he's been staring

at his phone, too. The thought makes me smile for the first time since coming home.

I know you will, he writes back.

How are things with you and your mom? I type quickly.

Better. She came by before she left the Harlow, and we talked. She talked to Daphne, too. I think we're all in a good place now.

I'm really, really glad.

My thumbs hover over the keyboard. On my screen, the three dots appear and disappear. I can practically hear the awkward pause between us even though we're not in the same room. But it's hard to know what to say next. I wish he was here so we could really talk. So I could tell him everything and ask him if what he said in Oasis is still true.

His next message pops up on my screen. **Someone beat me to it.**

I wrinkle my eyebrows in confusion, but then he sends a link to an article. I don't read the title at first because I'm staring at the accompanying image. It's of the chalk drawings we saw when we went to visit Professor Hoffman—the first one we spotted, sketched onto the winding sidewalk next to the pond. I finally read the title: "The Surprising Truth About the University of Colorado's Chalk Drawings."

I click on the link immediately, which takes me to the University of Colorado's student newspaper.

The truth about the chalk drawings, I discover, isn't as outrageous as an alien takeover or as practical as a pizza discount. It's that the drawings were done by a freshman named Hannah Persaud, who was "never that into art," but then she randomly took a class on art history because it filled a gen ed requirement. Then she became fascinated with Greek geometric art, and the chalk drawings were inspired by that. According to the article, she chalked homages all over campus as a way to "remind people to keep an open mind because you never know what you're going to fall in love with."

I rest my phone on the bed when I'm done reading. Before, the truth that the chalk drawings were done by a random student who was super into Greek geometric art might have seemed disappointing. But now, it just makes me think of what Leander said in the tunnel. How he wants to take a bunch of classes in college and figure out what he loves. How it could be anything.

I glance at my bookshelf, at the green spine of *Arcadia* resting on the bottom. I think of Imogen in my room that day, telling me I should audition for the play, her eyes bright with belief.

You'd be amazing. I'm serious.

And as I pick my phone back up to browse the University of Colorado website, that sparkling feeling is beginning to expand in my chest, the one I was trying so hard to feel a few nights ago.

And before I even get out of bed, I click on the Admissions button, create an account, and scan through the first-year application. Then I text Leander back.

I miss you.

The dots come and go again. And then: **I miss you, too.**

I stare at the words for a long time, until the soft, familiar sound of voices and clinking mugs reaches my room. When I go downstairs, Mrs. Matsuda and Mom are sitting at the kitchen table, drinking tea and eating mizu yokan.

"Morning, honey," Mom says, giving me a thorough inspection with her eyes, like she's done every morning since I've gotten home. "Did you sleep okay?"

"Yeah. I slept great, actually. Hi, Mrs. Matsuda. It's good to see you."

"Good to see you, too, Natalie," Mrs. Matsuda says, smiling warmly, her face barely wrinkled even though she's in her seventies. She puts a slice of yokan on a plate and pushes it in my direction. "Have some."

I've never had yokan for breakfast before, but I feel like I deserve it. I take a bite, savoring the light, clean taste as Mom gets up to make me some tea. It's then that I realize the last time Mrs. Matsuda saw me, I was flying down her street on a unicorn bed. I glance at her, wondering if she's thinking about that right now, too.

Mrs. Matsuda's mouth turns up in a small smile, and then she winks at me. I remember her doing that way back when I took piano lessons from her in sixth grade. If I hit a wrong note—which I did a lot—she'd wink at me, like *no judgment,* like it was a private joke between the two of us.

A question pops into my brain as Mom comes back to

the table with my tea. "Mrs. Matsuda, when I took piano lessons from you, was I really bad at it?"

Mrs. Matsuda looks surprised for a second, but then her face turns thoughtful as she shifts in her chair, brushing her long fingers over the smooth fabric of her floral skirt. "I don't know if anyone is really bad when they first start. Or else, everyone is really bad when they first start, which means that no one is better or worse."

"Right." When I started piano lessons, I knew I wasn't going to be as good as Imogen because she'd been playing for years. But still, it was hard not to compare myself to her. Hard not to believe that piano just wasn't for me when she was playing trills so fast they made my head spin while I was struggling through "Twinkle, Twinkle Little Star." But Imogen being amazing at piano didn't mean I couldn't be amazing at it, too. I gave up too easily. And I don't want to do that anymore.

A shiny new idea is forming in my head, and I already feel a rush of excitement. "Do you think I could start lessons again?"

Mom's face lights up.

"That would be lovely," Mrs. Matsuda says, eyes smiling at me over her mug of tea.

chapter twenty-seven

One day until the Spirit Ball

After another therapy appointment and another good night of sleep, my head feels clearer and my heart less hollow. But after another text exchange with Leander—where I planned on seeing where we stood relationship-wise but ended up asking him how the weather was in Estes Park—I also feel like the world's biggest wimp. Because I can work my way through a major emotional and psychological upheaval, but telling a boy I still want to date him is apparently too much.

When Mom announces after dinner that she wants to have a movie night, I'm glad for the distraction.

"It can even be horror if you want," Mom says, changing into her fashion jammies. "Just no home invasions or exorcisms, please."

"You can pick the movie. Any kind is fine." Horror is still the best, but I'm in the mood to branch out a bit. I pull up all the streaming possibilities on TV. "Just no love triangles or single-dad firefighters looking for love, please."

"It'll be difficult," Mom says, squinting at the TV like she's about to perform surgery. "But I think we'll be able to find something that meets both of our needs."

I check the cupboards and decide we need snacks. I let Mom browse through the options and head to Safeway.

I'm scanning the candy section, wondering if we need both Peanut Butter Cups and Peanut M&M'S, when I feel someone watching me at the far end of the aisle. I glance over but they're already moving. All I catch is a wisp of dark blond hair disappearing around the corner.

My heartbeat speeds up, but I focus back on the candy question. There are plenty of people with blond hair in Safeway right now. I grab both the cups and the M&M'S, plop them into my basket, and head to the frozen section for ice cream.

I'm holding the glass door open with my hip—the frosty air pricking my hand as I grab a pint of Half Baked—when I see them again. At least, I think it's the same person from the candy aisle. Their shape is fuzzy when I peer through the foggy glass door. But they're right there, standing still, watching me. And again, when I close the door to really look, they're gone.

I take a breath of chilly supermarket air. And then I make a beeline down the aisle to find out what's going on.

My heart is fully pounding now, but it doesn't feel the same as when I was on the Starlight Trail, chasing Imogen's ghost. I know this time that whoever's following me isn't Imogen. But they *are* following me, and I want to know why.

I take a sharp turn at the end of the aisle, and there, standing next to a display of chocolate syrup, is Bea.

"Hi, Natalie," she says, her face creased with embarrassment. "I thought it was you, but I wasn't sure. Sorry for being such a creep."

"Bea..." I think something will come out after that, but nothing does. I haven't seen her since after the funeral, when she asked if I wanted anything of Imogen's, and I said no. She looks better now than she did then. Obviously. Her green eyes are sharp and clear again, her blond hair flat-ironed into sleek perfection.

"I—You're not a creep," I say when I realize I've just been staring. "And hi."

She laughs through her nose and studies my face. "How are you?"

I think about what I should say. I don't know Bea that well. She was already in college in Maryland when Imogen and I became best friends, and even during breaks, she wasn't ever home for more than a week or two. After college, when she started living in Maryland permanently, she was back even less. But when she did visit, it was always memorable. Like when she took Imogen and me to see *The Ring*—what was known forever after as the holy monkey balls night.

I remember seeing her over Christmas break the following year, when the Lucases had me over for dinner. Bea asked me what was new, and I told her about getting my learner's permit. "Watch out for those old men drivers," she said with a wink. Imogen and I both laughed, and Mr. and Mrs. Lucas were confused and clearly wanted to know what Bea meant, but she just shrugged and said, "It's a proverb," which only made us laugh more.

Bea's eyes are roaming my face intently, and I realize she's not asking how I am as a formality. She wants the truth. "I'm better now," I say. "It comes in waves, though. I'm sure you know that."

Bea breathes out. "I do." She glances at the Starbucks kiosk at the front of the store. "Can I buy you a hot chocolate or something?"

I smile as the familiarity of it washes over me. Whenever she was home, Bea always treated Imogen and me to stuff. Hot chocolate and ice cream and popcorn and movie tickets. It was like she felt guilty for not being there that much, although we knew she had a whole other life far away. "You don't have to do that."

"I know I don't. I just really want to get you a hot chocolate. Please let me?"

I smile again and check my phone. It's only seven thirty, and it always takes Mom ages to pick out a movie anyway. "Okay."

I sit down at a small table dusted with crumbs, and a minute later, Bea plunks down two warm cardboard cups.

"Thanks for not lying and saying you were fine," she says, sitting in the chair across from me and running her finger in circles over the lid of her cup. "It's what my parents are doing."

"Really?" I've wondered a lot about Mr. and Mrs. Lucas. At the funeral, their faces looked so empty, like they were department store mannequins of themselves.

"They've got this whole new life in Arizona, which is good, but they think as long as they stay busy and keep their house spotless and go to all the right restaurants, everything will be just peachy. It drives me up the wall because I know they're not fine."

"Maybe it'll just take them a while to admit it," I say.

"Yeah." Bea nods. "Are you talking to someone about everything? A therapist?"

"Yup." I take the lid off my hot chocolate and blow at the steam. "You?"

"Yes. We talk about a lot of stuff, not just Imogen. But when the anniversary of her death came up last week, a ton of things came back. Mostly feelings of guilt for not being there enough. I mean, I figured she'd get out from under Mom and Dad's thumb in college like I did, so I didn't…" She trails off, shaking her head like there's no point in hashing through it all again.

"Anyway, I was talking about her in therapy, and I just felt this urge to come back here. I guess I wanted to be around the memories." Bea takes a long sip of her hot chocolate. "I was in Denver for a conference this week, and today I decided to come to Boulder. And it's been so *weird*. I felt her in all the used bookstores she used to go to. I practically heard her snort-laughing when I accidentally knocked over a display."

I'm nodding so much my neck hurts. "I know exactly what you mean."

"And then I see *you*, which is the ultimate reminder of her. You were so essential to her."

Bea's words warm me up more than the liquid chocolate in my stomach. I try to soak them in as much as I can.

"Imogen changed so much after she met you," Bea goes on, circling her finger around the lid again. "She'd always been so cautious and afraid of the world. But then she became friends with you and started coming out of her shell and getting so much braver."

"You..." I pause, the cup halfway to my mouth. "You think Imogen was getting braver? Because of me?"

"Oh, definitely." Bea looks a bit surprised. "You didn't see it? I guess you might not have noticed because it was gradual, and you were with her all the time. It's like how you don't notice you've grown until you measure yourself and see. But I only saw Imogen a few times a year, and I always saw a difference. She was stronger and braver each time."

I search my brain, sifting through all the memories again. Imogen had always just been Imogen to me—brilliant and kind and extraordinary and scared of basically everything, from bats to heights to saying no to her parents.

But then I remember that time she refused to wear her hair in a chignon even though her mom wanted her to.

You know what? I'm going to leave it down.

And the fierce way she argued with me when I said she was the smart one, and I was the brave one.

It doesn't mean we can't change or that I can't be brave and you can't be smart!

They might seem like small things—standing up to your mom, arguing with your best friend. But for Imogen, they were big. "I see what you mean," I say slowly.

Bea smiles. "Honestly, I think she was close to telling Mom and Dad off."

"What?" I sit up straighter. I can't quite believe that one. "No way."

"Mm-hmm. I FaceTimed with her the day before she died, and she seemed like she was gearing up to do something big. I kept asking her what the deal was, but she wouldn't say. I thought maybe she was finally going to put her foot down about not going to that piano camp she hated, but I don't know. I was going to ask her about it the next time we talked, but..." She breaks off, staring at the table. "Anyway," she says after a beat. "Did you notice anything?"

I rack my brain again, combing over the details of our last summer in Estes Park. But everything had seemed normal. As far as I knew, she was planning to go to piano camp.

"No." I smile regretfully. "I can't think of anything."

Bea nods, but I can tell she's a little disappointed. "You know, I don't think I ever told you how happy I was that you were Immy's best friend." Her eyes are bright with tears now. "She loved you so much."

"I loved her, too." My best friend who was brilliant and creative and bursting with possibilities. My best friend who wanted me to see myself as those things, too. I'm going to try my best to hold on to that always. I think of something that could help me remember.

"You asked me after the funeral if there was anything of Imogen's I wanted," I say. "I didn't think there was then, but..."

"You name it." Bea wipes a tear away, going into action mode immediately.

"We found this crystal hummingbird in Estes Park once. She kept it in the wardrobe in her dollhouse."

Bea glances up at the fluorescent lights on the ceiling. "I remember that hummingbird. It was gorgeous. But... I didn't see it when we packed up her dollhouse. I think Mom stored away a bunch of her special stuff before that. I'll call her tomorrow and get her to send it to you."

"Thanks," I say even though my heart sinks a little, wondering if Imogen's mom will want to let it go. If she doesn't, that's okay. I don't need the hummingbird to remember Imogen or to believe in myself. I have the memory of finding it, and if I've learned anything this past week, it's that memories can be the most powerful things in the world.

Bea and I talk for a while longer, reminiscing about

Imogen as we finish our hot chocolates. And when I drive back home, my mind wanders to what Bea said about how it seemed like Imogen was gearing up to do something big. I wonder if she really had been planning to stand up to her parents. Maybe she was finally going to insist that she wasn't going to piano camp.

I like thinking that she spent her last night knowing she was going to stand up for herself. It's hard to believe, but it's possible. And right now, that's enough to make me smile.

Mom falls asleep on the couch at the end of the movie. It's late, but after the talk with Bea and all the sugar I consumed, I'm wide awake. And I know exactly what I'm going to do.

I run upstairs and grab *Arcadia* off the shelf. I take a breath, open it, and start to read.

It takes me forever to get through each page because I have to stop and look up all the things the characters reference. Gothic architecture and poetry and complex equations.

It's both confusing and fascinating, and when I finish, my brain is buzzing with ideas and images. I flip back to a page near the beginning, to one of the lines I practiced for the audition.

> *When you stir your rice pudding, Septimus, the spoonful of jam spreads itself round making red*

trails like the picture of a meteor in my astronomical atlas. But if you stir backward, the jam will not come together again.

I remember talking about that line with Imogen. How some things are irreversible. When you stir jam into pudding, you can't stir it out. When you die, you can't come back. But Imogen said that even when you're gone, some part of you still infuses things. That ghosts are the ideas you put out into the world that people pick up and think about even when you're gone.

She was right. About ghosts. About us. I used to think we were so different. That I was the brave one and she was the smart one. But maybe that wasn't the case. Or maybe it was at first, but then we melded into each other so much—like jam in rice pudding—that it was impossible to separate us out anymore.

When I put *Arcadia* carefully back on my shelf, I'm still keyed up. So I open my *Ghost Chasers* footage on my laptop. I have this urge to turn it into something else. Something that captures the truth of what it was like to be at the Harlow Hotel, chasing Imogen's ghost.

I work on it for a long time. When I'm finished, I know exactly what I want to do with it.

chapter twenty-eight

The day of the Spirit Ball

"Are you completely and totally sure you want to do this?" Mom asks as I stare out the passenger-side window at the Harlow Hotel, a major case of déjà vu washing over me.

"I'm sure." I tug the white bead bracelet on my wrist, the new elastic strong and stretchy, as a wave of warmth and confidence washes over me.

Mom smiles. "Good luck, honey. You're going to do great."

And then I'm stepping out of the car, looking around at all the researchers here to present at the Conference for the Paranormal. Just like I am. Because I emailed Dr. B this morning, and she put me back on the schedule for two o'clock. I smooth out my satiny white blouse, making sure it's still tucked into the pleated black skirt. I'm glad I'm finally wearing the outfit, even if it's not for the *Arcadia* audition.

It's only ten in the morning, and I saw on the schedule that Leander's presentation is right before mine. We'll finally have time to talk face-to-face. I texted him this morning to tell him I was coming, and I'm speed-walking so fast to the dorms I'm already sweating, clutching the straps of my backpack, where I have my Terror in the Corn costume tucked in beside my laptop. Because Dr. B also reinvited me to the Spirit Ball. Hopefully, Leander will come with me.

As I walk down the hallway to his door, I take out my phone to text him again.

Turn off the Golden Girls and open your door.

I hear the scrape of a chair and a rush of footsteps before he throws the door open. For a second, he looks like he wants to sweep me into a hug. But then he just steps back and lets me in. All his clothes are packed up, his suitcase zipped and standing at the foot of the bed. "I'm glad you're back," he says.

"I'm sorry." I charge in because I need to get it out. I need to get us back to where we were in Oasis, before everything blew up. "I'm sorry I got mad at you for not believing what I said about Imogen being back. That wasn't fair."

"No, you don't need to apologize." Leander runs a hand through his hair. "I was too busy obsessing about facts—I wasn't listening to what you were telling me. Which was that you saw your best friend. I should have listened to you, and maybe we could have talked through it."

"Maybe. But I don't think you would have convinced me. I think I *had* to go see Madame Althea."

"You went to see Madame Althea?"

I nod and Leander takes my hand, directing me to the bed, where we both sit down, our hips touching. And I tell him everything. Everything that happened since I left Oasis up until now, watching his face shift from surprise to sympathy to admiration when I tell him about therapy and talking with Bea and finally reading *Arcadia*.

"And I need you to know," I say when I'm done because I have to get this out. "That I really like you. And I want to go to the Spirit Ball with you tonight. And I want you to be my boyfriend."

I cringe, realizing I should have practiced that part more in my head, but Leander is smiling like I just made the most eloquent speech in the world.

"Guess we should watch *Evil Dead II*, then," he says, shrugging. "Make it official."

"We really don't need to do that. You said you don't like horror movies."

"Oh, you're backing out now?" Leander raises his eyebrow at me. "So that later, when I annoy you, you can take back everything you said about me being your boyfriend on a technicality? Not happening."

I laugh, and keep laughing all through Leander grabbing his laptop, finding *Evil Dead II*, and spending $2.99 to rent it. But it's nothing compared to when we start watching the movie, because Leander Hall, Mr. Truth Hurts himself, is a horror movie lightweight. He flinches during all the gory parts, and when Ash cuts off his demon-possessed hand, Leander gags in a way that sounds like a joke but is completely genuine. I ask him multiple times if he wants to stop, but he shakes his head and says, "Nope, I'm doing this."

I give his knee a squeeze, remembering that the last time I watched *Evil Dead II* was with Imogen, right after we had our fight. It eased the tension between us because it's impossible not to be entertained by this beautiful, absurd movie. Even though I've seen it so many times, it still fills me with awe. The way the camera takes on the perspective of a demon and moves—rapid and wild—through the woods. The startling shifts between terror and laughter. The supernatural but still somehow human strength of Ash.

"This is a famous part," I say, when Ash attaches a chainsaw to his arm to replace the hand he cut off. He holds the chainsaw up to the camera in a true moment of campy, heroic badassery.

"*Groovy,*" Ash says.

When the movie ends, I look at Leander, who's still staring at the screen like he has no idea what just happened. "That was . . . ," he starts. "A lot."

"I know! They throw everything at you. Dancing demons, talking deer heads, creepy lullaby, et cetera, et cetera. But I love that no matter what, no matter how often the demons come back and tear things apart, Ash always comes out of it. He's bloody and missing a hand and sent back in time to the Middle Ages, but he's still him. He's still the hero."

Leander's mouth tips up even though he still looks a little pale. "I guess it's pretty inspiring when you think about it like that."

"I guess you're my boyfriend now," I say casually, reaching for his hand and lacing my fingers through his.

And Leander looks a lot less queasy now. "Yeah. Guess I am."

A shot of happiness bursts through me, mixed with nerves. Because in a few minutes, I'll walk into the Harlow Hotel again. Then I'll give a presentation in front of a crowd of scholars. Both things are really fucking scary.

"We should probably head out," Leander says, checking his phone. "You ready?"

I take a breath and lift my metaphorical chainsaw arm into the air. "Groovy."

The billiards room is as crowded as it was during Madame Althea's reading, but this time, the lights are bright and sun streams in through the windows. I'm watching Leander wrap up his presentation on Agnes Thripp, which was brilliant, like I knew it would be, even though it was technically a fake project all along. When he's done, a girl who looks about fourteen stands up and claps, the aggressiveness of it coming across as both ironic and genuinely proud. It has to be Daphne.

And then it's my turn. I smooth out my white blouse one more time, and when I'm up on the small portable stage, the same one Madame Althea used, I look out into the crowd of faces. Leander is sitting with his mom and Daphne. Dr. B is in the front with her clipboard. Mom, who rushed back here after she was done with work, is in the back, giving me an embarrassing but supportive double thumbs-up.

I connect my laptop to the projector, bringing up my *Ghost Chasers* footage, which plays on the screen behind me, showing eerie night shots of the Harlow. Then Madame Althea's voice speaks:

"If spirit energy is strong somewhere, if remnants of the past endure, then that is a haunted place. America is filled with them. The world is filled with them. And one of those places happens to be right here."

The night shot of the Harlow zooms up onto the porch, the empty wicker rocking chairs looking spooky, like they might start rocking on their own. But then the shot fades from the screen and a picture of me and Imogen comes up—us on the Harlow Hotel porch, squished into a rocking chair. The last picture we ever took.

"I was never afraid of ghosts until my best friend became one." My voice carries in the huge room. "I don't mean she walked through walls or popped up behind me in the bathroom mirror. It was a lot scarier than that."

As I speak, the footage behind me keeps switching

back and forth between night shots of the Harlow looking eerie and pictures of me and Imogen in Estes Park, horseback riding, hiking, eating ice cream downtown.

I ignore all the people looking at me curiously and let the words pour out. I talk about what happened to me over the past week at the Harlow. How real Imogen felt here, even though her presence was a product of my own memories. How metaphorical ghosts can be scarier than horror movie ones, because they don't follow rules or tropes. They aren't laid to rest with an ancient spell or object. They might haunt you forever. But maybe that's a good thing. Because being haunted doesn't have to feel scary. It can feel warm and familiar. It can be a presence or a voice, calling up memories, making you laugh, telling you to believe in yourself more than you do.

I end by trying to answer Dr. B's question about why people are drawn to haunted places. "I used to love the Harlow Hotel because it was fun to be scared. It was fun to believe, even just for a moment, that a ghost might drift across the lobby. But now..."

I think about how much I still feel Imogen at the Harlow Hotel, even though I know she's gone. How as soon as I put the white bead bracelet back on my wrist this morning, a warm glow spread through my body. How a few days ago, I walked into a classroom of people discussing *Arcadia*—which is the only thing about the past week I can't explain.

And I decide not to try. I decide to see it not as a random coincidence or as proof that Imogen's ghost exists. I choose to see it as a "what if?" moment. An open-ended question that isn't supposed to be answered but instead makes you less certain, less locked into one idea of the world. Because that's how Imogen would have wanted me to think about it.

"Now, I love the Harlow Hotel because it lets me believe—even just for a moment—that Imogen isn't gone. It lets me believe that when I come here, *her* ghost will drift across the lobby. Probably metaphorically. But maybe one day, it'll be real. In the end, it doesn't matter. I'll always be happy to see her, in whatever form she takes. Because she was my best friend."

As I step off the stage, I hear a smattering of claps that turns into a roar of applause. I see thoughtful faces and a few misty eyes and Dr. B looking at me with pride. When I sit back in my seat, Imogen's voice whispers in my head.

You're going to do awesome, important, world-changing things.

I smile, because now that voice feels like it's mine, too.

chapter twenty-nine

The Harlow Hotel lobby is filled with blood-spattered prom queens, skeletons wearing top hats, angry clowns, and sexy witches. I make my way through them all into the ballroom, where the music reverberates in my chest and eerie blue disco lights flash around the dance floor, illuminating a rag doll dancing with a nineteenth-century vampire, a woman in a corseted Victorian gown holding a frighteningly realistic cast of her own head twirling around, her skirt billowing around her.

It's amazing. I don't think it can get any more amazing until I feel a tap on my shoulder and spin around.

And there's Leander, dressed in full cowboy gear—wide-brimmed hat, bandanna, vest, and boots. My jaw drops open.

He tips his hat and leans in close to my ear. "Howdy, pardner."

I throw my head back and laugh, the bass drowning most of it out. Then I fling my arms around his neck and kiss him, glad Mom already left, giving Leander permission to drive me home as penance for saying, "Oh, so *this* is a Leander Hall" and winking when I introduced her.

Leander and I break apart when a flailing pirate bumps into us. Daphne, jumping up and down, swinging her head aggressively from side to side and thrashing her arms.

"What are you doing?" Leander shouts over the music.

"This is how people dance in clubs," Daphne shouts back.

Leander gives her a look that's a mixture of amused and sarcastic. "What clubs are you going to?"

"You've never seen a movie where they go to a club? Oh yeah, *your* movies are boring."

I knew it when I first met her after the presentations, but this seals the deal. I like Daphne. So I join her. Jumping, flailing, throwing my head up and down until I feel a little dizzy. After some peer pressuring, Leander does it, too. People make room for us, cheering us on as we leave it all on the dance floor.

After a little while, Daphne goes home with her mom, and Leander and I head out to his car because the Spirit Ball goes twenty-one and over at 8:30 PM. We didn't see anything wild happen at the party. The music played the right way, and the lighting fixtures stayed mounted to the ceiling. I thought I was going to be disappointed if nothing theatrically haunted happened at the Ball, but it's kind of a relief.

As Leander and I walk across the front courtyard, the sun has already sunk below the mountains, leaving behind a pinkish-gray sky. I shift my bag on my shoulder and take in the pine-covered mountains surrounding us, the smoky scent of the air, the buzz of hummingbirds. I don't know when I'll be here again. Maybe next summer, maybe not. But I know that when I do come back, Imogen's ghost will still be here.

I glance across the courtyard to the edge of the woods, the gap in the trees that marks the beginning of the Starlight Trail.

The urge to take one last walk down the path glimmers through me. I won't be chasing Imogen's ghost this time. I'll be remembering her. Saying goodbye, even though I know now that saying goodbye is a long, maybe never-ending process.

"Do you mind if we take a walk?" I ask, pointing to the trail.

"Not at all."

When we start along the Starlight Trail, the roar of the creek blows over us. I take in the yarrow swaying at the edge of the path, the green moss covering the rocks, the moths clicking as they zip by. I breathe in the sage smell and smile when I see Harvey the Aspen's cartoon grin. I tell Leander about Buttview so he laughs along with me.

When we finally reach Agnes Tree, we stop, craning our necks back as far as they'll go, blinking at the dark hollow high up in the trunk.

I still wish I could go back to the night Imogen died and climb it. I think I'll always wish that. But maybe I can do it now. It'll hurt to climb Agnes Tree without Imogen standing at the bottom, cheering me on, believing against all logic that a ghost left something for us to find in the hollow. But a voice inside me says I should do it. To finally make good on my promise to be brave and believe.

"I'm going to climb it," I say, and Leander casts his eyes up at the branches dubiously.

I half-expect him to try to talk me out of it, but all he does is take a deep breath. "Be careful up there, pardner."

I step onto the rock, putting my knee on the low branch and leaning my hands against the trunk for balance. I push myself up. My pace is quick and steady. I've climbed Agnes Tree so many times that even though I skipped last year, I still remember the distance between each foothold, the spring of the branches, and the butterscotch smell of the bark.

I glance down at one point to see Leander watching me closely, his feet planted in a wide stance, his arms slightly outstretched, like he's getting ready to catch me if I fall. "Don't look down," he shouts.

"Don't look up," I yell back, and keep climbing. A minute later, I'm right underneath the gaping hollow.

I take a breath. "I'm sorry I didn't do this last year," I whisper to the tree, to the sky, to the picture of Imogen that lives in my head, standing at the bottom of Agnes Tree, looking at me expectantly. "I'm sorry I didn't believe."

I reach my hand inside to complete the ritual, my fingers running over gritty dirt and tiny rocks. And then they brush against something cold and smooth.

I yank my hand back at first but then grasp on, my whole body shaking as I pull it out.

The crystal hummingbird, its emerald body sparkling in the dusky light.

It's a pretty good ending for a ghost story, I realize as I sit at the base of Agnes Tree, turning the hummingbird over in my hands. The last-minute twist that upends the rational explanation. The final, eerie "what if?"

"Okay, I'm sorry...," Leander says beside me, the side of his body leaning into mine. "But I have to know what you're thinking."

I've been quiet for a while, just staring at the hummingbird.

Truthfully, I'm thinking about a lot of things. Some of them rational and some of them not, but they all try to answer the question of how the crystal hummingbird Imogen and I found six years ago in the hollow of Agnes Tree ended up back there.

What I keep coming back to is Imogen shouting during our fight about the *Arcadia* audition, when I said she was smart and I was brave.

But that was one situation. It doesn't mean we can't change or that I can't be brave and you can't be smart!

Yeah... But it doesn't mean that you'll climb Mount Everest and I'll get my PhD in physics.

You might! I might! Again, I wouldn't climb Everest because it's unethical, but I could climb something tall!

"I'm thinking," I say slowly, still watching the hummingbird sparkle as the last bit of sunset pink fades into gray. "I'm thinking that Imogen was afraid of heights. But last summer, she climbed Agnes Tree anyway and put this back in the hollow."

"Why?" Leander asks, his voice quiet.

It could happen! It's possible!

"Because she wanted me to believe. Not in ghosts. She wanted me to believe in her. In me. In the idea that we could do anything we wanted to do, be whatever we wanted to be."

I'll never know for sure how the hummingbird found its way back into Agnes Tree. But this is what I believe.

I believe that last summer, when Imogen was getting ready to go to Estes Park, she took the hummingbird out of the miniature wardrobe in her dollhouse and packed it carefully in her suitcase. She snuck off through the woods at some point when I thought she was with her parents. She climbed Agnes Tree, clenching her jaw the whole time, maybe even swearing once or twice, sure this was a bad idea, certain she was going to fall. But she didn't.

She stashed the hummingbird in the hollow and

climbed back down, and when her feet touched the ground, when she was safe again, her face broke into an impossibly wide smile. She could hardly believe she'd done it. She bounced up and down on her toes. She snort-laughed as she pictured me climbing up the tree later and reaching into the hollow and finding the hummingbird. She imagined me looking down at her in shock and then realizing what it meant, what she'd done.

"So...," Leander asks, reaching out to run his finger along the smooth beak of the hummingbird. "Do you believe?"

I nod slowly. I believe Imogen climbed up Agnes Tree even though it scared her. I believe I can find a way to heal from Imogen's death, to be honest about how much I'll miss her for the rest of my life, even though that scares me. I believe I can do all the awesome, important, world-changing things I didn't think I could.

I lean against Leander, feeling the solid weight of the hummingbird in my hand. And as the mountain darkness falls around us, I realize I believe in a lot of things.

acknowledgments

I wrote this book during my first two years as a mom, which means there were many times when I thought I'd never finish it. To all the people who helped me see it through, I am deeply grateful.

To my wise and wonderful agent, Allie Levick, I am thankful every day that I have you in my corner. To my brilliant editor, Alex Hightower, thank you for believing in this story and helping me wade through its layers with insight and patience. I am so incredibly lucky to get to work with such smart, kind people who value both my work and my well-being. I am eternally grateful for you both!

Thank you also to Crystal Castro, Gabrielle Chang, Esther Reisberg, Patricia Alvarado, and everyone at Little, Brown Books for Young Readers who helped bring this book into the world. Thanks also to cover illustrator Max Reed, copyeditor Starr Baer, and proofreaders Dani Moran and Sarah Van Bonn for your amazing work.

Finally, I give so many thanks to my incredible family and friends who supported and helped me in numerous ways over the course of writing this book: Sue Nedved (thank you for your visits!), Hillary Bliss, Asmaa Ghonim, Michelle Quach, Kate Peters, and Casey Wilson. And as always, thank you to Mom, Dad, Adam, Natania, Hiro, Ronin, Andrew, and Mae—the newest extraordinary addition to the family.

Barb Colombo

Mariko Turk

grew up in Pennsylvania and graduated from the University of Pittsburgh with a BA in creative writing. She received her PhD from the University of Florida with a concentration in children's literature. Mariko currently lives with her husband and daughter in Colorado, where she enjoys tea, walks, and stories of all kinds. She is also the author of *The Other Side of Perfect*, a 2022 YALSA Best Fiction for Young Adults pick.

More from Mariko Turk

theNOVL.com

BOB1138